The only thing that matters to
her tenor sax. Stuck in a borin
who won't let her practise 't
sheep drowning in a bog', she hugs to herself the dream of becoming a musician. Then she meets Lester Mulley, an old 'pro' saxophonist. Tentatively, thrillingly, she is drawn into a whirl of gigs, tours, recording sessions. Lester becomes her teacher, an essential inspiration for her music – and perhaps just *too* essential to her life . . .

Brilliantly echoing the wail and blare of the tenor sax, Lorna Read writes with compassion of a special friendship that leads Chris to musical and emotional maturity.

Journalist, novelist and musician, Lorna Read was born in Liverpool in 1945. At the age of six she composed her first song on the piano and five years later started her own skiffle (folk) band. Swept into the music scene of Liverpool in the sixties, she sang and played her guitar in clubs and pubs until leaving for Bangor University where she gained a BA in English. In 1967 she came to London for the Richmond Jazz Festival and decided to stay and for the next decade found herself pursuing twin careers. By day she edited and wrote for a variety of pop music publications and by night she played guitar, keyboards and flute, singing solo and in bands on radio, for sessions and on many demo tapes. The last few years she has concentrated on writing novels, some of which are based on her own 'on the road' musical experiences, *Images*, *The Name is Zero*, *A Taste of Fame* (Pan). Now fiction editor of *Loving* magazine, Lorna Read lives in North London where she continues to write her songs.

Virago Upstarts is a new series of books for girls and young women. Upstarts are about love and romance, family and friends, work and school – and about new preoccupations – because in the last two decades the lives and expectations of girls have changed a lot. With fiction of all kinds – humour, mystery, love stories, science fiction, detective, thrillers – and nonfiction, this new series will show the funny, difficult, and exciting real lives and times of teenage girls in the 1980s. Lively, down-to-earth and entertaining, Virago's new list is an important new Upstart on the scene.

•CITY SAX•

LORNA READ

VIRAGO UPSTARTS

Published by VIRAGO PRESS Limited 1988
Centro House, 20–23 Mandella Street
London NW1 0HQ

British Library Cataloguing in Publication Data

Read, Lorna
City sax –(Virago upstarts)
I. Title
823′.914[F] PR6068.E2/

ISBN 0-86068-994-8

The lines on page 140 from 'Elegy Before Death: At Settignano', by C. Day Lewis, from *Collected Poems* 1954, reproduced by kind permission of the Executors of the Estate of C. Day Lewis, Jonathan Cape Ltd and The Hogarth Press.

Typeset by Florencetype Limited of Kewstoke, Avon
Printed in Great Britain by Cox & Wyman Limited
of Reading, Berkshire

Thanks to Jenni Jinx and Roy Carr
for help and inspiration

CHAPTER · I ·

'Too much air,' he informed her curtly. 'You're blowing too hard. Blow more softly. And your lips are far too tense. They should be like an elastic band, flexible, not too loose nor too tight. And there should never be any sounds coming from your mouth – that's what the instrument's for, to make the noise. Look, put it down for a minute. Flex your fingers, shake your shoulders, you're standing like a soldier at attention!'

Chris did as he said, feeling utterly depressed. There was nothing worse than thinking you were pretty good at something and then being told that you were doing it all wrong, she thought.

'Now pick it up again. Feel those fingers go floppier, more mobile . . . That's better. Now blow . . . No, still far too much air. You'll get dizzy and pass out if you continue to play like that.'

By the time she had paid her eight pounds for the hour's tuition, she was convinced that she would never make a saxophone player. That man; he'd played all his life, he was good, he was a teacher. She wanted to be good, too; she wanted to be in a hit band, make records, get famous. That was why, after playing all to herself for three years, with no guidance other than the records she listened to, she had sought professional advice. Now she felt she would never make it. To be right at the beginning, on the bottom rung, with all that study and practice and learning of technique ahead of you, was just too daunting. Yet, when she had been playing along to records in her bedroom, she had thought she hadn't sounded too bad . . .

With the tenor sax weighing down its case, and her spirit, like a lump of lead, Chris took the long way home through the park. It was a Wednesday in May and she had the day off to compensate for having to work on Saturday in the Oxford Street department store which she had joined shortly after leaving school.

The silver strip of pond in the distance grew larger and, squinting, Chris could just make out, somewhere near the centre, a dark blob followed by several tiny ones: ducklings. Her bad mood began to lift as she quickened her pace. She loved wildlife and these were the first ducklings she had seen this year.

The mother duck was dabbling at the edge of the pond, diving down head first, her dark-brown feet paddling the surface, while the babies, bright-eyed balls of brown and yellow fluff, scudded anxiously around her, making shrill piping sounds. Chris longed to scoop one out of the water and stroke it.

Her eyes left the ducks and scanned beyond, to a model yacht with white sails gliding soundlessly past a moorhen's nest on a tiny islet. Nobody seemed to be directing it. It was like a dinghy being sailed by a minute crew who were oblivious to the giants on the shore. For a moment, she wished she could scale herself down, like Alice after the medicine, and step aboard and experience the suburban pond expanding into a massive ocean of adventure.

Then she saw him. At first, she thought it was a fishing rod that he held in his hands. He was seated on a wooden bench and she went to step behind it so as not to become entangled in his line. She noticed that he held a black box with orange levers on it, and what she had thought was a rod was in fact an aerial with an orange pennant fluttering from the end, which she fancied might be some way of gauging the direction of the wind. As she watched, he pointed it at the yacht and it obligingly changed course, tacking to the left to avoid a pair of swimming geese; another pass with his magic wand and the graceful toy headed for the centre of the pond, skimming across the rippling wake created by the departing geese.

The man saw Chris watching. 'Would you like a go?' he asked. She considered. He was old – about her father's age, maybe even older for his hair had turned pure silver, though as the breeze ruffled it she could see a darker layer underneath. He smiled and it was a nice smile, not a creepy one. I'm young and swift on my feet, she thought, and there are other people around.

'It's quite easy really,' the man added, noticing her hesitation.

Chris made up her mind. Her urge to control the white yacht was irresistible. She put her saxophone case down on the gravel path, then sat down beside him on the peeling, graffiti-covered wooden bench. Briskly and eagerly, in the manner of two people dispensing with formality in the face of a common interest, he handed her the black control box which, she was relieved to discover, was quite similar to the remote control for a television or a video machine.

He told her how to use it and although she was at first terrified of capsizing the graceful and no doubt hideously expensive toy boat, she was soon slowing it down, speeding it up, tacking to left and to right, and describing a perfect figure of eight around a sign saying, *Danger – Deep Water*.

'I wish I'd had one of these when I was a kid,' she confided shyly, her first words to him that hadn't been said in response to a query or instruction of his.

'And I wish I'd had one of those.' He pointed to the bulbous black case.

'What? Do you know what it is, then?' She was used to having to fend off the rude suggestions of bunches of kids she passed in the street.

'Yeah. A sax. Correct?'

'Mm-hmm.' Chris wasn't usually interested in old people, but she suddenly was in him. He knew something, she could tell. Maybe he knew about music. There was something about his face, about the way his lines and wrinkles went, which wasn't sour and angry, like some older people, but spoke more of thought – of humour, even. She could tell that he laughed a lot. But there was something, not quite sad, but kind of melancholic, wistful; shadows. Things which you could express more easily through music than through words.

'Do you play?' she ventured.

His lines took the humorous path. He laughed, and at first she thought he was laughing at her, and drew herself up slightly, but then she realised he wasn't laughing at anything, really; he was just laughing.

'Do I play?' It was a rhetorical question. He turned his head and it was the first time the stranger had looked her directly in the eyes. They were a very unusual blue – bluer than the pond, less silver than the sky, warm, intense, sparkling. Chris had to look away.

'Of course, you don't know me. You're too young,' the man said. 'Lester. Lester Mulley. Mean anything to you?'

'Is it a place?' Chris asked politely. She had taken her thumb off the controls and the yacht was drifting with the breeze. She jerked her eyes away from it and back to the man, who was laughing again.

'Is it a place!' he repeated, shaking his head and smiling mischievously. 'My dear child . . . No, it's me. I am Lester Mulley. I play the saxophone. I've played it since I was nineteen years old. I wish I'd started much, much younger.'

Chris felt reproved. Thinking that she had put her foot in it and would be better off going, she offered him the boat controls back. He took them, thanking her. His 'my dear child' rankled. It was the sort of voice the teachers at school had used when they wanted to cut you down to size. Thank God she was away from all that now. Her eyes suddenly smarted. Something seemed to have a down on her today. For some reason it seemed desperately important that this man should like her and take her seriously, but she'd blown it. And all through a mistake which anyone could have made. Well, anyone who didn't know a lot about old music. He probably played jazz. That would explain it. She couldn't understand most jazz. It wandered about, not getting anywhere. Often, it didn't even have a definite rhythm. She felt out of her depth with it.

Skilfully, the man – Lester – called the boat to him, slowing it so that it floated in and nudged the bank.

'I – I'm sorry,' Chris faltered.

'What for? You didn't capsize my yacht.' Now he *was* laughing at her.

'For thinking you were a place.' An absurd desire to giggle twitched at the corners of her lips, but she beat it back.

'*I* wish I was a place – any place but here.' He began to hum some tune she didn't recognise, but it was catchy, the sort of thing which would sound good as a sax solo. 'Do you know that?' he asked.

She shook her head.

'Of course you don't. I'm only just composing it now.'

She stared at him. Was he pulling her leg?

He smiled at her; then, pocketing the radio control machine, he strolled to the edge of the pond, grasped his toy boat by the mast and pulled it, dripping, out of the water. Chris thought again of her earlier fantasy, about the teeny midgets on the boat. They would all be screaming now and spilling over the edge of the deck, smashing their limbs on the hard grassbank. She shook her head to clear it of the unbearable vision.

'I must go,' she declared, getting up herself.

'OK. I'll walk along with you,' Lester said. He was tall, about six foot, and thin, and walked with a spring in his step, as if he was still full of life. Chris was puzzled by him. He was old, yet not old. She had never met anyone like him. Sometimes he made her think of her granddad, at other times, her twenty-two-year-old cousin.

'I shouldn't really have teased you,' he apologised, shaking the boat so that glittering drops flew off in all directions. Some landed on her instrument case, but she made no attempt to brush them off. 'I belong to a different musical generation. How long have you been playing?'

'Nearly three years now. I played the flute before that and I can play the piano a bit, as well.' She didn't add that she tried to compose, too. For years she had been keeping a sort of journal, in a series of notebooks. 'The Collected Works of C. Lindsell', she had decided to call it. The title had been meant as a laugh, for she was convinced that her journal would never progress beyond a few pages. But now she had reached Volume 5. It contained poems which had rhymed when she had first started writing them but were now mostly blank verse, expressing her feelings and observations about things, such as how she had felt when Tigger, her much-loved ginger cat, had died, and how the big horse-chestnut tree in the park looked, silhouetted against the sky in winter. There were diary-type entries and also her attempts at composing tunes. She had never actually written one all the way through, but she had jotted down lots of musical phrases and ideas, a few bars each time, in her own musical shorthand which only she could understand. It was all far too complicated to explain to this stranger, even if she had wanted to.

'So you're really musical, eh?' he said.

Chris gave him a sharp look, wondering if he was teasing her, then decided that he wasn't.

'I'd never had any saxophone lessons, so I went for one today,' she confided.

'I gather it didn't go well.' His eyes twinkled but he smiled sympathetically.

'How could you tell?'

'I noticed your expression as you were standing by the pond, watching the ducklings. I thought for a minute that you were going to chuck yourself in and join them.'

'It wasn't that bad . . . Or maybe it is. I don't know. Did you –' She still felt nervous about asking him things. He was, after all, a complete stranger, and for all she knew, he might even be famous. In any case, he might think it a cheek.

'Go on,' he prompted. 'Anything about music I'll answer. Now, if you were asking about my bank balance . . .'

Chris had never understood why adults attached so much secrecy to money. She wouldn't have minded anyone knowing how much, or little, she had. Right now, it was about forty-eight pounds, minus the thirty-five pence she had spent on a choc ice before her lesson. She wished she had kept it as a reward for having come through an ordeal bravely.

'Did you ever find it difficult to practise – because of the noise level, I mean?' she asked him.

'Have you tried a sock?'

'A *sock*? You're having me on. You'll be telling me next that that's where the expression "putting a sock in it" comes from!'

'It probably is,' he replied with a chuckle. 'Trumpeters are better off than us because they can use a mute.' He explained about the device which fitted into the end and muffled the sound. 'They can't make one for a sax, though, it's the wrong shape. But a couple of woolly socks stuffed in the end don't half make a difference.'

'The last row I had with my parents about it, they told me I sounded like the Titanic going down,' Chris confessed ruefully. 'The trouble is, apart from my bedroom there's only one place I can play, my friend Shane's garage. He plays electric guitar and his parents have soundproofed it for him. But I don't like going there too often. I suppose all loud instruments create problems. I mean, how would you muffle a drum kit?' They were strolling towards one of the gateways that led out onto the road. Chris felt her spirits falling. This little interlude had been fun. More than that, it had been interesting. If only she could have found out about his saxophone playing, and what he did now.

'Play it under the bedclothes?' His inane shrug and comical expression made her giggle.

'That's better,' he said. They were out on the road now, no doubt going different ways. The sax in its case was dragging leadenly at her arm again. Maybe she ought to take it into a secondhand instrument shop and sell it, or swop it for something quieter that could be played through headphones, like an electric piano. But she didn't want to play piano. She wanted the bite, the edge, the gravelly bassnotes, the sky-rending, banshee soprano of the sax; the way it screamed, as she had always wanted to scream but didn't dare.

'Are you going back to that teacher?' he enquired.

She shook her head. 'No way. He –' She stopped. Maybe this guy was a teacher, too. She didn't want to insult the breed. Maybe there was a good one somewhere.

'Some teachers don't inspire you. I know.' He smiled sympathetically and paused, as if trying to make up his mind about something. Chris waited, shifting her weight to the other foot, anxious to get away now. Being in the park had relaxed her. The sun, the ducks and the water had spread a kind of magic about, enabling her to enjoy her conversation with a stranger, and sailing his toy boat. But now that there was pavement beneath her shoes, she felt a bit awkward and embarrassed. She was back in the normal world and, while she couldn't sense anything dangerous about this man, how did she know he wasn't some sort of mild local loony?

Before she could sidle off, he said, 'Don't think I'm just shooting you a line, but I give lessons, too. At the Institute on Thursday nights at six, and privately, at the Russell Rooms – you know that rehearsal place behind the music college?'

Chris nodded. His potential looniness receded and he assumed some importance in her eyes. So he *was* a teacher.

'Or you could come and hear the band. We've got a gig next Sunday lunchtime at the Haycart in Mill Lane, though I don't suppose you're quite old enough to drink yet?'

Just in time, Chris caught the teasing twinkle in his eyes and bit back her retort. He fished around inside his grey jacket and found a card which he handed to her. 'It's got my number on, in case you change your mind about lessons. Give me a ring if you do. The class at the Institute's been going three weeks, but you might be able to catch up. Or maybe see you Sunday?'

Chris nodded. The man waved and went off down the road, his yacht clutched beneath his arm. Lop a couple of feet off his height and he would have looked like a ten-year-old kid, she thought. A white-haired kid.

She glanced at the card. *Lester Mulley, A.R.C.M. Saxophone. Teaching, sessions* it said. There was an addition in pen: *Soundwaves, available for gigs. Ring* . . . and then a local phone number. It must be the name of his band, she thought. Soundwaves. The name gave no impression of what kind of music it was, but she had an awful suspicion that it was the smooth, technical, emotionless jazz that she hated.

The rest of the week, she was back in her dreary job in the department store, sorting small grey socks and white vests into the correct sizes and arranging the displays in the Childrenswear section. As she served her customers, answering questions mechanically, directing them to the section they required, telling them which floor the cafeteria was on, making out a refund slip on a shirt bought for a nephew that turned out too small, Chris often found her mind following the white sails of a model yacht, and recalling the quizzical expression in a pair of blue eyes set beneath a thatch of silver hair.

She knew she would go on Sunday. Just out of curiosity, that was all. Maybe he would be hopeless. But somehow, she knew already that he wouldn't be.

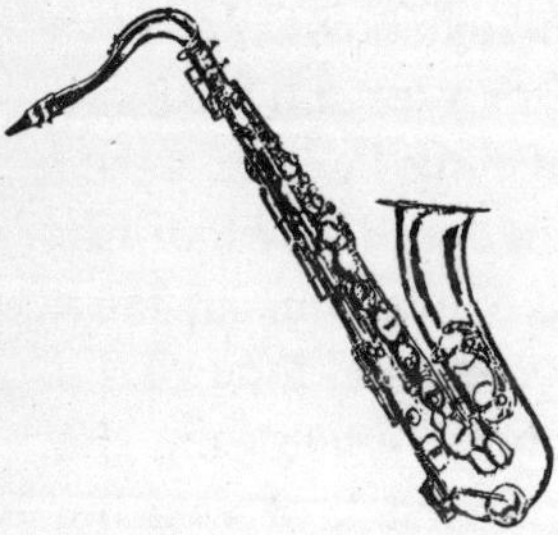

CHAPTER • 2 •

Sometimes Chris thought she was fully alive only when she was playing. It was all she had ever really enjoyed, or wanted to do. It was bliss to walk home down her narrow, hilly road in Clapham, south London, and find the house empty, as she had on Saturday night, a note from her parents informing her that they had gone out for birthday drinks with some business friend of her father's. Her father managed a furniture warehouse on a large industrial estate in Park Royal. Chris had been there a few times with her mother and had found the place bewilderingly big and confusing, with its stiffly formal room sets full of laminated teak and anaemic, cheap pine, and dark, oxblood-coloured horrors with brass and leather trimmings that she couldn't even put a name to, let alone would wish to live with!

She glanced at herself in her dressing-table mirror as she walked from her bedroom door to the shelving system to pick a tape to listen to. She wasn't usually the type to spend a long time examining her appearance but, for some reason, tonight she came back for a second look. Her hair was annoying her. The hairdresser at the store where she worked – Chris took advantage of her staff discount as often as possible – had cut the front much too short, so that Chris felt that she showed an unflattering amount of pale forehead which contrasted oddly with the sprinkling of tiny dark freckles across the bridge of her nose. In contrast, the back of her hair had been left long, with a wispy tail at the centre to which she often attached a clip or a bow.

It's a mess, she thought, wrinkling her eyes and nose in a scowl. *I'm* a mess. She hated the brown eyes which stared back at her. They were too dark. They were just like her father's, almost impossible to read an expression in. How could eyes as dark as hers be described as 'windows of the soul'? She hated her shape, too. Surely, at seventeen, she shouldn't be so flat and lanky? She was sick of wearing baggy clothes to try and make herself look more rounded than she was.

Giving her hair an angry tweak, she paced restlessly across the room and dived her hand into her tape collection, pulling out and discarding one after another. She didn't know what mood she was in, that was the trouble. She didn't fancy hearing anything boppy or funky. She knew the sound she wanted to hear; something that pulled at your guts and sucked at your soul and made you want to cry. But she had nothing like that in her collection, and it made her feel angry and bottled up inside, trapped with a feeling which she couldn't explain or express.

Her parents were always accusing her of being moody. 'What do you mean?' she would yell at them. 'We all have moods, don't we? We're all happy sometimes, angry sometimes, or down, or quiet, or bouncy and full of energy . . .'

Her mother would mutter darkly that that wasn't what she meant, but Chris knew that what she meant was that

Chris's mood was clashing with her own. With her mother, she often felt that she was on a see-saw. When she was down, her mother was up, and *vice versa*. They rarely seemed to coincide about anything. Just thinking about it gave her a surge of that angry frustration that came over her whenever she was up against a situation she could do nothing about. Swooping down, she grabbed a pillow off her bed and hurled it to the carpet, then picked it up again and smashed it back onto the bed, enjoying the violent draught its flying passage created, which made the picture on the wall at the foot of her bed, a print of an unknown man playing the saxophone, swing and creak.

Feeling slightly better, she picked up her own instrument from where it had been leaning against the bookshelves and, taking a huge gasp of air, placed the mouthpiece to her lips and blew . . .

From the recorder at age seven to the flute at ten: Chris was pleased now that she had made the transition. Being able to read music was a great boon, and her years of flute playing had helped her control her breathing and had developed her lungs. She had taken five grade exams on the flute and had then exasperated her parents by giving it up.

'All these lessons we've paid out good money for!' her mother snorted. 'You can get tunes out of that flute, you're good at it – even your teacher says so. It's a crying shame. You could have been another James Galway. What beautiful music *he* plays . . .'

'Mum, that's exactly what I don't want to be,' she had pointed out. 'I don't want to play nice, pretty tunes. I want to . . . to *express* myself.'

Her mother shook her head and gave Chris a sarcastic

look which infuriated her. 'Express yourself? Is that what those strange noises like a sheep drowning in a bog are, that I've heard coming from your bedroom lately? So it's this experimental rubbish you're into now? Well, I don't want to hear it in this house, so you can take your sax and find yourself a nice sheep field to play in.'

Having her tonal experiments compared to a drowning sheep upset Chris a lot more than her mother realised because, unwittingly, she'd hit exactly on the source of Chris's current dissatisfaction with playing the flute. The range of sound wasn't deep enough. She felt the flute was like her own voice – high, sweet, mellow or sharp, flowing or piercing, but always high, from the head rather than the belly. A flute could only sing, it couldn't shout; it could shriek but it couldn't wail. If her mother had likened the noises she had been making to an expiring cow, Chris wouldn't have been so upset. But a *sheep* . . .

Chris's friend Carol was mad on Bruce Springsteen and thought he was the sexiest male on earth. Chris had been round visiting her one night when Carol had insisted that she watched a video of a Springsteen concert with her.

'Aha! So he's got to you, too! The way he wears those Levi's . . .' Carol had sighed adoringly.

'It's not him, it's the sax player I'm looking at. He's incredible. What's his name?'

Carol had tossed her an album sleeve.

'Clarence Clemons,' Chris had read out.

'You're mad!' Carol had sneered. 'Fancy listening to saxophones when Bruce is on!'

Chris didn't care what Carol thought. She had located her ideal instrument. She just had to get a sax. And when she heard Raphael Ravenscroft's brilliant solo on Gerry Rafferty's 'Baker Street' single, she was doubly sold on the idea. She just had to make that sound. It was *her*!

Now, standing in her bedroom with the window closed, she blew a soft, husky note, then changed the air pressure and blew a string of tighter, punchier ones. How long would it be before she could reproduce all the sounds she heard in her head? Sometimes she thought they weren't even in her head, but floating somewhere outside herself and she was drawing them down, pulling them through the instrument, pushing them out.

It almost made her blush now to think that, when she answered the ad for a saxophone for sale in a local shop window, she had no idea that there were several kinds. She had bought a tenor, the correct instrument for the sounds she wanted to make, with its B flat to F sharp range – or higher, if you could manage it. But it had been pure luck and she could easily have ended up with an alto – or even a soprano or baritone, though she hoped she would have realised at a glance that they were the wrong shape and size, and not what she wanted.

The guy had asked for £200; she had offered him £180, all she possessed, and he had reluctantly accepted. So she had withdrawn the money from her building-society account, hoping she wasn't being ripped off.

Now, three years later, she knew first, that it had been very cheap, second, that the instrument wasn't a very good one, and third, that it had had all kinds of annoying things wrong with it such as leaky pads, which made the lower notes difficult to play. These things, and how to cure them, she had found out by trial and error, by reading books and asking around until she had found a boy at school who also played the saxophone.

The phone was ringing downstairs, but Chris went on playing and ignored it. Then, as it continued, she found herself using the rhythmic *breeps* as an accompaniment. She found their note and played a third, a fourth, a fifth interval away from them, then mingled them in a run. It was fun. When they stopped, she found she missed them. For a couple of minutes, that telephone bell had become her band.

The Haycart was built like a mock country farmhouse, with a dark brown imitation thatch roof, white paintwork, heavy brown timbers round the windows and under the eaves. It sprawled in a concrete car park which was shiny with puddles, a heavy shower having begun and ended while Chris was still on the bus.

As she walked between two rows of squat, ugly concrete flower tubs in which tall pink tulips thrust valiantly up through a mulch of crisp and cigarette packets, Chris felt her footsteps dragging. People pushed, chattering, past her and disappeared through the carved wooden door with its huge metal latch. All of them were with somebody, but here she was, underage and alone. She was terrified of going into a pub by herself. Although she had visited pubs with friends, she had seen only too often what happened when a girl was left on her own even temporarily; some drunken, paunchy, overweight yobbo would reel leeringly up and refuse to take 'no' for an answer. It had happened to her twice but each time she had been rescued by a friend returning from the bar or the ladies' room in the nick of time.

Today, though, she was entirely on her own with nobody to rescue her but Lester – if he remembered her and wasn't too busy playing. She had deliberately dressed inconspicuously, in jeans and a baggy black sweatshirt, though she had dashed on some lipstick to try and make herself look as if she was old enough to be there. Well, she was only three months off the magical birthday which would enable her to drink in pubs legally. Not that she would want to very often – noisy, smelly, smoky places. The only thing they were any good for was meeting boys – and she was right off them at the moment, thanks to Ian Fowler, her very-much-ex boyfriend.

Sounds of a drum roll came from inside the pub and Chris's breathing quickened. She heard some piano notes, a quick, complex run which reminded her of the trilling of a blackbird. She *had* to go in! If anyone tried to talk to her, she would just ignore them, pretend she was a foreign tourist or something. She had done that before.

Almost without realising she was doing it, she pushed the heavy swing door open and stepped into a low-ceilinged interior with pseudo-rustic furnishings and a dark-red, rather stained carpet. Without glancing round, for fear that anybody might think she was looking at them, she marched to the bar and bought herself a Coke. Then, with her hand chilling around the glass, she turned and surveyed the L-shaped lounge bar with its enormous stone-flagged hearth and the iron grate heaped with unlit logs. Every table appeared to be occupied. Nervousness clouded her vision and she clutched her icy glass more tightly. She couldn't see the band, there were too many people standing in the way. Squaring her shoulders, she walked determinedly forward and forged her way through the crowd. She could see the drummer now, a fat, balding man who looked older than Lester. The pianist was a thin man, West Indian or African, with a pointed beard, dressed in a stunning lemon and lime-green jacket. He and the drummer were lost in a quiet, private world of warming up. Deep, plucked bass notes joined in and Chris spied another man, half hidden behind the piano, his stand-up string bass almost larger than himself.

She couldn't see Lester. Perhaps he wasn't turning up today; he was ill, or the booking had been changed and this was not his band. Then the couple standing directly in front of Chris started clapping and Lester appeared, walking between the tables on the left, and following close behind him was a girl, young, in her mid-twenties maybe; olive-skinned, slightly Oriental-looking, with a halo of shiny black hair; skinny, hip and collar bones protruding through her tight blue dress.

Chris shrank back. She didn't want Lester to see her yet. Not until she had decided whether she wanted to be seen or not.

The girl hopped onto a stool and took up a position sitting on top of the battered upright piano. Lester grinned around his band, snapped his fingers in a 'one-two-three' and the muted playing of earlier on was abandoned as the drummer set up a lively beat. Sixteen bars, then Lester raised his saxophone to his lips, the bar lights gleaming warmly on the metal so that Chris was oddly reminded of Christmas-tree ornaments and candles.

A fusillade of sound-bullets piercing the ears, then an almost sensuous swoop down, then up. Bat-squeaks, then a rounded cascade, like fountain drops. Chris stood entranced, forgetting her self-consciousness. He was good – more than good. The number ended and the next one was a slow blues. Poignant piano chords counterpointed Lester's rough-edged runs. The girl started singing. Her voice was husky-light, and tinged with sadness, blending beautifully with Lester's playing. Chris felt something within her midriff start to melt and open. This was the kind of thing she had been craving to hear the other night, when she had felt so restless and frustrated. Music like this would have been the perfect outlet. Her face relaxed into a jubilant grin.

The number came to an end and everyone clapped and called. Lester smiled out into his audience and upended his sax to drain out the saliva that had collected there. Spit was the only thing Chris didn't like about the sax. She felt that it must be really unhygienic to play somebody else's; you would catch all their germs.

Suddenly Lester spotted her. 'Hi!' he called, and waved. 'Glad you could make it.'

Chris blushed crimson, aware that people were staring at her. The couple in front of her turned round. The girl smiled and her companion, a guy of about twenty-three with cropped fair hair and wire-rimmed glasses, asked, 'Are you a friend of Lester's?'

'A very new one,' she admitted. She liked the pair of them. 'I met him in the park the other day.'

The bass player was tuning one of his strings. 'I'm a student of his,' the guy explained. 'I'm Nick and this is my girlfriend, Julie.'

The girl, shorter than Chris, with curly ginger hair and a glittery scarf twined round her neck, nodded and grinned. The band launched into their next number, putting paid to any further conversation, but Chris felt far more at ease for having met them, and when Julie went off to the bar, she came back clutching three drinks, one of them a Coke for Chris.

After the set was over, Lester joined them, and Chris noted that he looked distinctly younger than he had the other day, with his hair tousled and his face flushed from playing.

He chatted briefly to Nick and Julie, then asked Chris if she would like to meet the band and she agreed eagerly. The bass player was called Steve, Neil was the bulky drummer, the lively pianist was Kal and the singer was called Marijke, pronounced Marayka. She told Chris that her mother was from the Dutch East Indies, which was where her unusual name came from.

'You all sound so good together. Is all your music written down?'

'No,' Marijke told her.

'Then how do you know who's going to play what when, if you know what I mean?' Chris asked, fascinated.

'We've been playing together for about four years, apart from Steve who's only been with us for a year, so I think we're almost telepathic by now,' Kal put in. 'Musicians get like that, if they all get on well. I can sense when Lester is cueing me in, and he knows just when to come in over the rhythm section. It's a sort of sixth sense you get from experience.'

'Would you like to play a few bars?' Lester invited out of the blue. 'We'll pick something you know . . .'

'Oh, no!' Chris said, shocked. What? Play in front of all these people? She wasn't nearly good enough, she would make a total idiot of herself! 'Sorry, I just couldn't, I've never played in public,' she gabbled, but she was seething with frustration. This was the kind of golden opportunity you read about in books. If she were a fictional heroine, she would step up there with the band and take the place by storm. A record executive would bound out of the audience and offer her thousands of pounds to sign a contract. Wembley Stadium would be on the line, saying that all the tickets for her concert had sold in the first minute. It was the stuff of her wildest dreams.

And here she was saying no, her lips trembling, her feet weighted to the floor.

'OK, you don't have to. But you must let me hear you one day. You've still got that card I gave you?' She had, tucked in the flap at the back of her purse. 'Give me a ring.

Maybe I could advise you about teachers and books and things. Chat to Nick . . .'

He waved a hand at the group of them, then accepted the pint of beer being pressed on him by some men at the bar. Nick was talking earnestly to Julie. Feeling suddenly alien, Chris slipped between the knots of people and headed through the door. It was still raining.

By Wednesday, she had decided that she had nothing to lose in ringing. She dialled, but all she got was his voice on an answering machine stating that she should leave a message. Struck dumb, she hung up.

She tried again in her lunch hour on Thursday. Thursday was the worst day of the week in the store, the day they stayed open until seven. It was eight before the cashing-up was over and the counter staff could go home. Being one of the youngest members of staff, she was sent on the hated first lunch sitting, which took place at the ridiculous hour of a quarter to twelve. Chris realised it made sense for the sales assistants' lunch hours to be staggered – after all, they got the bulk of their customers at lunchtime, so it would be crazy if this tidal wave coincided with a total exodus of staff – but how could she possibly be expected to feel hungry at that hour? Apart from that, it made the afternoon seem so interminably long, especially on Thursdays.

She went to the staff canteen with a group of girls from her floor, and dutifully picked at a ham salad, extracting all the crunchy bits such as celery and lettuce heart, and leaving the boring, floppy things. Then, making an excuse, she left the conversation, which was about men as usual, and went in search of a phone.

This time she was in luck and Lester himself answered.

'Chris! How's things?'

'I just wanted to –' Wanted to what? Say hello? That sounded rather a tame reason for bothering him.

'When are you going to introduce me to that saxophone of yours?'

She giggled. 'Just don't expect me to be a genius.'

'I don't. *I'm* not one. Anyway, most of the geniuses are dead.'

'Oh?' His remark puzzled her. There were loads of brilliant live sax players. She hoped he wasn't a musical snob who didn't like anything modern.

'I'm giving lessons until eight thirty tomorrow. How about after that?'

'OK. Where?'

'I'll meet you outside the Russell Rooms in Caton Street, main entrance.'

Caton Street was only about ten minutes' walk from where she worked.

'All right, then. See you . . .'

'Chris! Er-hmm, *Miss Lindsell*!'

At the sound of her supervisor's voice, Chris shot round, her elbow knocking a neatly folded heap of size-graded kiddies' T-shirts onto the floor. She coloured. 'Sorry . . .'

'We can't have this daydreaming,' Liz Walsh, the supervisor, snapped. 'There's a customer over there's been trying to catch your eye for a long time. Run along and serve her.'

'Jumped-up git!' muttered Syl Roche from the till. 'Bloody graduates swan in and think they can order us around like slaves just because they've got a BA. Management trainees . . . *huh*!'

Chris smiled her automatic smile as she agreed to search in the stockroom to see if they had the emerald sweatshirt in a size larger than the one on display. If she took her time and dawdled, with a bit of luck her customer would give up and go away, then she and Syl could start cashing up early. She wanted time to go home and change before meeting Lester. Time to practise for half an hour, too, if possible. A sax was cold for the first few minutes. It needed warming up, like her fingers. A musician . . . he was a real musician. If he thought she showed any talent . . .

But why should he? Compared to him, she was an untrained beginner who, according to that other teacher, hadn't even got her *embouchure*, her mouth position, correct. Lester would notice instantly. She was about to make an absolute fool of herself.

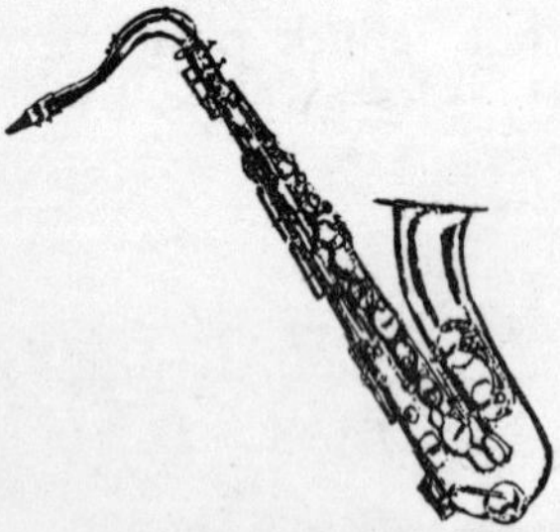

CHAPTER • 3 •

As she lay underneath the striped duvet in her narrow bed, listening to the raindrops tapping on the sloping loft window above her head, Chris was hugging the knowledge to her, like a cosy hot-water bottle. He thought I was good. *He* thought *I* was good! And she couldn't stop smiling, even though she should have been asleep at least an hour ago, in order to have the energy to get through another tedious day's work tomorrow.

She had asked him about that. 'Did *you* ever do a job you didn't like?'

He had laughed and she had been fascinated to see that he had hardly any fillings in his teeth. Not like most people his age. She didn't think his teeth were false, either. 'Plenty,' he had replied. 'Where do I start?' He had listed a whole heap of jobs he had done after school, in between college courses, during his time in bands: removal man, hospital orderly, bus driver, barman, even a spell at a private zoo, cleaning out the bird cages.

'I had a mate once who took a temporary job in a mortuary. One night he was there on his own and one of the corpses suddenly sat up! He nearly died himself, of fright.'

'Ugh!' Chris grimaced. She hated anything to do with death and bodies. She couldn't bear reading about murders or war. She knew that if she ever had to live through the kind of war her grandparents had lived through, she would simply go mad.

'The thing about jobs is, you have to do them until you can make enough money to live by doing the thing you really want to do,' Lester said.

'I suppose so,' she had conceded with a grimace, thinking: but for how long?

Lester had played at American air bases in Germany. 'I picked up a lot of good jazz records there. Opened my eyes a bit – and my ears.'

He had played on his first record when he was twenty-two. 'The label doesn't exist any more. We were doing experimental jazz-rock, all flash, no soul. You'd probably hate it.'

She had felt sure she would have done.

They had gone back inside the rehearsal place, to one in a row of identical rooms off a long corridor. It wasn't very well sound-proofed because she could hear a cacophony of instruments and vocalists, not very loud, but still loud enough to be off-putting.

She knew he would think it very feeble and wimpish of her if she made a great fuss about playing in front of him so, after muttering brief apologies, she had played one of the pieces she learned off an LP.

He had asked her if she knew the tune to Paul Simon's 'Diamonds On The Soles Of Her Shoes'. Hesitantly at first, then with more confidence, she played it from memory, and he suddenly joined in on his own sax, his melody lines twining in and out of hers, making her stretch herself with improvising. When she at last called a breathless halt, she was laughing and puffing.

'That was fun, it really was. Do you know, that was the first time I've ever played along with another sax player?' she had told him.

As he smiled delightedly, she could suddenly see him on stage with a rock band, as he must have been twenty years before, whip-thin, with longer hair, in denim and leather, with girls chasing him. She could recognise that boyish attractiveness, that hint of sexiness, despite the folds and furrows his face now fell into, and it disturbed her. She had no right to find a man of his age fanciable and sexy. Luckily, the dangerous moment passed and he was persuading her to play something else. And at the end of it he told her that she was good, that she had a lot of talent and if she wanted to be in a band, she should go for it.

'Surely I haven't had enough experience?' she challenged him.

'Nearly eight years, if you count the flute,' he pointed out. 'I've known musicians join bands with only a couple of years' playing experience. You just need to work on becoming more self-confident. And that means having the nerve to play in public, and developing your own style. You need to listen to a lot more records, a lot more tenor players. I can lend you some records. But you must practise – lots and lots.'

That was when Chris's dreamy smile faded and she ceased to hug her dreams and memories to her. Practise . . . it was the one thing she was more or less forbidden to do in her saxophone-hating household. Why couldn't her parents be easier on her? Why couldn't they turn the television up, or wear earplugs? Yet, even though she realised she could be creating further problems for herself by booking a course of lessons, Chris went ahead and arranged one for three o'clock on Monday afternoon, her next day off.

All the next day at work, she found herself brooding. Lester would give her exercises and scales to play, no doubt about it. She didn't want to let him down, yet her situation was hopeless. Maybe she should think of moving into a flat, but she wasn't eighteen yet, her parents could raise objections. In any case, even if she could find a place she could afford, the odds were greatly against her finding neighbours and flatmates who were any more tolerant about saxophone practice than her parents were. How did Lester manage, she wondered? Maybe he lived in a detached house, or had a soundproofed room. It was so much easier if you were older, with lots of money.

Chris imagined herself and saxophone installed in Lester's house. How wonderful it would be to live with somebody who understood music, who played themselves, especially somebody who could guide her own playing and help her to get better. Her imagination went one step further and appointed her a member of Soundwaves, playing duets with Lester and making records. That would be the ideal life, worlds away from sticking prices on pairs of small socks and dodging Liz Walsh's acid tongue.

Lester had said that some teachers inspired you and others didn't. She felt positive that he would inspire her. There was some kind of strange rapport between them that had started that day on the bench in the park. Why else would he have been so friendly and encouraging? Surely he wouldn't work that hard just to net himself another pupil? With the career he had behind him, he couldn't possibly be hard up unless he had gone mad with his cash in his rock days and let it all slip through his fingers . . .

That evening, after battling home on the tube, she decided to ask Shane for the loan of his garage. Sometimes he played along with her on guitar, and that was fun. Nearing his house, she could hear muffled electric-guitar chords coming from the garage. Damn! she thought crossly. If he was in the middle of practising he mightn't want to be disturbed, but she banged and yelled all the same, until there was an amplified thud as he put the guitar down.

He stuck his slightly pimply face round the sliding door. 'Oh, it's you,' he said ungraciously.

'You're growing a beard!' There were some dark clumps on his chin. 'Great!'

'What you mean is, it covers up more of my face. Go on, be honest,' he challenged, hauling up the sagging waistband of his dirty jeans. 'Don't try to flatter me.'

Shane was lanky, and his clothes always looked as if they were falling off him. Chris had been assured by some schoolmates that one day his games shorts had fallen right down, but she hadn't been around to witness the spectacle – fortunately, in her opinion.

'Wanna play?' He jerked his thumb over his shoulder. He'd swopped the clear, 100-watt garage light bulb for an atmospheric red one and the light on his amplifier glowed scarlet to match, reflecting in two dark patches of spilled oil like devil's eyes.

'With you, you mean?'

'Any time, baby.' He leered amateurishly, then swiped his greasy hair back from his forehead, leaving a grubby mark on his brow.

'Actually, I was wondering when you *weren't* going to be playing and whether your folks would mind me having a go.' Chris parked her black-denim-clad backside on an old packing case.

Shane immediately rushed at her, flapping his hands. 'Don't sit on that! It's the new parts I ordered for my motorbike. Some of them are breakable.'

'OK – sorry.' Chris stood up again and brushed off the seat of her jeans. The packing case, though supposedly newly delivered, had looked a bit greasy and cobwebby. There was something about Shane and his immediate environment that reminded her of Fungus the Bogeyman.

'I've just met this great new saxophone teacher and I need to practise, and there's no way I can do all I want to do at home. Mum would have a nervous breakdown. That's if Dad didn't leave her first. You're my only hope.' She hooked her thumbs into the waistband of her jeans and stared at him. She'd known Shane all through school. He was still there. He was a bit of a boffin and taking his A-levels any day. He hoped to go to university and study electronics, and end up working in a recording studio. Music was the only thing she and Shane had in common. She certainly didn't fancy him, and so his next remark fell on ears that were not just deaf, but pre-programmed.

'I'll trade you for a date. Come to the cinema with me.'

Chris's interjection of '*What*?' was intended to fill out some time until she could come up with a put-down which not only would not hurt him, but would also still allow her access to the only free practice room in the vicinity.

Shane's mouth flickered downwards at the corners and he cocked his greasy head to one side. 'All right. A kiss then . . .'

A *kiss*? That was even worse! She had kissed a few boys before, notably Ian Fowler. He had been her first real boyfriend and they had gone out for eight months. All the others had lasted just one or two dates. She had met Ian at a school disco to which fifth- and sixth-formers from a couple of other schools had been invited. He played football for his school team and Chris fell for his neat dark hair, his hazel eyes, his powerful shoulders and rocklike thighs which strained at the seams of his stone-washed jeans. For months she had gone faithfully to matches and practices – and then she had caught him out two-timing her with Tracey Watts, of all people. Everyone knew Tracey was a tart! How could he? As well as feeling heartbroken and furious, Chris cringed at the thought that maybe he had only gone with Tracey because she let him go further than Chris would have done. Of course Ian had hinted about sex, but, at sixteen, she just hadn't felt ready for it. She felt scared. If you got into sex, you were into an entirely different sort of relationship, something much more serious and committing. That's what she thought anyway. No doubt boys could do it one night, and then not want to speak to the girl the next day, but she knew that, for her, sex would involve far, far more than just her body, and she didn't want to give that much to Ian. He wasn't the right person. Whatever love was, she was positive she had never felt it for him.

She was in a nasty predicament right now, though. Kiss Shane Wallace? She would rather kiss a tarantula, and she was someone who couldn't stand spiders!

'Oh, come on, just a little one,' he wheedled and snaked an arm round her. He groped for her breast and squeezed it.

'Get off me!' Chris screamed, lashing out at him. But he caught her arm, yanked her towards him and brushed wet, rubbery lips against her cheek. Then he let her go, as if suddenly scared of his actions, and Chris chose that moment to grab her case and run for the door.

'You're a real pig!' she hurled at him.

'Takes one to know one,' he replied cheekily. Picking up his guitar, he struck two loud, jangling chords and Chris shut the door on him.

Taking long, angry strides, she struggled against a cold wind and was glad of its cleansing sting against her face as she pushed towards home. When was she ever going to meet a bloke with sensitivity, who knew how to talk to her and touch her? One who would encourage her with her music, and love her for herself, one whom she could trust, who would make her feel so good that she would never need to look at another man for the rest of her life? Was it too much of an ideal to hope for? She couldn't believe that it was. Somewhere, a soul-mate had to exist. But she wouldn't find him in Shane Wallace's garage, or in the Childrenswear department.

When she got in, her mother told her that her friend Carol had rung. She envied Carol, wishing she were on the dole, too, and could practise all day, while her parents were at work. Chris's mother had a typing job at a local solicitor's office.

'Oh, hi!' Carol greeted her when she dialled. 'What have you been up to? Johnson Kendrick's having a party tonight. You'd better come. Bruce Conroy might be there and we wouldn't want to miss *him*!'

Bruce Conroy was a real 'local boy made good'. He was extremely handsome and had been taken on by a model agency and had already appeared in some fashion spreads in magazines and a TV commercial. He was the nearest thing any of them had met to a star (except for Chris, who now knew a real star in Lester, and who also thought Bruce was very big-headed), and news had got round that he had finished with his girlfriend and was on the hunt for a new one. So no doubt Johnson's party would quickly degenerate into a 'who's going to get off with Bruce' session.

Chris talked to Carol until her father appeared and started tapping his watch, a sign that she had been using the phone for too long. Once her father had gone back to the Western he was watching on telly, Chris stole up to her bedroom and got out her sax, reckoning she could get away with a good few bars while the gunfire was blasting.

She even managed to sound a bit like Lester, for about two minutes . . .

The trouble about working on Saturday was that you were so tired when you got home that you didn't feel like doing much in the evening. This Saturday was no exception. It was her feet that hurt most, Chris acknowledged ruefully, as she prepared to step into a hot bath into which she had sprinked a liberal measure of herbal bath salts 'guaranteed to take away those tired aches and pains'.

Her father had offered to iron her party outfit for her. He had been in the merchant navy and claimed actually to enjoy ironing which, as Chris and her mother both hated it, was a good thing. They had a pretty good division of labour in their house, Chris thought. Her mother did the shopping on her way home from work – she finished at four – and most of the cooking. Chris vacuumed and dusted, and loved polishing woodwork, enjoying the rich gleam that emerged under her duster, and Dad ironed, washed up and took his turn cleaning the bathroom. She was always astonished to find that no similar system reigned in her friends' houses.

'Catch my dad helping with the chores?' Carol had said once. 'You must be joking! You might as well ask him to swim the Channel!' As Carol's father had a famous hatred of water and only ran about two inches of it into the bath, it made her point very well. In fact, if they weren't so bolshie on the subject of saxophones, and a little less concerned about what time she came in in the evenings, Chris reckoned she might just have ideal parents.

She was very grateful to her father for pressing her dress for the party. Chris didn't often wear dresses and skirts, except for work, as she didn't like revealing her legs.

'Don't be daft,' her mother would say impatiently, 'you've got a real model girl's figure. Many girls would give anything to be as slim as you.'

'I'm *not* slim, I'm skinny!' she raged defiantly. 'And I don't know why. I eat enough . . .' She had a good appetite, especially for her mother's puddings. It was a wonder she wasn't as overweight as her father. But then, he did drink rather a lot of beer.

The dress had been bought with some Christmas money from an aunt. It was blue and a bit fifties-looking, with a cinched-in waist and a swirly skirt. Chris loved it. Maybe Bruce Conroy would notice her in it.

Johnson lived in an apartment block and it sounded as though his wasn't the only party going on that night. Agitated dogs were barking as she and Carol walked briskly across the bare concourse to hide their nerves, clutching their bags tightly to them. Johnson's mother had been mugged there only three weeks back. The police had said that there was no hope of catching the culprit, who probably lived on the same estate. Though, as Chris's father had commented when she had told her parents about it, you could get mugged just as easily at your own front gate as you could in a slightly more dubious area like Johnson's.

'If they want it, they'll get it,' Mr Lindsell had declaimed, stubbing out a cigarette butt in the ashtray with the ring-pull of his drink can. 'That's why I've got plenty of insurance.'

There were lots of people Chris recognised, but no sign of Bruce Conroy. Little Jimmy, Johnson's brother – their father was Big Jimmy – appeared in front of Chris and Carol as they were discussing Bruce.

'What's he got that I ain't got?' he demanded cheekily, puffing his chest out and flexing his biceps, then making some rude gestures with his thirteen-year-old hips in time to the music.

'Plenty,' sniffed Carol scornfully. 'Buzz off, will you?' But Jimmy was persistent, although the top of his curls only just reached Carol's collar bone, and insisted on claiming her for a dance first.

Chris looked on in amusement, then got talking to one or two old school cronies about how everyone was doing.

'You still playing that horn of yours? I expected to see you around the clubs by now,' drawled Lee Tennant. Six feet four tall, he was dressed entirely in black apart from the striped Rasta cap he had taken to wearing.

'What about you and the drums?' was Chris's riposte. She was by no means the only aspiring – or failed – musician she knew. Everyone knew Lee had great ambitions for himself.

'I've been doing some sessions for a funk album, over at a studio in Westbourne Grove. You should come along. Do you like black music?' he asked, taking a long gulp from his lager can.

'Yeah. I can't say I know a lot about it, but I've heard some reggae and funk that I like.'

'Don't tell me you like Michael Jackson, please!' grimaced Lee, shaking his lager can to see how much was left. 'I'm sick of going round to girls' places and getting *Bad* and *Off The Wall* played to me all night. How they can like a guy who's had about five hundred facelifts, I just don't know.'

'It's OK, you're safe,' Chris assured him. 'Anyway, tell me about the band.'

'They're called Jalova. We've been together a few months now, played a few gigs, got a guy who's sort of managing us. That's the guy who runs the studio. He lets us record there when nobody else has booked it. We're putting together some demo tracks in the hope of getting somebody interested. Hey, wanna dance?'

He tugged Chris's hand and they both began to move to the beat.

Lee was an incredible dancer and Chris felt she must look stiff and wooden by comparison. Someone changed the tape and she became aware of a tenor sax cutting through the din of party noise.

'Hey, that's good,' she remarked to her partner. 'What is it?'

'You've never heard of Grover Washington before? Oh, my!' Lee wagged his head in remonstration. 'You do need some educating, don't you?'

'Grover Washington,' she repeated out loud, making a mental note. 'Who else ought I to listen to?'

He reeled off a list of names, most of which she forgot instantly. 'Slow down! I need to write these down. If I come to the studio, will you tell me again?'

'Sure. But I forgot, you're one of these boring people who works in the daytime, aren't you? We're at the studio most afternoons, though we often work through till two, three in the morning, whenever we drop.'

'Are you there tomorrow?' she enquired, wondering if there were any laws which stopped musicians recording on Sundays.

'Depends what happens tonight!' He grinned impishly.

Chris guessed he was trying it on with her. He was always trying it on with someone. She liked him a lot, but not in that way. How could any girl fancy someone who seemed to change his girlfriend every week? You'd never know where you stood with a boy like that, you'd worry every time you caught him glancing at another girl.

Fortunately, Gemma, whom she hadn't seen for three months, came over just then, dying for a chat, so Lee made a few cheeky remarks and left them to it. They talked for ages, then went and grabbed some bread and cheese before it all vanished.

Carol seemed to be getting off with a boy Chris hadn't seen before, a mate of Johnson's, she guessed. They were dancing draped all over one another. About an hour had passed and the place had filled up. Glancing round, Chris saw Lee in a close embrace with a fair-haired girl, and nudged Gemma.

'He's always at it!' Gemma commented knowingly.

'Trouble is, I need to ask him something. I don't like butting into the budding romance,' Chris complained.

However, Lee showed no signs of disengaging himself, so in the end Chris tapped him forcibly on the shoulder and made a very ostentatious throat-clearing noise.

Lee turned his head, laughing. 'Oh, it's you, Chris. I thought it was Helen's feller come to reclaim her,' he said.

'I only wanted to know where the studio was. I've got to go in a minute,' Chris told him. It was still early as parties went, but dancing in high heels had made her feet ache more, and she wasn't really in the mood for being chatted up even though there were a few spare guys.

'Look for a wall with a big mural on it. There's a blue door right by the woman on the motorbike. You can't miss it.'

Chris said she was sure she wouldn't. She said goodbye to Carol, who was still dancing with Grant, the guy she had met almost straight away and been with for the last three hours. Grant looked nice. Lucky Carol, Chris thought a bit enviously. She wished she could meet somebody who really interested and excited her. Where were they, all the potential Mr Rights?

Gemma said she would walk to the bus stop with her. 'Pity about Bruce,' she said.

'Mmm,' Chris replied absently.

'Do you think you'll get away anywhere this summer? A couple of girls from my course and I were thinking of going to Ibiza. Would you like to come?'

'*Sunshine*!' gasped Chris. 'What an amazing thought! The only trouble is, I'm saving all my cash up for a new saxophone. My teacher –' she said it with a flourish, proud to call Lester her teacher – 'says I really need one. The old one's falling to bits.'

'Wouldn't you rather have a fabulous, hunky, suntanned Spaniard with sexy eyes and great long eyelashes and –'

'Stop it – you've convinced me!' Chris said, grinning. They had arrived at the bus stop and Chris saw her last bus bowling down the street. 'I'll think about it. 'Bye!' she called as she got on.

She got a seat next to the window and closed her eyes, feeling tiredness wash over her. But her mind was spinning with images – faces, words, music. She hadn't drunk much, just two glasses of rather horrid white wine, but her impressions of the party were forming a pattern in her head, like a series of film stills accompanied by a funky rhythm and bursts of sentences in different voices . . . different keys. It was turning into a piece of rather weird music, she could hear it all in her head, hear sound effects on the saxophone, and percussion and synthesiser.

If only she knew how to orchestrate it and write it down properly. Perhaps Lester could teach her. But by then, she would have forgotten it. She tried to impress the ideas on her memory, but she knew she was tired and lacking in concentration. If only she had had a small tape recorder with her, though people would think it very odd if she suddenly started humming and squeaking into the microphone! She had read about one songwriter who managed to scribble a whole song idea on the back of a bus ticket. She hadn't even got her notebook with her. Lyrics and single notes were simple, though, compared to the complicated arrangement in her head. She would just have to see if she could remember it in the morning . . .

When she woke up next morning, she had forgotten all about having an amazing inspiration on the bus home from Johnson's party.

CHAPTER • 4 •

Some days are cut out to be super-ultra-mega days, only you never find out until the day is over and you can look back on all the events which took place.

Chris's day off started with a luxurious lie-in. Then she went over to see Linda for lunch. Linda had been her second-best friend at school, frequently becoming 'best' when Chris had a falling-out with Carol. However, Linda now had a seven-month-old baby girl called Danielle. Danielle's father was a boy with whom Linda had had a one-night stand at a party, when she was drunk.

'I could hardly ask him to marry me when we'd only known each other for five hours, could I?' she said afterwards. She had been hoping to stay on and take A-levels, but now she knew that to continue with that idea would be a laborious process involving one subject at a time, one evening class a week, because it wasn't fair to ask her mother to baby-sit all the time.

As soon as she had discovered she was pregnant, she had told everyone that she couldn't consider an abortion. Linda loved children, and had several younger brothers and sisters. There was scarcely room for her and the baby in the family's already crowded flat, but she had her name down on a list for a flat of her own and had been told she wouldn't have to wait long.

'I'll baby-sit for you if you ever want a night out,' Chris had offered. She loved Danielle, who was a chubby, gurgling bundle when visitors were around, although Linda had revealed that her daughter had a distinctly antisocial side to her, too, involving lots of screaming.

'Anyway, if I go out, I want to go out with you, Carol and Gemma, so it's no good if you're baby-sitting,' Linda had pointed out.

'I think Carol's going to be out of circulation for a while,' Chris said. Linda's eyes brightened. She loved hearing gossip about her old schoolfriends.

Chris told her all about Johnson's party and Lee's popularity and Carol meeting Grant.

'She rang me up yesterday and told me she was in love.'

'That's not like Carol,' Linda commented. 'It usually takes her *three* days to fall in love, not one. It *must* be serious!'

'Gemma's asked me to go on holiday with her . . . I don't think I can go, though.' Chris told her about the fund for the new saxophone.

Linda's face took on a faraway look. 'I wish I could go on holiday, even if I had to take Danielle. I think my summer's going to consist of one day in Brighton, unless Dad wins the pools . . . Anyway, what's wrong with you? Why didn't you meet anyone at the party?' she added, changing the subject. 'You haven't been out with anyone since Ian, have you?'

'No, but I've been kissed by Shane Wallace!' She proceeded to give Linda a lurid description of the garage incident.

'Do you think you'll die an old maid?' Linda giggled.

'Probably,' Chris said gloomily. 'Lester says I should practise the sax three hours a day. That doesn't leave time for boyfriends.'

'You *are* serious about it, aren't you? You always were, even at school. When are you actually going to do anything about it, like join a band?'

'Soon,' Chris promised her. 'I've decided to give it till Christmas and if I've got nowhere by then, I'll give up and let my parents' ear drums recover.'

'I can just see you in *NME* . . .'

'Oh, don't be stupid! I might get in a local band that no one's ever heard of, but I'll never be a star. I'm not good enough, and I'm not that sort of person –'

'Who says?' interrupted Linda.

Who indeed? thought Chris, as she made her way to the tube station. Only she herself. If she could just remove her self-made barrier of shyness . . .

Three o'clock, Lester had said. He had told her which room he was using for teaching. When she got there, there was a handwritten note Sellotaped to the door. *Two o'clock lesson cancelled. Gone home*, followed by his address.

Blast! She had come all the way into town on the train for nothing, when she could have stayed in her own area and gone five stops on the bus. Chris debated whether to go to his house or not. Maybe the note wasn't an invitation, merely an explanation of why he wasn't there. But if so, why should he have given his address? Unless it was for his *four* o'clock student . . . ?

Her sax was an annoying weight over her shoulder and she shifted it to a more comfortable position. As she walked back towards the station, a series of questions and one or two answers ran through her mind. Question: why hadn't he rung her? Answer: perhaps he had when she was round at Linda's. Question: why hadn't he gone for a coffee or a walk, then returned to the appointed place at three? Answer: maybe he could save an hour's rent on the room if he wasn't using it. Alternatively, perhaps he had just felt like going home, or maybe, with that lesson cancelled, he hadn't had to come into town at all. Oh, if only she had stayed at home and not gone to Linda's!

As she sat on the train, another question formed itself in her mind. Should she keep her appointment now? She was so late, maybe he wouldn't expect her. But curiosity won. She knew his road. It was one of the ones which skirted the park where they had first met. His house backed onto it. Boldly, she rang the bell, then was tempted to run away, dive down the pathway into the park before he came to the door. It was too late. Footsteps were approaching. Was it him or his wife? Was he even married? Perhaps he had children . . .

'Hello, Chris.' It was him. 'I wasn't sure if you'd see the note. That sticky tape's stick was going. I thought it might drop off the door. Come in. Mind out for Charlie,' Lester said as he ushered her in.

Charlie turned out to be a one-eyed, one-eared tabby tomcat – 'Named after Charlie Parker, but not nearly as tuneful,' explained Lester.

'Who's Charlie Parker?'

Lester's face took on an expression of utter incredulity as he led her into an untidy lounge which reminded her rather of her own bedroom as it had records and magazines scattered on the carpet. 'You've never heard of Charlie Parker? My dear girl, you need educating!'

Two hours and several coffees later, Chris felt considerably more educated. What was more, she hadn't played a note. Lester had taken her on a guided tour, via the stereo, of all his favourite jazz saxophonists. Chris still wasn't sure if she would ever get to like some of the more modern stuff, but there had been one album in particular which had completely taken her over as she listened to it. Lester had written down the details for her. *Kind of Blue*, featuring John Coltrane on tenor sax and Miles Davis on trumpet. It had been recorded in 1960, nine years before she was born. She had told Lester that.

'Good heavens, that makes me feel old! I was already a year older than you are, then.' He grinned ruefully. 'God, it makes me feel so old! What's it like to be seventeen, Chris? I can't remember!'

'It's not so hot,' she muttered. 'Nothing special. I feel in limbo-land. Roll on eighteen!'

To go from jazz to funky dance music in the space of one hour was actually not as difficult as Chris had feared. She found the large mural shortly after six, located the blue door next to the muscular, snarling, nine-foot-high woman biker, and rang the bell.

It was Lee who let her in. 'Great! I'm really glad you could make it. We're all here, bogged down in creativity. In fact, we're getting on so well that Don, the guy who owns the studio and is doing our engineering for us, has gone shopping. Come in . . . I see you've got your horn with you. Maybe I can persuade you to play something.'

Chris's heart sank as she followed Lee into a large, unfurnished room, in which everything was painted grey. Why did people keep asking her to play before she was ready for it? In a few months' time, maybe . . .

There were three other people in the room, two boys and a girl. 'We were just taking a break,' explained Lee.

'Yeah, one hour of recording and two hours' break, that's how we like to work,' chipped in one of the guys. Chris couldn't work out who played what, as the instruments were strewn around the floor haphazardly.

'That's Curtis, he plays guitar,' said Lee, indicating the young West Indian who had just spoken, who was wearing shades indoors and a black leather jacket.

'And who are *you*?' The speaker had hair so curly that it looked like a corn-coloured afro. Chris wasn't sure whether he was leering at her or just teasing. 'I'm Howie and I play bass.'

'And I'm Bonnie. I'm the singer, and I play a bit of percussion, too,' said the girl, and smiled at Chris. She had skin the colour of milky coffee. Chris thought how stunning she looked, with her thick cloud of dark hair.

'I hate to sound ignorant, but where is the recording done?' Chris asked a bit nervously.

Lee threw back his head and gave a snorting laugh. 'See that window?' He pointed to the far side of the room. 'The other side of there.' He slid heavily off the table. 'C'mon, I'll show you.' Taking Chris's hand, he led her back through the door by which she had just entered, across a vestibule decorated with posters of black bands, and through another door.

'Wow! Techno-land!' Chris whistled as her eyes took in banks of sliding levers, monitor speakers on the walls, things which looked like microphones on bendy stalks, like the desk lamp in her bedroom.

'It's only sixteen-track,' Lee told her, sounding apologetic.

'Looks more like a hundred and sixteen,' Chris observed admiringly. 'What does it all do?'

'You'll have to ask Donny when he gets back from picking up his dry-cleaning,' Lee said.

Chris started to giggle. The contrast between the technology before her eyes and something as mundane as dry-cleaning really tickled her.

Lee laughed too, reading her mind. 'Donny's dry-cleaning is serious stuff. No one's got more suits and jackets than he has. His laundry bills are so heavy, that's why he charges us so much to use the studio.'

'He owns it, does he?' Chris enquired. Her fingers were itching to move one of the levers down just a bit, but it would be no good if there was no sound coming through.

'Mm-hm. And a couple of clubs. I've played in them. This band's my third since leaving school.'

And I haven't even managed one, Chris thought despairingly.

'Here –' Lee flipped a lever and all at once Chris could hear quite plainly all that was being done and said in the other room. 'I've made the mikes live. Hey, Curtis –'

Lee had leaned forward and spoken into the microphone with the curly stem. Peering through the windowpane, which was made of very thick, obviously soundproof glass, Chris saw chunkily-built Curtis, who had been sprawled on the floor reading a music paper, look up.

'Grab that axe, man. Give me a few bars. I'm just showing Chris round the console.'

Grumbling, Curtis stood up and shambled towards a red guitar which was propped against the wall. He slung the wide, matching scarlet strap round his neck, played a couple of soft chords, then launched into a fast, rhythmic riff, his left hand sliding up and down the neck of the instrument, his right held like a claw around his pick.

'Keep it up – that's fine!' Lee called encouragingly. He

placed Chris's right hand over a line of identical sliders. 'Try that one,' he suggested.

Chris followed his instructions. The sound she was listening to changed. It split. Instead of one guitar, she was hearing two, then four, then so many that the individual notes were lost. She moved the lever back into a neutral position and, without Lee's guidance, tried another, and another.

'This is fun,' she said. 'Will I make a recording engineer?'

'Not until I can afford to pay one,' boomed a voice from behind them. Donny was back, his arms piled high with clothes in cleaners' wrappings. Chris leaped forward to catch two which were slipping from the skinny man's grasp. He *was* skinny. His face was only half the width of a normal face – 'He's the only man with three profiles,' Lee joked later – and exaggerated by a mournful-looking beard. His shoulders and hips were painfully narrow and even his feet, she noticed, were long and pointed like the feet on medieval paintings.

Donny placed his clothes across a chair. Half the polythene-wrapped heap promptly slid off to the floor.

'Leave them, leave them,' Donny said wearily. 'Let's get down to some serious music – and let's get some serious music seriously down.'

'Turn it up, don't turn it down, I'm the megawatt kid and I've come to town.' Curtis's spoken words were followed by a high-speed guitar run which took Chris's breath away.

'Who wound him up?' Lee groaned. 'He won't stop all night now. Donny's right. We should get back to work!'

'Shall I go?' Chris offered. She was worried about staying too long, in case Lee tried to continue what he had hoped had started at the party.

'If you like. Or stay. We don't mind. Or even play. Fancy some horn on 'Shoalin', Don?'

'Could do . . .'

Chris Lindsell's first appearance on vinyl was on the track 'Shoalin' on the LP Wave Hello *by London funk-rock band Jalova. The session took place on 8 June 1987.*

That was how Chris wrote it in her diary. Though Lee's band, even Donny, seemed far too relaxed and disorganised to see an album through to release. It stood about as much chance of appearing, in her opinion, as Donny did of getting his cleaning home without dropping any more of it. But she had played and been recorded. The laid-back atmosphere had cured her of any nerves, and Bonnie had given her wide-eyed, admiring encouragement. Chris enjoyed the experience so much that she lay awake half the night, unable to sleep, her fingers still twitching on an imaginary sax.

'Someone rang you. A man. He said his name was Lester.' Mrs Lindsell gave Chris a suspicious look. 'Who is he? A boyfriend? He didn't sound very young.'

Chris sighed deeply. It was Tuesday evening and she had just got in from work and certainly didn't need all this. It was great that Lester had phoned, but why couldn't her mother just give her the message and have done with it?

However, Mrs Lindsell ground remorselessly on in that complaining tone she used so often, which completely got on Chris's nerves.

'You didn't tell us you were seeing someone. You're very secretive lately, my girl, always in and out of the house and hardly ever saying where you're going. What are you up to?'

'Nothing!' Chris squared up to her mother defiantly.

'So who's this man then?'

'I told you. He's the saxophone teacher who I met in the park.'

'How do you know he's what he says he is? You shouldn't

go round talking to strange men. You don't know what might happen.'

'Oh, *Mum*!' Chris snorted exasperatedly. 'I'm seventeen, not seven! Men don't offer me sweeties any more. I make my own judgements about people. Anyway, I know he's on the level. I've seen his group playing and I've already had one lesson from him. He's brilliant.' She felt tempted to add, *so there!*, but having just plugged the bit about being seventeen and adult, she decided against the show of childish petulance.

Her mother frowned grimly. 'You didn't tell your father and me any of this –'

'Why should I?' Chris replied, feeling cool insolence creep into her voice. Shutting off, pretending she wasn't affected, was the only way she could deal with her mother when she was in this kind of mood, determined to have a go at her and find fault with everything.

'*Why should you*?' her mother echoed. 'Because we're your parents and we're responsible for you and we care about what happens to you –'

'And you love being nosy.' Chris was losing her own temper now. She could feel it going, taut threads snapping. In a second, the black cannonball of grudge and frustration and fury would be hurtling towards her mother. With a supreme effort, she held it back. 'Sorry,' she said.

'I should think so!' Her mother looked mollified by Chris's sullen apology. 'I've said my piece now. We can't stop you having saxophone lessons, but I'm entitled to my opinion. And your father and I would appreciate the courtesy of being kept in the picture, thank you. Now, do you want anything cooking?'

'No,' grunted Chris. She wasn't hungry. After the tremendous high that the recording session had left her on, a day's foot-wearying work at the store had left her feeling low and grumpy. Added to that, there were rumours going round that someone had seen the payslip of one of the salesmen in the Menswear department, and he was getting more money than the girls in Separates, for the same work. The union was to be informed, and the women staff were up in arms, wondering how widespread the practice was in their store.

So when she rang Lester back and he asked her if she would like to come round for a glass of wine and a proper lesson the following evening, she jumped at the invitation.

This time, with her nervousness gone, she was able to take a long, leisurely look round at her surroundings. His choice of a colour scheme in the lounge and hallway was neutral – beige, darker brown, a touch of peach in the curtains and lampshades. Where he really expressed himself, Chris decided, was in his choice of art and pottery, which had obviously been picked because he liked them, not as items of decor. Chris hated the kind of people who chose a picture for its colour scheme alone. She had an aunt like that. Furniture art.

He came in carrying two glasses of chilled white wine and caught her peering closely at a landscape. The foreground consisted of long grass of which every blade seemed to have been drawn separately and painstakingly.

'That's a Paul Bisson. It's one of my latest acquisitions. Once or twice a year I can't resist, and go mad in an art gallery or a print department. Of course, I can't fit them all on the walls at once. You should see what I've got in the attic!'

Chris gave a tiny, suppressed snigger. His last remark had sounded almost like an invitation to come up and view his etchings, as the old joke went.

'It must have taken the artist weeks to paint that,' Chris observed.

'He didn't paint it, it's an etching. Slightly different process, but just like you say, it must have taken ages. What's wrong? What's so funny?'

Chris had to fight not to burst out laughing. Etchings . . . he'd said it!

'Nothing,' she gasped when she had control of herself again. Lester looked quizzically at her as she perched herself primly on the edge of a green armchair. 'It's just . . . Do you know,' she said, appearing to change the subject but actually following her own train of thought, 'if you'd been closer to my age, I'd never have dared come here.'

Then it was her turn to wonder if she had said the wrong thing, as his brows drew together, But he said nothing and busied himself with taking his sax out of its case.

'Wine OK?' he asked.

'Mmm. Nice.' Her parents went in for very sweet wines and sherries, which she found a bit sickly. This was less sweet and a lot more pleasant.

'Good. Now, what were you saying on the telephone about some recording session?'

She told him about it, her face shining with animation.

'Looks like the big time might be coming faster than you'd expected,' he remarked, and she wondered if he was teasing her.

'Nonsense,' she replied, looking down at her saxophone which she had leaned against her knees.

'What if they ask you to join the band?'

'They wouldn't. I'm not good enough.'

'Don't keep putting yourself down, or you won't get anywhere. You'd be like the singer I knew once, who used to hide behind one of the stage monitors half the time. A bit stupid, really, because he wore a shiny silver jumpsuit and it was impossible to hide in that.'

Chris tried to picture Lester in a shiny silver jumpsuit, and failed. 'Did you ever wear anything outrageous on stage?' she wanted to know.

He cleared his throat. 'Er . . . I'm ashamed to admit it, but one band I was in, I used to wear skintight pink Spandex jeans, real spray-ons, a bright yellow T-shirt with red glittery stars on it, and a hat.'

His lips were compressed, his eyes sparkling as he awaited the obvious next question.

'What kind of a hat?'

'A top hat. A big black one.'

Chris burst out laughing. 'I . . . I don't believe it. *You*?'

'I can show you some pics if you like . . .'

'OK,' she accepted eagerly. What *had* Lester looked like when he was young? Spandex and red glittery stars? She would never be able to keep a straight face!

'It'll take me a while to find them. Tell you what, you start on your scales, thirds and fourths while I'm out of the room.'

Her exercises were almost finished by the time he came back, carrying a battered brown suitcase.

'You asked for it,' he warned her.

She laid down her instrument carefully. He knelt on the carpet and opened the case. As he bent his head to rummage in the packet-filled interior, Chris noticed that the hair on his crown was still thick, unlike her father, who had a patch of shiny scalp with strands of hair laid carefully across it. It was very thick hair, the top layer such a pure silver in colour that it almost didn't look like hair at all. In the dimness of the twilit lounge, it looked a kind of misty blue.

Lester started grinning to himself. 'Here, how about this?' He handed her a glossy black and white ten-by-eight photo of a line-up of musicians, all wearing shoes with high stacked soles, extremely flared jeans and scruffy T-shirts. There were six of them, all sporting long hair and beards.

Chris stared at the one holding the saxophone. 'That's never you?' she exclaimed doubtfully. His hair and beard were jet black, but the lean build was the same. How come Lester, unlike most older people, hadn't put on loads of weight?

'I'm afraid it is. But there's a better one here. This went on one of our album covers.'

Chris found herself wondering yet again why she had never heard of him, if he had been that famous and had made so many records. It had to be because, quite simply, he was from a different musical generation, and by the time she had started listening to pop and rock, he had moved on to jazz. After all, her parents often talked about 'stars' she had never heard of.

She took the proffered picture and hooted with glee. Dark hair way past the shoulders, but clean-shaven this time, sitting on a tree branch with a cheeky grin. Four other guys were similarly perched, and a girl wearing a short satin nightdress was lounging against the tree trunk. He really had been pretty good-looking then, she admitted. *The Chestnut Valley Band*, it said beneath the photo, and in the bottom right-hand corner was a record-company logo and a date, 1973. She had been four, then!

'I can't seem to find the really crazy ones right now. I need to have a proper sort-out. Here's one taken live on stage, though,' Lester said, handing her a page from a glossy music magazine. The colour photograph was quite clear, and she spotted Lester on the right of the stage, nearest the camera, leaning slightly backward, holding the sax almost horizontally in front of him.

'I wish I'd seen you in those days,' Chris said, feeling slightly sad.

'I think you might have enjoyed it. I'll play you a few records one of these days. Now, I think we ought to be getting on with this lesson,' Lester said firmly, but at that moment the telephone rang out in the hall.

After he had gone out to answer it, Chris got up and strolled around the room. It had grown quite dark and she put the main light on, then snapped on one of the table lamps, the one on the small table by the sofa. French windows led onto a long, quite narrow garden which ended in a fence, beyond which was the park.

There were some shelves to the left of the French windows, containing books and pieces of glass and pottery. Some framed photographs were scattered among them. Chris paused. She could still hear Lester talking, although she couldn't make out many of the words. She caught something about a van and sound checks, so no doubt he was fixing up another booking.

Sure she was safe for a short while longer, she began to examine the pictures, convinced she would discover some of Lester's secrets. Her curiosity was fired by one of Lester standing with some mountains in the background, his arm around the waist of a pretty blonde woman. She was leaning her head on his shoulder and they were both smiling at the photographer. Chris stood on tiptoe for a closer look – the photographs were on quite a high shelf – and yes, that definitely looked like a wedding ring on the woman's finger.

There was another photo of two young boys of about nine and seven, by her reckoning, though she wasn't much good at guessing ages. When her auntie Susan had asked Chris once how old she thought she was, Chris had grossly insulted her relative by saying, quite positively, 'Forty-five,' when poor Susan was a whole ten years younger. Chris's parents – Susan was her father's sister – had laughed and joked about it for months.

There was one picture of a different woman, younger than the blonde, dark-haired, with unruly curls. She was lying on a towel on a beach, dressed in a bright red one-piece swimsuit. She had just decided that the blonde was his wife and the dark girl his sister, when she heard approaching footsteps and sprang guiltily away from the shelf and was staring fixedly at her manuscript book when Lester came back.

He was a good teacher, no doubt about that. He mingled praise in with his criticisms, always finding little boosts to make her feel better after he had savaged her *embouchure* or her creaky lower notes.

When they paused, over an hour later, Lester told her, 'If you didn't have talent, I'd tell you now so that you wouldn't waste your money on lessons. But you've got something special, girl. You've got a better than average grasp of harmony and counterpoint, your sense of rhythm's excellent, your tone is coming along well. But there's something more. I'm sure you will be able to compose. You've got a creative spark. You're a different person once you start playing; you light up.'

Chris stared at him in embarrassed amazement. From someone who was as experienced and talented as he was, these words were praise indeed.

'When I first saw you that day in the park, I thought, what a solemn little thing. You were so self-contained, so held in, somehow. But now, seeing you play, I can see you putting your spirit into it, your essence. You come alive with that saxophone. Damn it, girl – you're very, very good, and I'm going to try and make you even better. *You wanna be a star*?' He put on a mock American accent and Chris laughed, glad about the lightening of the atmosphere. She didn't think she could take any more compliments. She wasn't sure if she believed them. How much wine had he drunk?

'Have you got time to have three lessons a week? I usually charge ten, even twelve quid an hour, according to how rich I think my pupils are –'

'Thirty pounds a week?' squeaked Chris. It was impossible. Her good mood began to evaporate.

'I don't really want to charge you at all, but I can tell that you've got a lot of pride and wouldn't take anything for nothing –'

'Right!' Chris chipped in. She would feel most awkward about accepting free tuition. It would, in an odd way, put her in his power and she didn't like the feeling that at any time in the future, he could call in the debt, ask her to do something for him in return. She didn't know him very well yet, she realised, and suddenly felt a twinge of nervousness about being alone in a house with him – a nervousness which was quickly dispelled when he said, 'Seven pounds a lesson and each third one free. How does that sound?'

It sounded extremely reasonable, and put them back on an official footing, which she liked. He was her teacher, not a would-be friend forcing her to accept charity. Maybe in time he would become a real friend, but that needed time to grow. Chris had always been suspicious of instant friendship. There had been too much of it all through school, people trying to be your best buddy the day they met you, then running out on you for someone else three weeks later.

Yet, she thought, she could do with more friends. Or one special one . . . She would need it if she ever became a real star. Which was highly unlikely, of course.

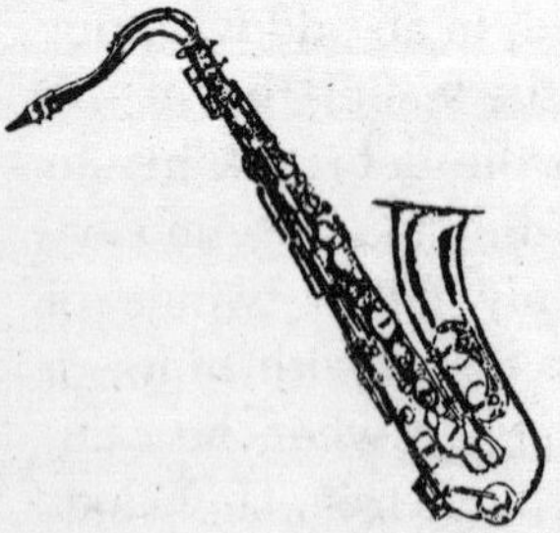

CHAPTER • 5 •

'You've got natural musical talent, my girl. Why are you throwing it away on this awful rowdy pop stuff when you could be playing proper, decent music?'

Chris glared at her father. It was two weeks since Lester's order for practice, practice and more practice, and never had she been up against such opposition.

'It's driving me and your mother mad, all those squeaks and honks on that wretched saxophone. Why don't you sell it and play the piano or the flute again? That would be a pleasure to listen to.'

'I'm not doing it for you to listen to!' she shouted passionately. 'Why don't you just switch the telly up louder?'

'The people in the top flat next door can't hear their television as it is, when you're playing. It's driving them distracted. Your mother and I have been getting complaints from Mrs Levy.'

Mrs Levy was the landlady from next door, who lived in the basement flat. Several of the houses in the street were divided up into flats, and Chris had often thought how lucky her family were to have a whole house to themselves, especially as there weren't many of them. She had had a brother, John, who had died when he was four. Chris had been six then. Nobody ever spoke about John now. It was as if he had become an unacceptable part of the past. There were many times when Chris would have liked to bring up the subject of her brother, but she was worried about upsetting her mother. She realised that it partly explained why they were so picky and exacting with her. She knew she had let them down academically, but she didn't need a college education to play music. There had been a time when she had toyed with the idea of applying for music college, but when she had thought about it seriously, she had realised that a formal, structured music course would kill both her enjoyment and her creativity. She wanted to play like an individual, in her own style, not as a member of an orchestra, playing every note as it was written. She wanted to play what was in her own head.

She was fighting for the right to achieve her own goals now, and she wasn't going to give in. The worst they could do would be to throw her out of the house, and she was mentally prepared for that. In fact, if they took the initiative, it would be far easier for her than to have to say goodbye and leave.

But her parents didn't throw her out, they just went on nagging and needling her, and it was really getting her down.

'Did you ever have problems like mine with *your* parents?' she asked Syl Roche at work. Syl was twenty-three, shared a flat with two girls and a guy, and was engaged to Eddie, who was working out in the Middle East on an engineering project. They were to be married when he next came back.

'Not exactly the same, but I did have fights with them. It was about boys in my case, not musical instruments. They never liked anyone I went out with, thought they were all unsuitable in some way. So I ended up leading a double life, pretending I was going to see a girlfriend, then meeting the latest flame round the corner.' Plump, pretty Syl giggled.

'Then someone told me of the room going in the flat. That was four years ago. It's been fine. We all get on well, and –'

While Syl had been talking, an idea had been forming in Chris's head. Syl and Eddie were getting married and she was going back to Dubai with him. That meant . . . 'Who's going to be taking over your room when you go?' she asked.

Syl gave Chris a direct look, then bit her lip. 'Er . . . if you're thinking what I think you're thinking, then no,' she said, rather awkwardly. 'It's not that I don't like you, or think you wouldn't mix in, Chris, it's –'

'It's the saxophone, isn't it? The bloody saxophone!' There was a lump of frustration and pent-up exasperation in her throat. What did other musicians do? Maybe Lester would know.

The lessons he was giving her were brilliant. Chris felt she had never learned so much so quickly. If *only* she were able to practise more! Some of her lessons took place in the rehearsal room and some at his house. She always preferred going to his house. She felt more relaxed there and it was less formal, even if they seemed to spend more time chatting and listening to records and looking at more of Lester's old photographs than they did working.

She went to hear Soundwaves play again. This time it was a Saturday-night concert at a large polytechnic. She was interested to see that a guitarist was incorporated in the line-up this time and when she asked Lester about it, he replied that Ricky, the guitarist, was a regular member of the band but had been ill on that first Sunday Chris had visited the Haycart.

She felt proud to know the band, and Lester in particular, when, after the gig, an eager crowd of music fans sought them out to praise their music and ask questions.

One bloke, who was doing an interview for the college magazine, asked Lester earnestly, 'Would you say that your music was an experimental synthesis of modern jazz and power rock?'

Lester looked amused. 'I don't know,' he responded. 'I just call it music.' He winked at Chris, who grinned.

She overheard a girl ask Marijke, 'Are you married to Lester?'

'Oh, no – he's never even asked me out!' Marijke gave a peal of laughter, then confided, 'Actually, Steve is my boyfriend.' Steve was the bass player. That answered one question which had puzzled Chris, and yet she was still puzzled. Surely Lester must have some relationship in his life? After all, he was good-looking and in good shape, and musicians normally had followers who chatted them up. What about the women in the photographs? She felt sure one of them must be his wife – and yet there were no signs of a woman around the house. Perhaps he was divorced. She hardly knew him well enough to start asking him about his private life, even though she was desperately curious. She would just have to wait for the information to surface in its own good time.

She hadn't seen Lee for a couple of weeks. He had come into the store one day and told her that they had been unable to rehearse or record for a while as another band had booked the studio. Then one evening he rang and said the other band had finished, and would she like to come down and add some sax to another track? Chris went gladly. She was particularly happy to see Bonnie again. She liked the vivacious singer, with her wild clothes and irrepressible sense of humour and her unusual voice, which went from deep contralto to highest soprano. Bonnie told Chris that lots of people had likened her to Linda Lewis, who also had an incredible vocal range. Chris said she had never heard Linda Lewis, so Bonnie promised to lend her a tape. She also confided that she and Curtis had just started a passionate romance, and none of the others knew yet!

On her second meeting with Lee's band, she felt far more at home with them. She had been a bit fazed by Curtis's cool, tough image and the freakishly skinny Donny, but this time she found herself chattering unrestrainedly with them, and swopping wisecracks. Everyone put themselves out to be friendly except Howie. Chris didn't know what to make of him. He seemed very quiet, in a world of his own.

Donny played the tape of the track they were thinking of putting sax onto, then Chris tried out a few things until she felt she had got it right. Then they did a 'take' and Chris was fascinated to hear how Donny had altered the sound levels and even put on a bit of reverb in places, so that her playing sounded entirely different, and blended in perfectly with the rest of the music.

'Would you like to play a gig with us some time?' Lee asked. 'Just come on stage and play for one or two numbers, the ones you've recorded on? We'd far rather have you than some session player we don't know.'

'Well, I . . .' That day when Lester had invited her to play with Soundwaves, she had never felt more terrified. They had been much older and more professional than her, and sounded so together. But Lee's lot were different. She had known Lee for years at school, they messed around and had fun with their music and she felt she genuinely had something to offer their sound. 'OK,' she heard herself saying. She felt quite excited. If she were ever to join a band, this way was far better than having to pass a formal audition.

Her chance came the following Friday. Jalova had been booked to play in a club. They weren't due on stage till eleven at night and Chris had trouble with her parents who reckoned they knew all about the sort of dark and dreadful things that happened in clubs late at night.

'Look, I'll be eighteen in August,' she reminded them. 'Old enough to vote. I'll be an official adult. And anyway,' she added, 'if I was living away from home, you wouldn't know what I was doing, or what time I got in at night.'

'Maybe it would be better for all our sakes if you did,' muttered her mother darkly.

'Did what?' Chris asked sharply.

'Lived away from home.' Her mother jerked her square chin up and looked her daughter straight in the eye. 'It might make you nicer and more civil to talk to. You're nothing but a grouch lately, not a good word to say about anything, particularly us. You're all moans. If you're so keen to leave home, then the sooner you do it, the better, as far as I'm concerned. At least we wouldn't have to listen to that ruddy saxophone any more! That'd be a blessing.'

Chris felt as if she had gone up too fast in a lift and left her stomach behind. She couldn't believe her mother meant it. So much for imagining herself mentally prepared! Despite all the occasions on which she had longed for freedom from nagging, freedom to play without hindrance, she now felt like a fledgling which was being pushed out of the nest before it felt quite ready to fly. Yet, in spite of her pain, a hot anger was flickering inside her.

'OK, I will!' she spat defiantly, and was pleased to see her mother flinch slightly, though she soon recovered her own hard, challenging look. 'Just as soon as I find a place. And don't think I won't be glad to see the back of this house with all its stupid restrictions. Oh, and another thing,' she hurled over her shoulder as she held the front door open, preparing to stamp out, 'don't expect me back at any particular time tonight. We might go on somewhere after.'

Mrs Lindsell muttered something which Chris didn't quite catch, but she didn't turn round before slamming the door as hard as she could.

She was still full of anger and fire when it was time to go on stage. With hardly a twitch of nerves, she strode to the microphone, waited for her cue, then blew out a compressed, furious stream of air and was pleased to hear the edgy, cutting sound she made. She had been practising with a harder reed than usual, a three instead of her normal two-and-a-half; and it produced a significantly firmer sound. Lester had shown her how to cut and smooth the reeds to suit her lips, and that was another bonus.

She noted the glances she was getting from the other band members. Good! They had expected her to curl up and die of nerves and instead she was smouldering with fiery energy.

Then she went for a high note and cracked on it and felt terrible, but everyone else went on playing around her and, after a quick nerve attack, which was like vertigo and left her legs feeling wobbly, she recovered her composure and carried on playing.

It's not so bad, she thought as she improvised. Playing live's really good. I can see people looking at me, moving to the rhythm, enjoying themselves. A guy in the packed audience smiled at her and she responded, facing his way, playing a few bars just for him. It was as if she were catching energy from the audience, processing it through her music and throwing it back at them. What was that expression she had heard in biology at school? 'A symbiotic relationship' – where two organisms lived as one, each doing the other some good, feeding it, helping it. A musician and an audience were a bit like that.

Bonnie started singing. That was when Chris wished, just for a moment, that she played the higher horn, the alto sax, then she could have better mimicked Bonnie's voice, playing musical lines behind her.

After the number was over, while the clapping was still going on, Chris walked off the tiny stage, back to the cramped backstage area. She was dripping with sweat, her hair was wringing wet, and it wasn't just from the heat in the basement club, but from nervous tension, effort and adrenalin. Unlike a lot of her contemporaries, she had never tried drugs, she had never seen the point of experimenting simply for experimentation's sake. But the only word she could find to describe how she was feeling was high.

She had to wait out a couple of numbers before she was due on stage to play again. She spent some of it sitting in the dingy dressing room, where she could hear the music coming through the wall in a muffled fashion. Then, carrying her sax so that it wouldn't get stolen, she went back through the door and lingered at the side of the stage, from where she could watch both the band and her very first audience.

There seemed to be an awful lot of them and they obviously loved music. Some had found a space and were dancing. A cluster of guys hung round the bar at the back. There were lots of couples, and though the average age seemed to be about twenty-five, there were some people who looked well into their thirties, or even older. She tried to imagine Lester there, but found she couldn't. It wasn't his kind of scene. She could imagine him turning his nose up at reggae, funk or soca. The thought of his possible disapproval both irritated and dismayed her. She wanted him to like what she was doing. It would be awful if he decided not to teach her any more simply because he didn't like the kind of music she was playing. It was stupid. As he had said himself, music was music. But she knew how snobbish some people could be about it. Her uncle would only listen to Beethoven and Mozart and thought anything else was rubbish, even other classical music.

The number was coming to a close. It was time she went back on again. The thought gave her a jolting thrill, like an injection of fear and excitement mixed. She wanted to shine: She wanted people to go home that night remembering her, thinking how good she was. But *was* she good? Was she any good at all?

Suddenly, it was difficult to breathe. Her palms felt clammy as Curtis introduced the number and when she lifted the sax to her lips, she found that her hands were shaking.

As she blew her first notes, the sound that emerged was thin and reedy, not at all what she wanted to play. She sounded just like a beginner. She was standing next to Howie and saw him scowl.

Pull yourself together! she admonished herself fiercely. But her heart was pounding almost as loudly as Lee's drumbeat and she felt sick and drained of all her earlier energy. She just wanted to run off the stage and hide from this sea of alien faces who were just waiting for her to falter and break down.

She took a deep, ragged breath and tried to pitch her thoughts far away. She was on a distant beach, standing on the sand, facing the sea. It was dawn. A golden sun was lifting itself over the horizon and a cooling breeze was blowing off the water. There was nobody there, not even a bird. Nobody to hear her play, so she could make the instrument ring and wail and scream, as loud as she liked. Then she blew, and her fantasy had worked. The sound was clear, strong, OK. She felt the audience was relieved, too. And the old symbiosis started working again, the energy flowing. She had them – they were with her, following every note. She felt uplifted . . . supreme. She could do anything in the world with that power. Anything.

'That was great, Chrisso. Really good.' Lee gave her a hug. He often called her Chrisso and she quite liked it.

'Yeah. You must play some more with us,' said Howie, grinning for once.

Bonnie gave her slightly shy smile, her eyes dancing. 'Why don't we ask Chris to join us properly?' she put to the others.

Lester must be psychic, Chris thought wryly. What would she do if some band asked her to join them, he had enquired, and she had never replied, because the truth was that she didn't know. Now, though, she was being forced to come up with an answer.

Something blindingly obvious occurred to her. 'I've got a full-time job, I wouldn't be able to rehearse as often as you.'

'Oh yeah, of course . . .' Bonnie's face fell. 'I'd have liked another girl in the band, too, for moral support against this lot.' She winked at Curtis.

'I'd have liked you in it as well. We'll have to find a way round it,' Lee said, sneaking his arm around her waist again. Chris pushed him away. It was far too hot and sticky to be that physically close to someone. Besides, she had a pretty good idea that he still had the hots for her.

Curtis snapped his guitar case shut. He had stripped to the waist and had a towel draped round his shoulders.

'Maybe you could carry on just playing on some of the numbers, not all of them. Learn a different one every week, make two or three rehearsals,' he suggested.

'Just . . . just let me think about it for a bit,' Chris said, suddenly feeling her euphoria deserting her and weariness creeping in in its place. She had done a day's work before this, after all, and it was now past one a.m.

'Take as long as you want, so long as it's not more than twenty-four hours.' Lee grinned. 'OK?'

'What say we go to that all-night Chinese in town and then go back to my place for a jam?' suggested Howie.

Chris's heart sank. She had been relying on them and their van for a lift home. After all, as long as she wasn't a member she wasn't getting any money for playing.

'I hate to be a spoilsport, but I'm shattered. I need to get home, but I haven't got enough for a cab. I'm sorry to be a party pooper.' She shook her head and glanced appealingly at them. They all looked at one another, then started digging in their pockets, one after the other. Lee donated three pounds, Bonnie one, plus an apology, and Howie and Curtis came up with two pounds each.

'It'll have to be one packet of fish and chips between four of us now. Good job Don isn't here,' Howie grumbled, handing her his contribution.

'Don't make me feel worse. I feel guilty enough as it is,' remarked Chris. She was so tired, she could have cried.

Lee gave her shoulder a squeeze and for once she was glad. 'Don't worry about it,' he told her sympathetically. 'You were fantastic tonight, especially as it was the first time you'd ever played in public. You should have seen me the night *I* first played. I couldn't get off the toilet. The others had to come and –'

'Spare us the details,' Curtis said dryly. 'Go and ring a minicab for the girl.'

Fifteen minutes later, Chris was nodding on the back seat, her instrument case beside her, as the cab sped through the night. She didn't notice if anyone had waited up for her, as she went through the hall and up the staircase, following the familiar route with her eyes tight closed . . .

Chris's days off became Linda and Lester days. Lester sometimes had rehearsals himself in the afternoons, or else had to set out early to play a gig, so she went over to his house at elevenish, then arrived at Linda's in time for lunch with her and Danielle.

The day after the gig, a Saturday, just as she was about to leave, there was a ring at the doorbell and when she went to answer, she found Bonnie and Curtis standing there.

'I've brought you that tape at last,' Bonnie said.

'And we were wondering if you'd had time to think since last night about joining the band,' Curtis chipped in.

Chris glanced at the tape. It had Linda Lewis on one side and David Sanborn on the other. Lester had mentioned David Sanborn as a saxophonist she must listen to, but she hadn't got round to buying a tape yet. Bonnie had to be psychic!

'That's really good of you. Thanks,' she said. The two of them were gazing expectantly at her. Her innards gave a little lurch, as if she had temporarily lost her balance. She was in confusion. She had always wanted to be part of a band and here were two people who were fast becoming friends of hers, offering her a golden opportunity. Surely she shouldn't have to think twice? Yet she was doing, and she thought it had something to do with the style of music they were playing. Funk was fun, but she wanted something freer, something a bit more melodic, rather than just punching out riffs. Yet maybe she ought to play with them a bit, for practice, if nothing else.

'I can't really stop and discuss it now, I'm afraid. I've got a lesson and I'm a bit late as it is. Can I . . . could I let you know later? Ring you at the studio or something?'

'We're having a day off, but you could ring Lee,' Curtis suggested.

'OK. Sorry I can't ask you in. Are you walking towards the High Road?' asked Chris.

'We're in Curtis's car. Can we drop you off?' Bonnie grinned.

'Would you like to meet him?' Chris asked, when they got to Lester's. 'Just say hello. I'm sure he'd like to be able to fit faces to the names I've been telling him about.'

Lester went one step further and invited them in for coffee. When they had gone, she told him about their offer and asked his advice.

'What do *you* want to do?' He turned the question back onto her.

'*I* don't know! That's why I'm asking you. Would it be good experience? Would it do my playing any good?'

'It would certainly improve your nerves and your stage presence, and the experience of playing with other people would be invaluable. I think you should do it, just for a while. Now, you said you were having trouble with one of your pads. Let's have a look at it.' He took the gleaming brass instrument from her and turned it over in his hands. 'It looks as if you've sprayed it with Mr Sheen,' he commented amusedly.

Chris bit nervously at a fingernail. 'I have . . .'

'You'd be better off polishing the family silver than working on this piece of tin. They don't need it, anyway. A rub-down with a soft cloth will do. But you really must get a better instrument than this old horn. It was never much cop to start with, and it's more than had its day. Here . . . try mine.'

Chris gently accepted the saxophone from him, with an awed feeling of receiving a great honour.

'Go on, go on, you won't break it. It's not the only one I've got. Have a go,' he urged, smiling kindly at her trepidation.

She bobbed her head through the broad neckstrap, then placed her lips around the mouthpiece and tentatively, soundlessly, fingered the keys. She had been attempting – and failing – to learn Raphael Ravenscroft's 'Baker Street' solo and now she played the first four bars, not quite getting the required sleazy, slidey sound, but she had to admit it, the instrument was not only easier to play than hers, but had a more vibrant tone. She liked it a lot. She twisted it in her hands until she found the name stamped on it: Yamaha.

'Are they expensive?'

'Quality doesn't come cheap. This and my old Selmer Mark 6 – that's the one I played when you saw me at the Haycart – are my favourites. The Selmer's the perfect jazz machine. Lots of the old jazz geniuses played them. But I like the Yamaha for certain numbers, and for rock. It's all down to personal preference, really. You'll soon pick it up.'

'I wish I could pick one of these up – preferably for twenty quid off an eccentric millionaire who'd decided to take up croquet instead.' Chris unstrapped herself and handed it back to him. 'I really am going to start saving. Money from gigs would come in useful.' She remembered she owed money from the previous night, and felt bad that she hadn't mentioned it to Bonnie and Curtis.

'Tell you what,' Lester said. 'Take my sax again and just run through those bars you played before. When you get to the end, I want you to hold onto the last note for as long as you can, OK?'

'Got it.' She took the Yamaha and began playing. As she held onto the last note, she had the feeling he was counting. When she felt she was running out of breath, she collapsed into giggles.

'How did I do?'

'Sixteen seconds. Room for improvement. You really must practise a lot of long notes, because they'll improve your tone. You need to work on that, Chris. Think about each note. Is it a high one, a middle, or a low? They each need producing differently. Try this . . . Think of the word *he* when you're pitching those top notes. Then *who* for the middle ones, and finally, *ho* for the bottom ones.'

This way of thinking about her music was new to her and she took to it eagerly, suddenly realising, with a shock, that she was late for Linda's.

'Doing anything tonight?' Lester asked casually, as she was struggling to get her arm through the sleeve of her denim jacket. 'If you're not, come along with us. We've got a gig at the 100 Club in Oxford Street. You might enjoy it.'

Chris felt a happy glow. It was a privilege to be invited along as his guest. Was he taking anyone else, she wondered?

'I'm going by car. I'll pick you up at nine, if you give me your address.'

She gave it and it wasn't until she was halfway to Linda's that she wondered if staying out late two nights running was likely to cause ructions at home . . .

CHAPTER • 6 •

The answer was so simple that she was surprised she hadn't thought of it before. She would ask Carol to come with her. She had only seen Carol once since Johnson's party. Ever since, her friend had been completely wrapped up in her new romance with Grant, the boy she had got off with at the party. They were together practically every night. Carol tended to be like that, Chris had found; cutting herself off from her friends while she was embroiled in the first throes of a new relationship, then gradually looking up her old mates again once the heat of love had cooled from 'boil' to 'simmer'.

Her parents liked Carol. If they knew they were together, they weren't so likely to object to Chris getting home late as they would realise that they could get a cab together. No need to tell them about Grant going, too . . .

Having rung Lester to check that it was OK to bring two friends along, she then rang Carol. Luckily, Grant liked jazz. Carol herself wasn't so sure, but when Chris reminded her that she was only just getting into it herself, Carol said she was sure she would like some of it.

'All I'm really coming for is a chance to meet your new boyfriend,' Carol teased.

'He's not my boyfriend,' Chris proclaimed hotly. 'He's old enough to be my dad!'

Carol made a rude snorting noise down the phone. 'What difference does that make? There are plenty of men who are about thirty years older than their wives. My uncle Dan's just married for the second time, and he's in his fifties and she's only twenty-four.'

'I've heard you call him "Dan, Dan, the dirty old man",' Chris reminded her.

'There's nothing dirty about true love,' said Carol dreamily.

'OK, I'll see you and lover-boy later. Your names will be on the door.'

'I'm off to meet Carol now,' Chris announced shortly after eight thirty. She was going to have to lurk in the street and intercept Lester's car. She couldn't risk her parents being rude to him. Her mother acted as if she detested the very sound of his name and held him personally responsible for Chris's saxophone assaults on her eardrums. She would be certain to say something caustic and insulting. No, it was best to keep them well apart, even if it meant a long cold wait in the street.

As she hung around about six doors down, a little cat stepped briskly out of the shadows and rubbed itself against her ankles and she was so absorbed in stroking it that she almost didn't look up when the car came slowly up the road, the driver peering at the house numbers. She straightened up and waved frantically and he hooted the horn, making Chris hold her breath in case her front-room curtains twitched. She shot into the passenger seat and closed the door. Lester glanced at her amusedly.

'Am I late?' he enquired.

'No. I'd . . . been out for a walk and was just on my way back to wait for you.' She thought how lucky she was to have recognised his car. She had seen it parked in the driveway of his house, a silver hatchback, ideal for carrying instruments. There were two sax cases in the back now, and a pile of sheet music.

As they drove into the city, Chris felt as if he were taking her on a date. A proper date, to go and have a meal in a posh restaurant. There'd be low lights, candles on the tables, and the waiters wouldn't bother them, just silently bring the food and disappear. They'd talk about each other, and she would have her hand resting on the tablecloth as she talked, and all of a sudden he would place his hand over it and she would know that this was just the beginning of the bonding between them.

'I was wondering how you felt about playing with us tonight? Just on one number? Just a few fill-ins? That number we've been practising . . .'

He had dragged her out of her daring fantasy so abruptly that she gave a little jump. 'I – I don't know,' she stammered. 'I'll see how I feel.' It was the Jalova situation all over again, but with a difference. The two bands belonged to different musical cultures and she wasn't sure if she was capable of spanning them.

She glanced at him but he was staring straight ahead, concentrating on driving. He had a very good profile, she thought. Though his eyes were a bit crow's-footy at the corners and the smile lines dug rather deeply into his cheeks, in the gloom of the car's interior, his silver hair darkened by shadow, he looked at least ten years younger. If he were thirty-six, that would make him only eighteen and a bit years older than her, which didn't sound nearly so bad as twenty-eight!

As they sat separated by their seats and seatbelts, Chris

thought how separate they really were as people. She wished she could build a bridge between them and walk across it into his life. Who was he? He couldn't have been that famous in the sixties and early seventies, because he certainly wasn't a household name now, and he didn't live like a star. Yet, even in her few brief years of following pop groups, she had seen how quickly some of them came and went. And so often you only really identified with the singer and the lead guitarist, and hardly noticed the rest of the band. Lester had obviously been in the 'rest of' category. Often, people could have written loads of hit songs, too, yet their names still didn't ring a bell. She had read about some guy in the *New Musical Express*, a millionaire, the article said, who had made his money composing advertising jingles and hit songs. Yet she had never heard of him, though he was obviously very highly thought of by other musicians and the music business.

Lester must fit into this category, she decided. Maybe he had had a big fan following because of the band he had been in years ago, but now he was one of those behind-scenes people. He had obviously had some success in the past because once, when she had been having a lesson at his house, she had visited the bathroom and passed along a landing, on one wall of which hung three framed gold discs with his name on. She knew you could buy joke gold discs, but Lester wasn't the type go in for gimmicks. What had he done with his money, then? Booze? Drugs? Or had he simply spent it all, which was why he was reduced to giving lessons now? It was so frustrating not to be able to find out.

They reached the club and Chris soon found Carol and Grant. It was a muggy July night, the underground room was packed out and suffocatingly hot and a solo guitarist was on stage, playing some rags which had originally been composed for piano. His agile fingers danced so rapidly up and down the fingerboard that at times his movements were blurred. Would it be possible to adapt the tunes for the sax . . .?

'Fantastic, isn't he?' commented a boy standing next to her.

'Yeah, great!' Chris agreed, glancing absently at him and noting the great, dark patches of sweat around the armholes of his green T-shirt. The heat was almost unbearable. Even though Chris's hair was short, she could feel it sticking to her forehead and the back of her neck. She was glad she had worn black. How on earth did musicians manage to play in such hot, wet conditions? The club where she had played with Jalova hadn't been this hot. It was just as well that saxophones couldn't go rusty! At least, she hoped they couldn't.

In the break before Soundwaves came on, Grant battled to the bar to get them all a drink and the boy who had spoken to Chris kept up the conversation. Carol stood by listening, occasionally giving Chris a surreptitious wink or a dig.

'Are you a jazz fan?' he asked.

'I like rock, too,' she answered cautiously, not wishing to classify herself as a fan of either type of music.

'Have you heard Soundwaves before? I think they're amazing. That Lester Mulley can really play. He's one of Britain's best session tenor players. I've got eight albums with him on. All the band are good, but he's something special.'

'Yes,' Chris agreed thoughtfully. 'He is very good. He's my sax teacher, actually.'

'He's what?' The boy gazed at her in utter incredulity, as if she had just announced that she was Princess Diana. 'Hey, you couldn't get me his autograph, could you?'

Carol gave Chris a little kick on the ankle and stifled a snigger.

'I . . . I don't know. I might be able to . . .' This was like one of those parties where you were trapped in a corner by some utterly boring wally who was ranting on about his home computer, while the guy you really fancied was asking some other girl to dance. In this press of people, there was little chance of escape. She would be stuck with him all night.

Which was why, when Lester announced from the stage that there was a young lady in the audience who might be persuaded to come up and guest with them for a number, she overcame her nerves enough to go.

Marijke whispered encouragement as Lester handed her his Yamaha. He was playing the Selmer.

Neil, the drummer, tapped out a brisk rhythm on the snare and Steve took it up on string bass. The keyboards and guitar joined in.

'Every time I play a line, I want you to copy it,' Lester hissed. 'Then, when we get to the part you know, you carry on with the top line and I'll play around you, OK? Here we go!'

He had clipped a tiny Barcus-Berry electronic pick-up to her sax, like the one he used himself. As she played, Chris revelled in the freedom of being able to move around on the stage without having to think of where you were in relation to the microphone all the time, even though that moving about was on legs which trembled with stage fright.

She copied his musical lines faithfully, mimicking his grace-notes and slurs. Then, suddenly, she was on her own, playing the winding melody while he wove around her, sometimes above, sometimes below. It required tremendous concentration to stick to her notes and not wander off onto his, but she managed it and they ended with a glorious run, experimenting, joking about, landing up on the same note, an octave apart. And Chris could hear applause – loud, and lots. And shouts of 'More!'

She dashed her hair out of her eyes and peered into the sea of faces. She could make out Carol and Grant and the green-shirted boy, all leaping up and down and yelling. She gave a little bow of acknowledgement, feeling, for the very first time, like a real performer. With Jalova, she had felt like a bit-player, like someone who comes on with an orchestra, bangs a triangle once or twice, then lapses into obscurity.

Here, she felt like a star.

When she walked off stage and back into the audience, fighting her way through a sea of hands which were patting her on the back and squeezing her elbows, she was waylaid by Greenshirt. 'Would you mind giving me *your* autograph as well?' he begged, and dug a notebook out of his pocket, which Chris signed with a flourish, adding the date.

'That will be worth something one day,' Carol told him.

He gazed at Chris with shining eyes. 'I can believe it. Can I be your first fan?'

She had noticed a couple of girls staring at her. One came over. She had a striking hairstyle, her hair cut in a long bob with a deep fringe, dyed jet black, but with an inch at the bottom, and the whole of her fringe, bleached silver. She faintly resembled a panda.

'Are you with a band at the moment?' she enquired.

Chris told her about Jalova.

'That's a pity. Reet and me – that's her over there – are looking for people to form a band. I play drums and trumpet and Reet's a keyboard player, but she can play alto sax quite well, too. Originally, we thought of doing something like the Fairer Sax – you know the all-girl sax band? But I think it's a bit too gimicky. Men seem to find girl sax players kinky. Have you found that?'

Chris shook her head. 'No. But then, I haven't played a lot of gigs yet. Perhaps I've got horrors like that yet to come . . .'

'Look, it's too noisy to talk in here. Why don't you come round? I'll give you my number.' She wrote down her name – Jan – and a number which Chris recognised, from the exchange, as being in Wandsworth, not far from where she lived. She was glad when Jan went back to join Reet as she had been missing an incredible solo by Lester. And this time she joined in as the crowd went wild.

The band, plus Carol and Grant, and Greenshirt, who was determined to meet his idol, all went to a late-night pizzeria. The fan, whose name was David, made little conversation, seemingly struck dumb by being in such illustrious company. He only came out of his shell when Marijke took pity on him and started to ask him about himself. To Chris's amusement, he was studying computer science. Having got the autograph of everyone there, including Carol and Grant who could not convince him that they weren't musicians, too, he went off to catch a late-night bus, pausing briefly to assure Chris that he would be following her career avidly.

'You've made a big hit there!' Lester remarked, as the door swung shut behind the departing green T-shirt. 'How will you feel when there are hundreds of them lining the street by the stage door and trying to climb the drainpipe to your hotel room?'

'I'd pick the best-looking ones and tell the rest to come back tomorrow,' said Carol, oblivious to Grant's jealous scowl.

'It won't happen to me. I'm never intending to go on stage looking like Madonna,' Chris said. 'I shall shroud myself in a yashmak.'

'How will you play a saxophone through the veil?' asked Marijke.

'Why not bandage yourself like an Egyptian mummy and just leave a hole where your mouth is?' suggested Kal, the pianist.

'Just imagine the bandages coming undone and getting tangled in the keys.' Carol laughed.

'She might end up being the first woman who's strangled by her own saxophone, like Isadora Duncan and the scarf!'

Having seen a film of Isadora's life on TV, Chris was quite an admirer of the tragic dancer. But all the same, the image of a mummy and a sax entangled in bandages was very funny and Chris burst out laughing. She caught Lester's eye and they both became quite helpless with amusement. The more they looked at each other, the more they laughed, until Chris had to wipe tears out of her eyes.

Lester managed to calm down first. Chris only managed it by taking a long swig of her orange juice. Then she looked at Lester again. He was turned away from her, talking to Grant, but, as if he felt the power of her stare, he inclined his head and met her eyes and suddenly, she couldn't pull hers away. His eyes were like two ice-blue magnets, locked with her own. Chris felt something strange happening to her. She felt frozen in position, like in a game of statues. Her heart was pumping so violently that she could almost hear it. Everyone else's chatter seemed to have faded away as if someone had turned down the volume knob on the television.

It was Lester who broke the grip-gaze by turning his head again sharply and resuming his conversation with Grant. The incident had left Chris quite shaken. She sat in silence, then heard Marijke trying to attract her attention from across the table. She couldn't quite hear what she was saying, so she got up and went over to her, mouthing, 'What?'

'It doesn't matter,' Marijke said.

'Yes, it does. I want to know what you said.'

'I said, "Watch it, you two!" '

'What do you mean?' Chris had her hand on the back of Marijke's chair and was bending over her. She doubted whether anyone else could hear their exchange.

Marijke looked thoughtful. 'I saw the way you were looking at Lester just now. Be careful, won't you?'

That was all she had time to say before Lester himself called something to Marijke from his end of the table, but it left Chris puzzled and a bit uneasy. She felt that she would like to talk to Marijke; just the two of them, and find out the reason behind her warning . . .

'I'm sick of you using this house like a hotel. We never see you these days. All I see is your dirty dishes in the sink, and your laundry. Why not leave the maid a tip sometimes? That's all I am to you, isn't it? You don't care about us. All you do when you're in is make that bloody racket!'

'Shut up! Shut up!' Chris jammed her hands over her ears as her mother shouted at her from the top of the stairs.

'You'll lose that job of yours too, my girl, if you keep getting in late in the mornings. And I can't see that saxophone ever earning you any money . . .'

'God, I'm sick of this!' Chris's words came out in a kind of slow motion, her muscles jammed up with sick frustration. How much more of this could she take? Being at home was getting to be a nightmare. Yet every time she threatened to leave, her mother would change her tune and become the tragedy queen being deserted by her beloved only daughter. Her father generally kept out of their rows, sticking to his beer and telly.

She was only too aware of the precariousness of her job. She was out late so often these days that it was difficult to get up in the mornings, and half the day she felt as if she were sleep-walking.

'I'll be in tonight,' she said sullenly.

'Good. I'll cook enough for three people, for a change. You're looking half-starved, my girl. Don't you go to the canteen any more?'

It was a fact that Chris rarely went to the canteen now, preferring to nibble an apple and a packet of crisps on a bench in one of the squares, if it was warm enough, or in the staff lounge if it wasn't. The money she would have spent on a proper lunch went into the fund for a new saxophone. She had seen just what she wanted in Bill Lewington's in Shaftesbury Avenue – a gleaming Yamaha, just like Lester's. It cost just over a thousand pounds. Every time she went to buy new reeds, she gave it a longing gaze. If only she could start earning more money . . .

The main reason why she was home so rarely was Jalova. An indie label had shown interest in the album so they were working hard in the studio, and Chris was working with them. She knew most of their material well by now, and played on three-quarters of the stage numbers. One afternoon, on her day off, when the house was empty, she had attempted to write down and play into her cassette recorder as much as she could remember of that musical idea she had had ages ago, on the way home from Johnson's party. Then, full of trepidation, expecting to get laughed at, she had played it to the band.

To her amazement, and their credit, they had listened attentively, and then asked if they could work on an arrangement and include it on the album.

'You're kidding!' Chris had accused them.

'No, we're not,' Lee had assured her. 'It's good. It's unusual. It's got something new about it. You must let us do it. What are you going to call it?'

Chris hadn't a clue. 'Well, it was written about Johnson's party –'

'How about calling it that, then?' Bonnie had suggested. So 'Johnson's Party' it became, and Curtis, Howie, Bonnie and Chris all added vocal effects, words and disjointed sentences meant to sound like snatches of party conversations.

When they weren't rehearsing and recording, they were gigging, or else Chris was at her lessons with Lester, and trying her best to run through her exercises at home.

She had been right about herself and Lester. Something had changed slightly. No, not a change, exactly; more of a subtle shift in their attitude to one another. He wasn't treating her like a kid student any more, but more like an equal. As promised, he had lent her some records featuring people like Charlie Parker and Lester Young, and rock sax players she hadn't heard before, like Mel Collins, Andy Mackay and David Payne. She had wondered at the time it was in the charts who the sax player was on Ian Dury's hit single, 'Hit Me With Your Rhythm Stick'. Now that she knew it was David Payne, she listened more closely to Dury's albums, with a technical ear now, as opposed to listening just for entertainment's sake.

Her father had been in the room once, while she had been listening to Mel Collins playing with the seventies band Camel.

'I know a thumping good saxophone player I bet you haven't heard of,' he said proudly. 'Listen to this. I bet you won't know whose band this is!'

He hadn't reckoned with the *Rock 'N' Roll Years* series on TV.

'Bill Haley and the Comets!' Chris cried triumphantly, as soon as she heard the first two lines. She recognised it even before Haley had got to the chorus line of 'Rock Around The Clock'!

Mr Lindsell's face fell, then brightened again. 'Bet you can't give me the name of the feller on sax, though.'

Chris couldn't.

'Bill Pompelli!' he crowed. 'Just listen to that.'

Chris listened. 'Dad . . .' she said, when two tracks of the LP had been played and her father lifted the needle off before the third, 'Dad, do you really mind me playing the saxophone? I mean, really *really*?' It was a long time since she had felt so close to her father. It was strange how easy it was to take people you lived with for granted, and never really communicate with them.

There was a short silence. Then her father said, 'You're very serious about it, aren't you?'

'Yes, you know I am.'

'Then I say good luck to you. Go out and do it, girl.'

Chris stared at her father in amazement. 'You mean, you don't mind – about my wanting to play in a band and make records?'

'You know something? Your mother wouldn't like to hear me say this, but I'm quite jealous. I wish I had had an ambition. Well, I did once – to go to sea, and I did that, as you know. I never wanted to be famous, though. I don't know where you get that from. There are times when I wish I'd done more with my life though. Sometimes I think –'

Chris never found out what he thought, because her mother walked in just then and scolded the pair of them about not having set the table for tea.

One day, about three weeks after that evening in the 100 Club, she was transferring the contents of her bag, which had a broken strap, to a new one she had bought, when, among the old sweet-wrappings, screwed up tissues, bits of fluff and old receipts, she came across a small, neatly folded piece of lined paper. Opening it up in curiosity, she found it to be the phone number of Jan, the girl with the panda hair, whom she had met in the club that night. She had promised to phone, and hadn't. Oh, dear . . . Chris hoped they wouldn't think that she had been too egotistical, too much of a superstar, to call.

She was about to go downstairs to the phone, when she halted in her tracks. What was the point in ringing Jan? Her life was filled to capacity with music as it was. She was only seeing Linda and Danielle once every two or three weeks now, instead of every time she had a day off, and it was fortunate that Carol was still being monopolised by Grant.

No, she wouldn't ring. Not right now, anyway.

This is the eleventh time I've played in public, Chris calculated as she came off stage in yet another hot, sweaty club. This one was actually in the back room of a pub, which meant the music had to finish at eleven. Chris didn't mind that. It would enable her to get a reasonably early night for once.

'This is a good way to lose weight!' Bonnie commented wryly, peeling off her wringing wet top and throwing on a dry baggy T-shirt. 'By the way, did Lee tell you about the guy who wants to manage us?'

'No, he didn't,' Chris responded, with a slight frown. They were changing in the group's van, the boys having stayed behind to sort out the equipment and their pay, which amounted to twenty-three pounds each, the bare union minimum for a gig.

'His name's George Wilson and he manages a couple of other London bands. Don played him our tapes the other week and he was really impressed – wants to get us a deal.'

'How about that label who were already interested?' All at once, Chris felt like an outsider again, rather than a proper group member. She was still only part-time with them, really, as her job prevented her from attending many of their rehearsals. Everyone else in the band was on the dole, except Howie, a self-employed electrician who worked his own hours.

'George reckons he can do much better than that for us. He's going to take the tapes to some bigger companies,' Bonnie explained. 'Isn't it exciting?'

'Mmm.' Chris was noncommittal. Surely one of them should have made the effort to ring her and tell her about this development? They were so casual and slap-happy about everything. Perhaps they did need a manager. The getting of bookings was conducted in a haphazard way, too. Although she liked them all, with the possible exception of Howie, who was in turn either withdrawn or sarcastic, she still wasn't positive Jalova was the right band for her. But, as Lester had said, she needed the experience.

'We're having a meeting about it tomorrow morning,' Bonnie informed her.

'But you know I won't be able to come!' Chris reminded her crossly. 'I am supposed to be a member of this band, aren't I?'

'Of course you are,' Bonnie said soothingly. 'It's just a pity you can't be there.'

'You're telling me! Look, Bonnie, would you be able to meet me at lunchtime? I really would like to know what's going on.'

'If he asks us to sign anything, you'd have to be there, anyway,' Bonnie pointed out. 'Mind you, I'm not sure if you can sign legal documents until you're eighteen. That's in three weeks' time, isn't it?' Chris nodded. How could she forget? 'OK,' Bonnie went on, 'I'll meet you if you like. Where?'

They arranged to meet outside the main entrance of Chris's store. Bonnie was almost a quarter of an hour late, which annoyed Chris, who could only take her exact hour for lunch. Chris was just about to give up on her when she came dashing through the Oxford Street crowds in a state of great excitement.

'Guess what? Oh, Chris, it's fantastic! We've been offered a deal on the album! XL Records want to take it and put out a single, too!' She hugged Chris round the waist and danced around with her.

Chris felt stunned, and rather put out. To think all this had happened while she had been behind the Childrenswear counter. Now, having missed out, she didn't feel really part of it. She had never heard of the record company, either.

'What's wrong? Aren't you thrilled?' Bonnie was staring at her, her face dropping.

Chris forced a smile. 'Of course I'm thrilled. I just wish I'd been there, that's all. I feel a bit left out.'

'Count yourself lucky to have a job. Maybe, if the album does well, you won't need one any more. Wouldn't that be something?'

She had to agree that it would.

Lester was jubilant at the news. She told him that evening when she met him at the Russell Rooms for her Thursday evening lesson at eight o'clock, after her late night in the store. She always felt tired then and they spent more time talking about theory and technique that evening than actually playing.

'Eighteen and your first record out. That's pretty good going! I think this deserves a celebration, don't you?'

'Don't you think it's a bit premature? We haven't even signed the contract yet,' Chris pointed out weakly.

'Be an optimist! Come on, there's a wine bar near here. We'll have a glass of champagne.'

Chris's eyes widened as Lester came back from the bar to the table, accompanied by a barman carrying an ice bucket, in which the frozen cubes clinked against a whole bottle of champagne.

'I hope you like shampoo,' he chuckled.

'Shampoo? Oh, I see – champagne, shampoo. I've never heard it called that before. I prefer it to genuine poo!'

Lester laughed and spilled a few expensive drops as he was pouring the sparkling liquid into their glasses. He replaced the bottle in its cooler, raised his glass to his lips and Chris did the same.

'To your success. May the record go straight to the top of the charts!' He clinked his glass against hers.

People were gazing at them as usual. Chris could tell they were mumbling to one another, wondering if he was anybody famous. He certainly had some kind of magnetism about him. She leaned back in her chair, feeling proud to be with him, wondering how many times in the past he had drunk champagne to toast his own success.

After two glasses, Chris was feeling light and floaty. As a rule, she didn't drink much. She knew that had partly to do with the fact that she didn't like her father drinking so much. She hated hearing him slur his words, seeing him knock into things and stumble around, and he looked so overweight and unhealthy lately. But tonight was a special occasion, after all. And 28 August, her birthday, would be the next.

Lester was talking about press launches for records, recalling one particular occasion when the record company had hired a boat to cruise down the river, carrying a group of journalists, the band themselves, photographers, record-company personnel, and also a full complement of instruments and amplification, as the band were to perform a couple of numbers from their album live, for the benefit of the press.

'There was a lot of booze going around and I don't know if anyone had spiked the drink of the man at the steering wheel, but all of a sudden there was a great yell, the boat lurched, and we collided with a concrete pillar. Everything fell over, instruments, drinks, people, and two people fell overboard. One of them was my wife, who had been leaning over the side trying to spot some fish. Some journalist guy who was a good swimmer jumped in and rescued her and it made a great picture on the front pages of the papers, though Cheryl was furious because she'd had a white dress on and it had gone all transparent!'

So he *had* been married. The champagne having removed all constraint, Chris enquired, 'Where is she now? Your wife, I mean.'

Lester pulled a face. 'It went the way of so many music-business marriages. I married a pretty blonde dancer, I was away a lot with my various bands, she got bored at home and started an affair. I can't say I'd behaved like an angel, either. We got divorced, oh, about eleven years ago now. Cheryl got the house, because of the kid. We lived in an enormous detached place in Buckinghamshire, with horses, swimming pool, the lot. I moved into town in disgust and bought the first place I saw, the house where I'm living now. You might call it a come-down after what I had, but I was sick of the whole image thing by then. I prefer to live in suburban obscurity. I know I could afford better. I'm still getting royalty cheques from the old records – and some of the new ones. I have my session money, my teaching money, cash from gigs . . . I'm not a millionaire, but –'

'Did you have a son or a daughter?' Chris interrupted, then immediately stifled a hiccup. The fizzy wine was getting to her.

'A daughter. She's grown up now. She's in America, working as a nurse. Cheryl was American.'

'Is your daughter the dark-haired girl who's in that photograph on your shelf?' Chris asked boldly.

Lester laughed. 'No, no, that's Mary. And those two boys in the other picture are Mary's. Well, one of them's mine *and* Mary's.'

'I see.' Chris didn't see at all. She was totally confused. Had he married Mary after his divorce from his first wife, and was the older boy her child from a previous marriage? Lester was obviously not going to explain. Instead, he had launched into a serious talk about managers and percentages and she tried her hardest to concentrate, but it wasn't easy when she was full of champagne.

The bottle was empty now. 'I don't think we'd better have another, do you?' Lester asked.

Chris shook her head. Then she yawned.

'I'd better get you back home, Missy. Let's find a cab.'

She followed Lester out, nearly tripping over the top stair.

'Steady!' He took her arm and piloted her out onto the pavement. Then, still holding her arm, he waved and yelled at a passing taxi, which screeched to a halt. He let go of her arm then, but Chris could still feel the impression of his warm fingers.

When they gave their destination, the cabbie shook his head and didn't want to take them at first, saying it wasn't worth his while because he couldn't pick up a fare the other end, to bring back into town.

'Oh, come on!' Lester argued. 'Are you telling me that there won't be one person in yuppified Clapham who doesn't want to get over the river to Chelsea or Pimlico? Don't give me that old bull!'

Reluctantly, the cabbie acquiesced, and they climbed in.

Chris was never sure what happened then. Either she passed out, or fell asleep. All she remembered was waking up and finding herself cradled against Lester, her head resting against his shoulder, his arm around her back. His hair was touching hers, intertwining with it. She could feel their hair pulling apart as she raised her head.

'Where are we?'

'Nearly there, lovey. I'm dropping you off first. It's been quite a day for you, hasn't it?'

'Mm.' She felt too weary to form a proper word.

The taxi halted outside her house.

'Thanks,' she said as she fumbled for the door catch. 'For the lesson, the champagne . . . everything.'

'See you at the weekend. Oh no, I won't. I forgot. We've got some out-of-town gigs this weekend so I won't be around. See you Tuesday, then.'

She was just stepping out of the cab when he leaned towards her, as if he was going to say something, but instead, he checked himself. As she hesitated, he kissed her lightly, high on the cheek, just missing her eye.

'Goodnight,' was all he said, but she felt as drunk as if they had had that second bottle of champagne, after all.

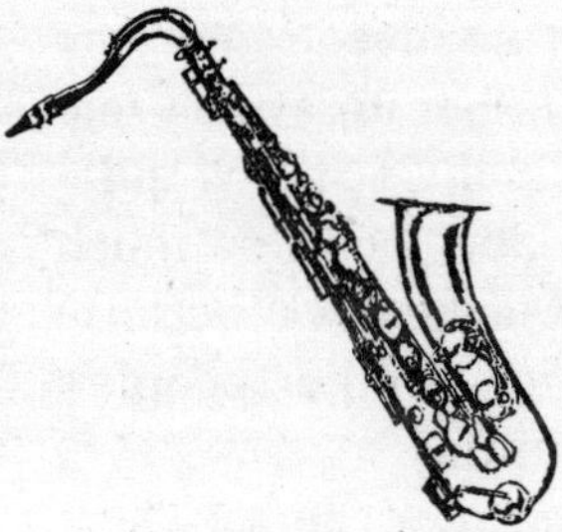

CHAPTER · 7 ·

'Wake up, Chris, Walshy's on the warpath!' Syl Roche prodded her and Chris came to with a start. She pretended to be sorting some notes in the till as their supervisor slunk by, hoping to catch them slacking.

'You've been in a dream all morning. What's happened?' Syl probed. 'Are you in love?'

Chris felt her cheeks flame. In love, indeed! With a man nearly thirty years older than her? It was unthinkable. She liked and admired Lester, that was all. Yet she couldn't pretend to herself that she hadn't been thinking about that kiss ever since last night. She had been over and over the feel of it, to impress it on her memory, along with the warm, firm touch of his fingers on her arm.

'No, I'm not in love, but I did receive the most gorgeous kiss in a taxi. It was really romantic,' she confided.

'Who is he? What's his name? Are you seeing him again?' Syl demanded excitedly. Since she had got engaged, she had developed an extreme nosiness about her workmates' affairs, now that she wasn't on the market for new romances herself.

'It's a secret,' Chris said, and Syl gave an annoyed tut.

'You could tell me, surely?' she wheedled.

'There's no point, because nothing can ever come of it.'

'Oh. Married, is he?'

Chris decided she may as well answer yes. It was probably true, anyway.

'Well, you're very wise not to get involved. Now, my friend Kerry . . .' Syl launched into a rather unsavoury tale about what had happened to Kerry and Chris was quite glad to be rescued by a customer. She found so much intimate detail rather embarrassing. Maybe it was because she hadn't started a sex life yet. Tales of other people's sexual goings-on made her feel a bit weird.

She had a long gap of doing nothing after she had dealt with her customer, and she found herself thinking about her birthday. Would her parents let her have a party? Or would it be better just to go out with a crowd, go to a wine bar and a disco? When she got home that night she sounded her parents out about the party idea and the result was a resounding negative.

'We'd never hear the end of it from Mrs Levy. She'd go to the police,' Mrs Lindsell stated flatly. 'She's bad enough about your saxophone.' So that left Chris's wine-bar idea.

Whom did she want to invite? There were Carol and Grant; Linda, if she could get her mum to baby-sit; Gemma; Johnson Kendrick and his new girlfriend; the members of Jalova and their respective partners . . . Syl Roche, of course, without her fiancé, who was still away in the Middle East, and quite a few people from school, whom she still kept in touch with. Then she remembered Lester. He was so important to her; in some ways – musical and creative ways – she felt closer to him than she did to anybody, even Carol and Linda. He wouldn't want to mix with a gang of teenagers, though, would he? And if she asked him, it would be nice to ask Marijke and Steve, too. But that would mean mixing up two lots of musicians whom she played with and perhaps that wasn't a good idea. She had never told Jalova that she had played with Soundwaves, and intended to again, and now that they were about to sign that recording contract and take on a manager, she was worried that it might complicate things legally.

So she decided, slightly reluctantly, that she'd better not invite Lester, a decision which was made even harder by her next meeting with him.

She took him a tape of 'Johnson's Party', thinking that her teacher would be interested to hear his student's first completed composition. He put it into the cassette slot on the stereo and as soon as the track started, he fiddled with the sliders on the built-in graphic equaliser, then sat down and concentrated, while Chris watched him hard, willing him to like it.

She couldn't read anything in his expression and when the track was over, he remained silent, staring into space. She clenched her right fist so hard that the nails made crescent-shaped indentations in her palm. Oh, God, he hated it – she knew he did. He was just searching for the right words in which to couch his distaste.

He seemed to move very slowly as he turned round to look at her. She knew her face must look pale and tense.

'That. Is. Great!' Each word separate and distinct, like a sentence in itself. Chris gasped. 'No, I mean it,' he continued. 'I can't believe that's the first real thing you've ever written. It shows real originality and maturity. And the arrangement is –'

'That wasn't just me,' she interrupted, unwilling to take the credit for Jalova's input.

'I bet most of the ideas were yours, though.'

She nodded. It was true. She had described the sounds she heard in her head and the other musicians and Don had experimented until they had got something which was as close as possible to her concept. It hadn't seemed particularly brilliant or unusual to her. In fact, it had come quite easily, once she had put her mind to remembering the ideas she had had on the bus.

Lester reached out and patted her hand and she jumped as if burned by the contact. 'I always felt you had something special, Chris; now I know. I feel privileged to be working with you.'

'*You* feel privileged?' she burst out. 'You're the talented one! All those groups and records, the gigs and travelling, the gold discs . . . I'll never manage anything like that.'

'Don't you believe it. I've a feeling you're going to be very big. You're going to make your mark on the music scene in no uncertain way. Though whether it will be with rock, funk, jazz, I don't know. I'm not sure even how to classify that number of yours. It's commercial, though, I'll tell you that much. Tell that manager of yours to push for its release as a single.'

All this praise was getting too much. Chris couldn't quite believe it. Maybe he was just humouring her. She *wanted* to believe it, of course. Who wouldn't? Yet to her, the piece she had written sounded a bit childish and amateurish, rather than mature and professional. Or was she too close to it to judge clearly?

He extracted the cassette from the maw of the machine and gave it back to her. 'What would you like to do now?' he enquired.

She knew he meant in terms of exercises. However, she had a completely different suggestion. 'Would you mind playing me something? Perhaps one of *your* compositions?'

Lester grinned. 'You've asked for it!' He strapped on his tenor and launched into a dazzling display of jazz-rock which had Chris swaying her head and banging her heels against the floor to the rhythm. She loved watching him play. He would remain in one place for a while, scarcely moving the sax, then he would suddenly take off, hauling the instrument about, stamping his foot, rolling his head, swaying from the waist, to the left, the right, backwards, forwards, in mobile mastery of his music.

A lump came into her throat and she closed her eyes, unable to look at him for a moment as feelings engulfed her. Her mind was the dam holding back a flood of emotions. It was essential that they should be kept back. She didn't even dare examine them for fear of being swamped. Only by ignoring them, by keeping that mental dam strong, could she stay sensible and sane. Otherwise she might do or say something daft and ruin their perfect, complicated relationship, teacher/pupil, musician/fan; though tonight, who was the fan and who was the musician . . . ?

'A tour? Wow!' Chris felt a shiver of excitement run through her. She and the other members of Jalova were sitting in George Wilson's office above a shop in Notting Hill. He still hadn't asked them to sign anything, which she thought was a little odd but in a way felt quite relieved about.

George was short and neat and about thirty. He was an ex-DJ, with a soulful moustache and a habit of weaving and dancing about which, she was told, was a result of the martial arts he was for ever practising.

The others were grinning and chattering about the eight dates he wanted them to play, in major cities like Liverpool and Birmingham.

'It'll coincide with the release of the album,' he explained. 'I've got a date from XL now – 28 August.' Her birthday! It was the best gift she could get! Polydor had signed the album on a one-off deal which allowed them to release a single from it, too. If the tour and the record went well, George said, he would ask them to sign an official contract then. But for now, he would take them on trust, and vice versa.

Chris's dizzily spinning brain was brought to an abrupt halt by two enormous problems that suddenly presented themselves. The first was that she desperately needed that new saxophone now if she was to do herself justice. (What a pity she couldn't have had a decent one for the recording, she thought wistfully.) The second was, how on earth was she going to get the time off work?

She had already had to fake a dental appointment to attend the meeting with George. When she finally got to work, she discussed the matter with Syl, who was all agog at the thought of her workmate becoming a superstar.

'Why can't you just give up work, if you've got this tour and a record coming out?' she said, with a slight note of envy in her voice.

'Because there's no guarantee we'll make any money,' Chris retorted. 'Anyway, there are five of us so whatever we do make has to be split between the lot of us. But the gigs he's got us are £300 a night – that's sixty each, £480 for the entire tour. But our expenses have to come out of that, and the rest will go straight into the saxophone fund. I wish we could be given it in advance . . .'

'Aren't you due any holiday? You've only taken a few odd days so far,' Syl pointed out.

'Yes, I am, but you know how much notice they want us to give. It's too late for that. If I asked them and they said no, then I just disappeared, it would look dead suspicious.

I think maybe I'd be better off faking an illness and hoping the doctor will believe me and give me a certificate when I get back.'

'I won't tell on you – promise.'

'Thanks, Syl. And by the way, you are coming on the 28th, aren't you?'

'You bet!' Syl replied eagerly. 'I haven't had a good night out for ages. Which wine bar have you decided on?'

'I'm not sure yet, but it might be the Cork and Bottle. I'll let you know,' she promised. Yes, this was how she wanted to spend her birthday. At a gathering of all her friends, organised by herself. She just hoped her parents wouldn't mind her not wanting to spend the evening with them. She had a horrible feeling they might want to come to the wine bar, too, which would put a real damper on things. She could just imagine her father getting drunk and cracking dirty jokes.

But there was another, far bigger hurdle to be got over before her birthday. The tour . . . How on earth was she going to tell her parents? They had both seemed quite impressed when she told them about the record. Her mother had even stopped going on at her so much about practising. But they might still try to stop her going. She had to go, no matter what they said. It was more important than anything, especially boring old work.

There was no time to hang about. She had to tell them that very night. She chose a moment when there was nothing worth watching on TV and her mother was reading a library book while her father filled in his pools coupon.

'Um . . . Mum, Dad – I've got something to tell you.'

Two pairs of eyes swivelled in her direction and Chris quailed.

'Well?' her mother asked sharply. 'What is it?'

'I'm not pregnant, if that's what you're thinking,' Chris put in quickly.

'Have you left your job?'

'No, Dad. It's something else. It's the band . . . Jalova. We're going on tour.'

'When?' demanded her mother.

'The week after my birthday. On the Tuesday. I've checked with work and I can take the time off. I'll only need four days, anyway.' It was a double lie, and Chris hated lying, but her musical future was at stake. She would probably have to take a couple of days off the following week, too. She would need to fool her doctor as well as her workmates, as she was going to have to pretend to be very ill indeed!

'You mean you'll be gallivanting round the countryside with a bunch of drug-taking weirdos? I don't like the idea at all,' her mother began, but Chris cut in.

'Mum! They don't take drugs . . . We've been through all that. They're serious career people, like me. We all want our record to be a hit and –'

'Look, love, we're proud of the fact that you've made a record –' began her father.

'Even though it's not really *yours*,' cut in her mother witheringly. She always managed to say something flattening. Chris glared at her.

'We just hope you've got your head screwed on, that's all,' continued her father. 'You've always been a sensible sort of girl. We'd worry about you far more if you were like that friend of yours, Linda . . .'

'Linda's not like that any more.' Chris knew he was referring to Linda's days of drinking far too much at parties, which had resulted in Danielle being born.

'No. She doesn't get the chance,' said Mrs Lindsell. 'We don't want to see you ruin your life, that's all. I can see it's a great opportunity for you and as long as you're careful, and make sure whoever's driving you drives safely . . .'

'Thanks, Mum.' Chris was profoundly relieved that her news had been accepted so well, with only a tiny amount of objection. Now she could really look forward to organising her birthday celebration, with only a few slight twinges of conscience about her job.

She had a secret hope that Lester might send her a card, but as it happened, he went off a couple of days before her birthday, on a short tour with Soundwaves, which solved the problem of whether to invite him or not. She felt quite upset when she opened all her cards and found nothing from him. She could understand how occupied he was, but still, he had known what date her birthday was.

However, enough compensations came her way to make her forget her moment of disappointment. For a start, her parents shelved their sax phobia and donated a hundred pounds towards her fund for a new one. Carol was waiting for her when she got home from work and presented her with a set of matching earrings and necklace in gleaming silver and brass. Chris thought how fantastic they would look on stage under the lights.

Chris and Carol went on ahead to the wine bar to organise a couple of large tables and some sparkling wine in ice buckets to greet their guests with. It was so exciting to be kissed and hugged by everyone, and given presents. Everyone she had invited turned up, and a few more besides, and Chris felt it was her best birthday ever.

When the wine bar closed at eleven, they all decided to go on to a club. Chris danced so much that her feet were in agony and she had to kick her shoes off and continue barefoot. Three blokes she didn't know asked her to dance, as well as some of her own crowd. She turned two down, but had a couple of dances with the third, extricating herself when he tried to pull her close to a slow record. She didn't need all that stuff. She had no time for it right now. A boyfriend would only get in the way of music. Bonnie's relationship with Curtis only worked because they were in the same band and saw each other at rehearsals and gigs. If only one of them had been a musician, they couldn't have seen enough of each other to keep things going.

Some time in the future there would be time for a boyfriend. When she fell in love. She was positive she'd recognise the feeling when she did. A sneaking, exciting little buzz inside her told her she might have done so already . . . How else could she explain those strange surges and plummets in her stomach which she always got when she was near Lester? And that kiss he'd given her on the cheek had affected her far, far more than any smooch on the lips from Ian Fowler. She had forgotten Ian now. She hoped he was happy with tarty Tracey. She never saw them around. How had she ever imagined that she fancied him? She knew so much more about herself and life now . . .

Chris started building up her alibi two days before the tour. She went to the extent of rubbing talcum into her cheeks to make herself look pale, and smudging dark shadows under her eyes with a kohl crayon. Even the hated Liz Walsh remarked that she didn't look well, giving her a golden opportunity for describing her symptoms: a nasty pain in the stomach and a shivery feeling, as if she had a temperature. She had decided to give herself a dose of summer gastric flu.

The morning she was meeting the rest of the group, to drive to Manchester, she rang work to say she was ill and wouldn't be coming in. Then, feeling far too excited to feel guilty, she slung her sax into the back of the van and clambered in for the long journey.

George had some friends in Manchester and had arranged for them to stay there. He had given them instructions and a scrawled map, but even so, they drove around the suburbs for three-quarters of an hour before they found the street. Bonnie got out and rang the bell of the shabby terraced house and was almost knocked over by the shoving, pushing gang of children who burst out the moment the door was opened.

Their mother, Brenda, greeted them warmly and apologised for the lack of facilities. They would have to divide themselves between the sofa-bed in the lounge, the floor, and a mattress on the carpet of the small back bedroom which their hostess used as a workroom for her dressmaking business.

Bonnie and Curtis's romance was out in the open now and, naturally, they would have liked the privacy of the boxroom, but that would have left Chris having to share with three men! So, reluctantly, the lovers decided that they would have to be apart for one night so that Chris and Bonnie could share the room.

They dumped their stuff, sorted out their stage clothes and drove to the enormous pub where they were to be appearing. They found it very well equipped, with an excellent PA system which would save them the trouble of having to set up their own gear. They also met up with Gerry, a friend of Don's who was joining them for the north and Midlands part of the tour, as an extra roadie, to leave Jim free to work the mixing desk.

Chris felt far too nervous to eat anything before the show. She was worried about the reception – or lack of it – that they might get. After all, they weren't that well-known in London, and outside the capital, nobody had heard of them at all, especially as there was no sign of their album getting anywhere in the charts.

'You'd think the record company, or George, would have organised some publicity,' Howie grumbled, stuffing a chunk of pork pie into his mouth. The company had asked for black and white photos of the group, and a brief personal biography on each of them, but although they had bought all the music papers for the last two weeks and read them avidly from cover to cover, they had been unable to find any mention of themselves, not even one lousy review. 'I bet no one will turn up.'

He wasn't far wrong. When nine o'clock came, the huge back room of the pub was only a quarter full.

From the start, their performance was decidedly lack-lustre. Chris found herself playing flat on a couple of occasions and was aware of one or two winces among the unenthusiastic audience. They were booked to play two sets of forty-five minutes each with a half-hour break in between, and when the break came, Chris had never been so glad to scuttle off the stage and slug back an ice-cold bottle of lager.

A scowling man from the pub management grumbled at them, complaining that they weren't pulling the crowds and he wasn't doing enough business behind the bar.

'That's not our fault, mate,' Lee countered. 'We've got a good record out. Blame the record company for not getting our name about.' They had brought a pile of albums with them, hoping to sell a few as they went along, but so far that evening they hadn't sold a single copy. Chris felt very despondent. She had been so elated when they had set off that morning, so looking forward to getting the crowds on their feet and moving to the music, generating that heat and energy that she had already become addicted to in her two months of stage experience. But tonight nothing was catching fire. The spark just wasn't there. If only she could see Lester. She felt like running to him, flinging her arms around him, hanging onto him, taking strength from him. The sudden realisation that she wasn't going to see him for a week made a gulf open up inside her so that she was empty, almost breathless. No wonder there was no power in her playing tonight.

He had rung her before she had left that morning, to wish her luck. Whom did *he* think about when he was on stage, she wondered? To what face did he dedicate his slower, more emotional numbers? It wouldn't be her, it was more likely to be that Mary, in her red swimsuit, lying on the sand. Chris sipped her lager without seeing anything around her, her gaze directed inwards, at her bleak thoughts.

When the call came for them to go back on stage, Chris almost felt like running out and hiding in the ladies', but Bonnie tugged her arm.

'Come on, cheer up. Just because there are only six people out there doesn't mean we can't enjoy ourselves.' It was a slight exaggeration – there were probably thirty-six. 'Just imagine it's a rehearsal. We've had some good times rehearsing, haven't we?'

Chris forced herself to smile. 'Sorry,' she muttered. 'I'm OK. I'll do better in this set, I promise. You sound good tonight. You look great, too.'

Bonnie was wearing a sleeveless jumpsuit in a stunning shade of blue, with a wide black elasticated belt which emphasised her tiny waist. She had an excellent figure and could get away with the kind of clinging outfits Chris would never dare to wear. Chris herself was sticking to her safe black, wearing leggings and a long, baggy T-shirt.

'Thanks. You and I'll have a talk later. Come on now, folks . . .'

Something happened to Chris during the number before 'Johnson's Party'. She was halfway through a sax solo between verses when she was suddenly transported in her mind to Lester's lounge. He was kneeling before the stereo, putting a record on and after he had closed the Perspex lid, he turned towards her and gave her a penetrating stare from those blue eyes. It was as if he had telepathically beamed inspiration to her, all the way from London. She felt a surge from deep within her which spilled into her playing, making her fingers dance, brightening her tone so that the run she was playing changed abruptly from pedestrian to playful.

It was as if the meagre audience sensed the change. All at once, she could see heads nodding and shoulders rhythmically jiggling. Howie glanced at her and Curtis moved alongside her and started to play a harmony to what she was playing. The fire was catching alight! It was hard for her not to grin as she blew.

A little way into 'Johnson's Party', the door opened and more people entered, filling the empty seats at the round tables. Some came right up to the foot of the stage, grinning encouragement and appreciation. At the end of the set there were shouts for more and a much happier-looking manager nodded that they could play one more number.

They chose something they hadn't rehearsed but they all knew, and jammed along and it was great. Back in the dressing room, Lee flung his arms round Chris and gave her a smacking kiss. 'Jee-*sus*! That was fantastic, Chrisso! Curtis – you ran rings round Eric Clapton tonight. And Bonnie – Tina Turner's got nothing on you, baby! God, I wish some journalists had been here.'

No critics had introduced themselves to the band but obviously someone had been there incognito, for next morning, Brenda, their hostess, drew their attention to a page in the local morning paper. There was a photograph of them that they didn't even know had been taken, together with a paragraph about the gig which called them 'a powerhouse of talent who deserve to be better known'. They went out and bought two copies each, and Chris was tempted to ring Lester, but there was no time as they had to pack up and head for Liverpool.

The newspaper item gave them the boost they needed. They played better from then on, and everywhere they went, reports appeared in the papers. It looked as if the buzz about Jalova was getting round. They even managed to sell a few records.

It was halfway through the tour, after their fourth show, that trouble started for Chris . . .

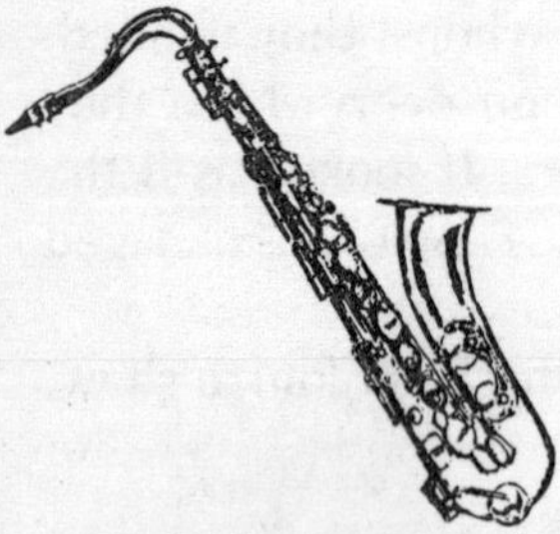

CHAPTER • 8 •

Chris had told nobody about her true feelings for Lester. She simply didn't think anyone would understand. Although Carol teased her about Lester, Chris felt that she would be shocked if she knew the extent of her fantasies and hopes.

Perhaps it was because she was so wrapped up in her world of music and imagination that she was missing things which were going on around her. At least, that was what she thought later.

They were on their way to Bristol, passing through some lovely countryside, when Bonnie had the idea of buying food and drink and having a picnic, as the weather was warm and sunny.

They parked the vehicles in a lane, up against a grass bank, and walked along until they found a gate into a perfect English meadow. The grass was long, soft and feathery and rippled in the slight breeze. The scent of wild honeysuckle growing in the hedgerows was almost overpowering in its intensity, reaching their nostrils in billows and floods, while their eyes feasted on the profusion of wild flowers, pink, yellow, white and blue, spotting the grass.

They had some blankets in the van, and took them out to sit on.

Chris was in heaven. She rarely got out into the country. 'Oh, look, a wren!' she cried delightedly, pointing to the tiny bird hopping in the hedge.

Howie was particularly enthralled. 'I've never seen one in real life before, only in books. It's got that funny, sticky-up little tail.'

The distant trees shimmered in the midday heat. Above them somewhere was the spiralling song of skylarks, visible only as faint, swooping specks against the blue sky.

Chris wondered if she could possibly sketch the scene in sound, the way she had done with 'Johnson's Party'. She put down her partly eaten apple and lay back, her hands clasped behind her head, gazing into the sky through eyes narrowed against the glare.

'Think Bonnie and I will go for a stroll, if that's OK by you folks . . .' That was Curtis.

'Sure . . . See you,' from Lee.

'That looks like a stream or a river down there. Coming to investigate?' Jim asked Lee. 'And you two . . . Do you want to come? Someone ought to stay and mind the things, though . . .'

'I'll stay,' Chris offered at once. 'I've got an idea for some music. I'll just lie here and think about it, if you don't mind.'

'And I'll stay and make sure she doesn't just go to sleep.' Howie laughed.

Chris wished he'd go with the others. He wasn't her favourite member of the band and she would much prefer to be left alone for half an hour. She could take just so much of company, then she craved some time to herself, in which to think and mull things over. But she couldn't very well tell Howie to take a walk . . .

'Are you fond of birds and animals?' he asked her, as Lee and Jim went swishing off through the knee-high grass.

'Yes,' she answered absently, without looking at him. Hadn't he got the message that she had some music to think about?

'I've got a dog at home. We've had him since I was six. That makes him fourteen now. Not bad going, eh? He's got all his faculties, still runs about. Good old Benjy . . . he's great. He goes mad when I go round to my parents, demands to sleep on my bed if I stay. Though he keeps me awake with his snoring.'

Chris grinned, despite her irritation. She was amazed at the way Howie was suddenly opening up. She didn't think she had ever heard such a long speech from him. Maybe her instinctive dislike of him had been unjustified. He was, after all, an extremely good bass player.

'Have you got any pets, Chris?'

'Only my saxophone. Hey, I was thinking of getting a silver one when I get my new one. What do you think? I don't think there's any difference in sound, but it would look great on stage under the lights, wouldn't it?'

'Anything would look great with you playing it, even a comb and paper.'

Chris's eyes blinked open. Was he pulling her leg? He was reclining on one elbow, smiling down at her.

Chris decided to try and make light of a potentially heavy situation. 'Thanks for the compliment,' she said.

'Oh, come on, you must get compliments all the time, you're a very sexy lady,' he said, in a slow, lazy drawl that made Chris's flesh creep slightly. Where had the others got to? She felt very uneasy. Although they had played together, been on the road together, for weeks now, she had never managed to get as close to Howie as to the others. He was so aloof somehow. Older than the rest of them, too. But he was OK . . . She was just imagining things.

If only it could be Lester alone in a field with her on a summer's day, gazing down at her like this, she mused. No, whatever was she thinking of? She must *not* think about Lester like that.

'Come on, Chris, don't you fancy me a bit? I know you've got no boyfriend. You must know by now that I fancy you like crazy, and you've given me the come-on once or twice . . .'

She had? How? When? She had no knowledge of it at all. What had she done? She was positive she had never led Howie on in any way. She wasn't remotely interested in him, apart from as a fellow member of Jalova.

'I've never led you on, Howie,' she said frostily. 'I'm not like that –'

'She's not like that,' mimicked Howie. 'Bloody little prick-teaser.'

'What did you call me?' Chris almost screamed it at him, she was so furious and hurt. How *dare* he? Why did she have so many lousy experiences with men? What was *wrong* with her? Was it inexperience – she couldn't read their signals? Men weren't that subtle, surely?

Then he launched his attack. He really did launch it, too, landing on top of her with a crushing blow which knocked the breath out of her. His lips crushed bruisingly down on hers and his hands started fumbling at her clothes.

'Come on, Chris, just a bit of fooling around,' he said, panting heavily.

She summoned all her strength and heaved him off her. She was trembling all over. 'How – *how* dare you?' she stammered, blinking back tears.

'What's wrong with you? Don't you like men, or something?' he asked coldly, brushing his clothes down. 'Frigid cow.'

'Just because I haven't got a boyfriend at the moment doesn't mean I don't like them,' Chris said stiffly. 'I just prefer to pick my own, rather than having them . . . thrust upon me!' She felt stronger now, more able to give him a piece of her mind, because she could see a car winding its way down from the top of the hill.

'You need to relax – take it easy. You'll never get a guy if you're so uptight about a little bit of kissing and cuddling.'

'Call that kissing and cuddling? I thought you were going to rape me!' Chris protested.

'You should be so lucky,' Howie said nastily.

Chris clenched her fists so tightly that her knuckles gleamed white.

'I suppose you read those romantic novels,' he went on relentlessly. 'You know, those ones in which some rich guy comes down in his private jet and scoops some silly cow up and whisks her off to a lifetime drinking champagne in the Bahamas. Come on, that's what you're saving yourself for, isn't it? I'm not good enough for you. *I'm* only an out-of-work electrician who plays bass in a no-hoper band.'

'Oh, so that's your opinion of Jalova! The others would be most interested to hear you say that!' Chris said, fighting back.

They were hailed by Jim and Lee. Thank goodness! Chris glanced at Howie, who was ignoring her now. She had the uncomfortable feeling that she had just made herself an enemy.

Later that day, before the gig, she decided to tell Bonnie about the incident with Howie. In a way, it involved the whole band, after all. Bonnie's eyes were like saucers by the time Chris had finished.

'It would be funny if he hadn't been so nasty. Poor Howie, stuck in a field with his nose well out of joint. But there was no need for all the rest. He'd certainly kept his adoration well hidden. Like you, Chris, I hadn't suspected a thing. It's a bit weird, isn't it?'

'How long have you known him?' Chris wanted to know.

'Oh, about eight months or so. Ever since we advertised for a bass player.' Bonnie paused, picked a blue flower and fixed it in her hair. 'He tried to get off with me once, ages ago, after we'd all been to the pub, but I told him straight that I didn't think it would work if two members of the same band started going out together, and he never tried again. He was very polite to me, though, just asked if I'd go to see a film with him.'

'What about Curtis? He's a member of the same band,' Chris pointed out.

'Well, anyone would make an exception for Curtis. He's irresistible!' Bonnie giggled.

'So in all these months you've never known Howie go out with anyone?' Chris persisted.

Bonnie thought, shook her head and said, 'No. He's not very sociable, really.'

'You're telling me! With an approach like his, he'd be better off joining a monastery,' Chris snorted.

'How about you, though? Is there nobody on the horizon at all?' Bonnie probed.

'Not really . . .' She toyed with the idea of mentioning Lester. But she would look such a fool if this Mary was someone big in his life. Besides, it would lead to all kinds of serious, awkward discussions about age-gaps and things, and Chris didn't want that. For now, she would rather carry her torch in secret, until the day came when he gave her some encouragement. Not until then could she release all the feelings she was holding back so hard. Feelings that, as yet, she could safely express only in music. My saxophone is my chastity belt, she thought, and laughed out loud. But when Bonnie asked what she was laughing at, she just replied, 'This crazy afternoon.'

That night on stage, there were definite hostile vibes coming off Howie and Chris kept well away from him. They were staying the night in a small, cheap, back-street hotel, and as there were three double rooms between the six of them, Chris thought of offering to share with Lee, rather than risk any trouble with Howie. Bonnie had begged her to be allowed just one night in comfort with Curtis, as they had passed the previous night in the back of the van.

In the event, Lee disappeared somewhere with a girl he had met, saying he would be back in the morning, and Chris was left with a twin room to herself. Even though she had locked the door, she still lay awake until gone two, waiting for the handle to begin rattling and turning. When she woke at seven, roused by a heavy lorry rumbling past her window, she felt heavy-eyed and worn out.

Lee rolled up for breakfast looking tired but triumphant. 'Great party last night – should have come back for you lot! And look at this . . .' He passed a music paper round the table. 'Here.' He jabbed with his finger.

It was a review of their album. 'It says that there are at least two potential singles on it,' he quoted excitedly. When Chris at last got a chance to read it, she saw that one of the two tracks mentioned was 'Johnson's Party'. There was a flutter of excitement in her stomach. What if the record company were to release it? She would feel so proud, on top of the world! It would be the best thing that had ever happened to her. Well, the second-best . . . No, there was no point in thinking about it and hoping. If you wanted things too much, they never happened.

'Sorry, what?' She dragged her vivid imagination back to the present, where Jim was talking about arrangements for the day's travel. Three more dates to go, that was all. Three more days and she would be back home, having to face her supervisor at work. She had rung Personnel that morning, with the lie that she was still ill.

Three more days of a scowling Howie, too . . .

It was worse than she could have imagined. He took every opportunity he could find to criticise her and put her down. Once or twice, Chris felt close to tears.

'I can't stand it,' she confided to Bonnie. 'I'm going to have to leave the band if he carries on like this.'

'I'd rather you stayed and he left,' said Bonnie. Then she shrugged. 'Talk about hell hath no fury like a *woman* scorned! Would you like me or Curtis to say something to him? I'll get Curtis to hit him, if you like!'

Chris thanked her for her kind offer but remarked that she ought to be able to fight her own battles. 'I'm just trying to think of the best way of dealing with him,' she explained.

'How about booby-trapping his bass?' suggested the irrepressible Bonnie.

Howie reserved his master stroke for the very last night of the tour. They were playing at an American air-force club in Cambridgeshire, after which the plan was to bat down the motorway and deliver everybody home. Chris wasn't looking forward to crawling into work in the morning after a three a.m. bedtime, though of course it would aid her gastric flu story as she would certainly look washed out!

The club they were playing in had the luxury of two backstage rooms, so the boys were in one and Chris and Bonnie were in the smaller one. Suddenly, Jim, their roadie, barged in without knocking, a look of panic on his face.

'It's your saxophone, Chris. I can't find it. It's not in the van!'

'Of course it's in the van,' Chris replied soothingly. 'I put it in myself this morning. It was wedged behind one of the drum cases.'

'You just come and look for it, then. Show me where you put it.'

Chris followed Jim out, with a quick, 'Oh, these hysterical men!' grimace to Bonnie, but when they reached the van and she had had a good scrabble around, she had to admit, with a horrible sinking feeling, that Jim was right.

'Did you leave the van unattended for a second?' she asked suspiciously.

'I might have done. There's only me to do the unpacking, after all. That lot haven't been much help tonight. I went and asked for a hand and they were all too busy playing Brag. Was it insured?' he asked, looking like a sympathetic Jesus with his long, dark hair and beard.

'Yes, thank goodness.' Her father, with his belief in insurance, had insisted that she pay fifty pounds for it to be covered for theft and damage.

Her bottom lip started quivering and Jim pulled her to him, scratching her cheek with his beard. 'Let's go and report it, shall we, chicken? No point standing out here all night. I'm sorry if it was my fault, but I did my best to lock the van every time I left it. I wonder if it could have fallen out during the day? How about that place where we stopped for lunch?'

'I don't think it could have just fallen out. The case was quite tightly wedged, I made sure of that. I didn't want it getting bounced about,' Chris said in a quavery voice. She felt quite weak and shivery.

'You'll have to come with me to the phone, to speak to the police, as you know the details of the make and serial number. Then I suppose we'd better ring George . . . No, we'd better tell the manager of the club first.' Jim went off to talk to the manager, leaving Chris to break the news to the rest of Jalova. But she got no further than Bonnie, and collapsed sobbing in her arms.

She was crying so loudly that at first she didn't hear Jim's voice.

'*Chris*!' he called from the doorway, louder and more urgently. 'I said, we've found it!'

She raised a tear-streaked face. 'Where . . . where was it?' she asked, her voice coming out all croaky.

'You won't believe this, but Howie offered to help me have a final search and it was right underneath the spare tyre. If Howie hadn't thought of looking there –'

Howie . . . of course! How easy for him to find it, if he was the one who had hidden it in the first place, thought Chris grimly. It was obvious what he was trying to do: crack her nerve so she would play badly on their last night, just when the record company had promised to transport a group of music journalists to the show. Her fright had left her feeling jumpy and drained and she was aware that her hands were trembling. Yes, it would be only too easy to play badly tonight. But why should she give Howie that satisfaction?

She had the saxophone case by her side. 'Bonnie?' she asked. 'Could I ask you a colossal favour? Leave me on my own for a few minutes, to get myself together?'

Bonnie gave her an understanding smile. 'Sure, babes. When you want me, I'll be putting on my fiftieth coat of mascara in the loo!'

She and Jim went out and the door closed behind them.

Chris stretched and took a gasping breath. She unclasped her sax case, took the instrument out and fitted on the mouthpiece and a new reed. They wore out quickly and she had gone through two in a week, at seventy pence a time. There was no point in trying to carry on with a worn-out one, it only took the edge off the tone and made it sound flabby.

She formed her lips around the mouthpiece, noting the scuffmarks her teeth had made on it. She had bought a new mouthpiece shortly after acquiring the sax, feeling it was more hygienic. Somehow, the teethmarks made it truly hers. She moved it a little further in and played half a dozen deep, resonant notes, then pulled it out a little and played an octave higher, all the while trying to feel a relaxing calmness flow through her.

It refused to come. She tried deep breathing, tried emptying her mind of all thoughts, yet still she felt wobbly and twitchy. Hell! Try a colour. Blue . . . Ice-blue eyes under snowy hair, set in a mobile, chiselled face. She recalled that time during the first gig of the tour, when thinking of Lester had suddenly revitalised her lacklustre playing. Could the same miracle be worked twice?

Lester . . . Lester . . . She whispered his name under her breath, like a talisman. And, like a candle lit in a dark room, she felt every gloomy bit of her begin to glow.

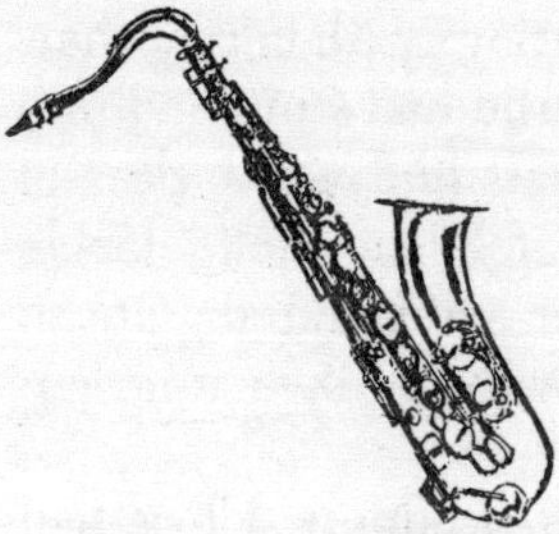

CHAPTER • 9 •

As Chris walked through the Childrenswear department on Tuesday morning, she was conscious of receiving some very strange looks which made the skin down her arms and up the back of her neck tingle.

Hurriedly, she swung through her door into the staff loo and found Syl combing her hair.

'Hi!' she greeted her. Syl turned round, but didn't smile. 'I'm better at last . . .' Chris said hopefully. Surely Syl wasn't angry with her? She couldn't be. Syl was her friend.

She tried again. 'This is really me, you know, not my ghost.'

Syl chewed her bottom lip nervously. 'I . . . I don't know how to tell you this. Oh, you'll see for yourself, I suppose. They've, er . . . they've brought in a replacement. They assumed you weren't coming back. Oh, Chris!' she said rebukingly. 'When Kenny Harris brought that copy of the *Post* in on Friday –'

'What do you mean?' The *Post* was one of Chris's local papers. 'What was in it?'

'Only an article on Jalova and the tour, and a big bit on you, as you're a local girl. Walshy took it straight down to Personnel, and now you're right in the shit. What your mother said didn't help, either. Ssh!' Syl suddenly put her index finger to her lips and glanced towards the door. 'Quick! Hide in one of the loos. I think it's Bat-Face!'

Bat-Face was Jean Philips, their departmental manager, the very last person Chris wanted to see before she had thought up a good story. She was furious with her mother. When she had seen her briefly, as she had stumbled into the kitchen to make a piece of toast and get a glass of orange juice, which were all she felt she could tackle after three hours' sleep, her mother had grunted, 'Oh, so you're back,' and had then got on with her own going-to-work preparations.

Pasty-faced and piggy-eyed with tiredness, Chris had fancied she looked a genuine post-flu case. She had known that, sooner or later, she would be asked for a doctor's note, but her plan had been to say that she would pick it up that evening and bring it in the next day.

As she quaked behind the locked door of the cubicle, she heard Bat-Face tell Syl to stop titivating herself and put the float in the till. The door banged – obviously Syl had scuttled out to do the boss's bidding – then she heard Bat-Face use the loo, flush it, wash her hands, and finally, after an aeon of tense silence, her heels clack-clacked across the tiled floor to the door, leaving Chris alone.

What should she do? As she sat on the closed lid of the toilet, her elbows resting on her knees, her chin on her hands, she stared blankly at the handbag hook on the back of the door as alternatives raced through her mind and her heart bumped with fear and uncertainty. She could go straight to Personnel with a trumped-up story, but they already knew it wasn't true. For all she knew, her mother had come straight out and admitted that she had gone on tour with the band.

How about if she were to get Bat-Face or Walshy on their own and try to win their sympathy? But she knew it wouldn't be worth it. They were far too straight and establishment-minded to bend the rules for her.

Cautiously, she crept towards the door and unbolted it, opened it just a crack and looked around. Then, finding no one had crept in undetected on soft-soled shoes, she walked towards the window. The Childrenswear department was on the first floor. Leaning across one of the basins, she unlatched one of the old-fashioned windows and looked down onto a network of cast-iron pipes and the tops of two walls. Yes, it might just be possible . . .

Scrambling on top of one of the basins, she edged towards the sill and squatted down on her haunches, working out the best route. She would have to be quick, before anyone came in and caught her. It was a four-foot drop to the top of the nearest wall, and there was a horizontal pipe about two feet below the sill. She took off her shoes and tucked them into the waistband of her brown uniform skirt; then, hanging onto the window frame, she swung her legs over the sill and began to edge along the pipe.

She heard the door of the ladies' bang, and froze. Her shadow was visible through the frosted glass, her hand was still clutching the window, and there was a good fourteen-foot drop below her! Chris crouched down, praying the pipe would take her weight, and let go of the window, grasping instead at a section of vertical pipe. The moment she heard the door of a cubicle click shut, she launched one foot into space and felt about for the top of the wall. Finding it, she reached down, took hold of the pipe she was standing on, swung sideways and got both her feet onto the top of the wall. But she was still holding the pipe and the rest of her body was spanning the drop. She was stuck!

What if somebody saw her? She was suspended over an area that, judging by the garbage cans and piles of boxes, was outside the ground-floor coffee bar. At any minute, a member of staff could come out to chuck something away, and see her. They would think she was a burglar! No, hardly. Not while she was still wearing her regulation skirt and blouse and staff badge. What would they make of someone who was breaking *out*, rather than breaking in?

Her position was growing uncomfortable. Maybe, if she gave a push with her hands and let go, she would be able to drop into a quick crouch on top of the wall and get her balance, before looking for footholds and climbing down.

There! She let go – but she had overestimated the power of push needed. With wildly flailing arms, she stood upright on the wall just for an instant, then found herself falling through space. Before she even had time to think of the injuries she might incur, she was landing with a bruising, breath-robbing crash on a pile of (fortunately empty) cardboard boxes.

Chris was up in an instant, gasping for breath, rubbing her arm and hip, which hurt. She had to get out of here before she was seen. She was in a kind of alleyway and could see what looked like part of an enormous shed at the end. Of course! At the back of the store was a council depot for refuse trucks and road cleaning vehicles. If she just walked down the narrow cobbled way, she would find herself back in the main street.

She undid the pin of her staff name-badge and went to drop it in her bag. But she had no bag! Her stomach lurched in panic. What had she done with it? Had she dropped it in her scramble from the window? With a sickening sinking feeling, she remembered putting it down on the floor of the loo cubicle. It was still there, complete with her purse, diary, doorkeys and Travelcard.

The sky seemed to swirl around her head. She felt herself sway slightly and had to stumble towards the wall, where she placed one hand on it for support. She could not go back into the store – no way! She would be walking right into what she had just gone to a supreme effort, and sustained numerous scrapes and bruises, to escape from. But without the contents of her bag, she was stuck. She couldn't even go home. She didn't even know anyone nearby from whom she could borrow any money.

Then she thought of the Russell Rooms. There was just a chance, a very, very slight one . . .

As she approached the reception desk, she was aware of what a picture she must make, in her dishevelled state, with her tights all holed and laddered, her right knee bleeding, the sleeve of her jacket torn. The man at the desk stared at her and frowned. 'Yes?' he said curtly.

'Er . . . I was wondering what room Lester Mulley is in? I'm a student of his,' Chris announced as coolly as possible, just as if she had stepped out of a limousine wearing a dress from the latest Next catalogue. If *she* ignored her appearance, *he* would have to.

The thin, anxious-looking man consulted the book. 'Sorry, Mr Mulley doesn't appear to be coming in today. Did you have an appointment with him?'

The knowledge took the wind right out of her sails. 'Oh,' she said, in a crestfallen tone and felt tears pricking at her eyelids. How *could* he not be here? Couldn't he have felt she was in trouble, and come to her rescue? Her battered limbs suddenly began to ache abominably, and her tears were too hot and big to hold back. They splashed out and down her cheeks.

'Are you in some sort of trouble, dear? You haven't been attacked, have you? I could ring the police . . .'

'No, don't do that, I'm OK. I've lost my bag and my money, that's all . . .' Chris decided to let him draw his own conclusions as to the circumstances.

The man tutted and pushed his glasses up his nose. 'I think it's wrong to let these fellows get away with it. Still, I suppose they'll be miles away by now. They never seem to catch them, do they?'

'I . . . I can't get home, I've got no money or keys,' Chris choked out between sniffs. 'I was hoping that Lester . . . Mr Mulley . . .'

'Do you know his telephone number?' the man asked in a kindly tone.

Chris told him. She had memorised it the first time he had ever given it to her. She had found it strangely easy, though as a rule she was very bad at remembering people's numbers. As the man dialled, she dug for a screwed-up tissue in her pocket and blew her nose. She prayed Lester would be in. He *had* to be!

'I've got a young lady here who says she knows you. She's been in a spot of trouble,' the man was saying.

Hooray, he was in! The man was beckoning her towards the phone.

'Lester? It's Chris – Chris Lindsell. You're . . . you're not in the middle of anything, are you?'

He was almost at the end of a lesson. He sounded concerned about her.

'I won't tell you about it now, but is there any chance you could come and get me? I'm stuck at the Russell Rooms and I haven't any money or anything . . .'

He said he would be with her in half an hour. While she was waiting for him, the man made her a cup of tea.

'It's so kind of you,' she told him gratefully. 'I don't know what I would have done . . .'

'You remind me of my granddaughter,' he said. 'She's got a smile like yours. Go on, let's see it.' His little ploy to cheer her up worked, and she found herself grinning for the first time that day. And then at last the door swung open and Lester came striding in, and it was all she could do not to fly into his arms.

Her tale of woe was punctuated by barks of laughter from Lester as he accelerated away from the traffic lights.

'You climbed out of the window of the ladies'? I've never heard anything so funny. You make it sound like escaping from Holloway Prison!'

'It's not far off that,' she retorted.

'I think the best thing I can do is take you to my place and let you call that friend of yours, what's-her-name – Syl? Perhaps she can meet you later with your handbag. Do you know, I think you should phone your record company, too. The story would be great publicity if they could get it into the press.'

'I'm in a lot of trouble which hasn't been sorted out yet,' Chris reminded him. 'I've probably lost my job.'

'I should think you have.'

'But I won't get a reference. What am I going to do?' she wailed.

'Have a hit record, it's the only answer.'

'Huh! Easier said than done . . .'

She rang Syl and arranged a lunchtime rendezvous. She wished she could get home and change out of her conspicuous outfit. Syl said she had lots to tell her. While she was on the phone, Lester started running her a bath.

'I've put a clean towel out on the chair. Take your time. Sorry I haven't got any of that stuff which sends knights on shining chargers galloping up to your window,' he joked.

'You'll do,' she told him, with a grin. He smiled back, and once again she felt that tug, as if someone was tightening a cord which strung them together. He had a blue shirt on which accentuated the blue of his eyes, so that they looked like the sea in summer. Those romantic stories always went on about drowning in somebody's eyes. She could drown in his all right and it would be a painless death.

He cleared his throat, and she snapped guiltily out of her reverie, fearing that he had suspected the theme.

'I'll, er, go and take that bath then.'

'I think you might need some antiseptic cream on those scratches. There's some in the bathroom cabinet,' he told her. 'When you come down, I'll make some coffee.'

The bath was wonderful, soothing both her aches and pains and her jangling nerves. It felt distinctly furtive, to be looking in someone else's bathroom cabinet, but he had given her permission. There was a tube of cream right at the front and she took it out, but couldn't resist a good peep at the rest of the contents. Deodorant, an electric shaver, headache pills, a packet of tablets for holiday tummy . . . so he got the gut-rot when he went on holiday, too?

Then she noticed the packet of tampons in one corner, and a bottle of red nail varnish next to a pot of moisturiser. The moisturiser could possibly be his, but not the other two items! Her heart beat a fast tattoo. Did that mean he lived with someone? Was that what Marijke had been trying to warn her about, that night in the restaurant? She had never noticed any female belongings around the place, but perhaps he tidied them up during the day while he had people in for lessons.

Chris reminded herself that Lester wasn't a tidy person. She also realised that a resident woman would have more things openly scattered around the bathroom. Scented soaps, bath oil, hair conditioner . . . This bathroom lacked a woman's touch, too. It was austere. No shells or dried flowers or pretty curtains. So maybe she only came for weekends . . .

It had to be that Mary, Chris decided. Did she bring the two boys? If so, then maybe one of the bedrooms was their room and she would find toys in it and spaceship posters on the walls, if she had the cheek to look. Not today, though. She had seen enough for now.

Chris didn't feel completely flattened by her discovery, she found as she towelled herself dry. If he had no woman living here, then he couldn't be deeply in love. He had told her himself that Soundwaves took up most of his evenings, so any relationship that had to be fitted around his schedule and rehearsals and gigs would have to be a casual one. She reckoned, from observing people like Carol and Grant, that when you were in love, you wanted to be with your partner every minute of the day. Any woman who fell in love with Lester was in for a lean time. *Unless she was another musician . . .*

Chris Lindsell, Soundwaves' second horn player, girlfriend of Lester Mulley; it was a wild, wicked, fabulous thought, and it made Chris feel as hot inside as the bath had made her feel on the surface. If she were to practise really hard for the next twelve months, and gain loads of experience of playing in public, might there be a chance for her to play full-time with Lester? Just doing fill-ins and backing riffs?

It would be an awful lot better than playing with Jalova. Although Chris had felt elated at being able to put Howie down by not cracking up during the final gig, she was nevertheless dreading their next meeting. As for the thought of another tour . . . There would be news from George today or tomorrow, all the latest on the record. She wanted the record to do well, of course. She wanted them to release her composition as a single. But she felt quite split over it, too. How could she carry on playing if she had Howie hassles all the time?

Another thing that was worrying her slightly, too, was that she was starting to find their style of music, with its predictable rhythms, just a bit restricting. It must be hard on Bonnie, too, she thought, always having to punch it out and move about with never a chance to sing with real feeling. But at least she had her romance with Curtis . . .

'Hey, Chris? Are you nearly out? Coffee's ready,' Lester yelled up the staircase. 'I've got Kal and Marijke coming any time now, to run over some new material.'

Chris groaned inwardly as she began hastily dressing. She had hoped for some time alone with him and now her plans were dashed.

When the doorbell rang, she was the one to answer it, because Lester had just gone out into the garden to retrieve some clothes from the line, as it had started spotting with rain. Marijke stood on the step and looked surprised to see Chris.

'How did the tour go? Shouldn't you be back at work?' she asked.

'OK. Not brilliant. One or two hassles,' Chris replied. 'And as for work . . . well, I think I've left!'

She told Marijke briefly about it as the two of them went into the lounge. Lester reappeared and greeted his vocalist. 'I'd make some more coffee but I've just run out of milk,' he told them. 'Hold the fort and I'll dash out and get some. Kal should be here any minute. About a quarter past eleven, he said when he rang me earlier.'

The front door slammed behind him and Chris was left alone with Marijke. She knew it was a golden opportunity to quiz her further about Lester, and that remark she had made about 'being careful'. She hoped Marijke wouldn't mind.

Marijke brought the subject up before Chris had had a chance to speak. 'I've been hoping we'd bump into each other soon, Chris. I wanted to talk to you.'

Chris instantly felt on the defensive. 'About Lester?' she said tightly.

'Mm-hm. I'm not blind, you know. I can tell you're starting to fall for him and I wouldn't like to see you hurt.'

'I can look after myself.'

'I'm sure you can.' Marijke sighed. In the slight gloom of the long room, her skin had a greenish tinge, giving Chris the sudden fantasy that she was a visitor from outer space. 'I'm worried about Lester, too. He's such an attractive guy. Women are always falling for him.'

Chris felt a stab of jealousy. Then something dawned on her. 'You sound as though you're pretty keen on him yourself.' She stared at the older woman.

Marijke shrugged her thin shoulders. 'I fell madly in love with him when I first met him,' she confessed. 'I'd just started going out with Steve and he was already Lester's bass player. I went to a gig, and *bingo*! I just had to look at him and . . . Well, you know. Then Steve suggested I sing with the band. It was torture, fancying Lester like mad, but going out with Steve.

'Steve guessed, of course, he's not thick. We had a row about it and Steve told me I'd never get anywhere because Lester had had some bad deals from women and was pretty cynical. I thought at the time that Steve was just saying it to try and put me off, but I've found out a lot about him since then, and I think there's a grain of truth there somewhere. He's a very sensitive guy, easily hurt. His emotions go deep and he doesn't talk about them. Even though he seems so friendly and outgoing on the surface, it's hard to get really close to him. But then, I'm no psychotherapist! I've got over my infatuation, anyway, and I'm happy with Steve, but I thought I saw you heading the same way I did–'

'He mentioned his ex-wife to me once,' Chris cut in, remembering that evening in the wine bar. 'What really happened?'

'Basically, she took him for every penny he had. Their daughter was young then, and she got the big house and he had to pay a fortune in maintenance. He was very bitter.'

Chris realised how little he had really told her that night. 'But didn't he go on making a lot of money out of music?' she asked. 'Surely he could afford a better house than this, in a posher area?'

'Don't forget that his old style of music, that very mannered rock with lots of equipment and effects, went out in the early seventies. Punk came in in '76. Lester had been getting keener and keener on jazz, so he studied it and changed over. But it's not so easy to make a lot of money in the jazz world. People play it for the love of it, not to have a top-ten single. He was still earning money from royalties on his old songs and records and he did some film scores and television soundtrack music. I don't think he was doing badly. He just went off the whole commercial pop scene. And then he met Mary and they started living together and had the little boy.'

'Why didn't they get married?'

'I think he'd probably – Oh, that's the door.' As Marijke got up to let Kal in, Chris cursed the interruption. As soon as Lester came back, she made her farewells, having borrowed enough from him for her fare into town so that she could meet Syl.

She had been waiting in the Wimpy for six minutes exactly when Syl came in, brandishing her bag.

'Oh, thank goodness!' Chris breathed, taking it and hugging it to her. 'If someone else had found it before you did –'

'I was watching the door and as soon as Bat-Face beat it, I dashed in to give you the all-clear, but you'd disappeared. It was as if Scotty had beamed you up and only your bag had been left behind. I must say I was totally baffled. How did you do it?' Syl gabbled eagerly.

When Chris told her, Syl's eyebrows nearly disappeared into her hair. 'You climbed out of the window?' she repeated incredulously. 'But why?'

'It seemed the only way of avoiding the inquisition. I panicked, I suppose. Anyway, did anything happen?'

'I'll say it did! Walshy went barmy and Personnel kept ringing your parents, to try and *find out what's happened to you*!' Syl shrieked, over the jangling of a fire engine's bell. 'That's probably on its way to rescue someone else who's trying to climb out of the window.' Syl sniggered, as it raced past.

'Bat-Face has probably jumped out and forgotten her broomstick!' contributed Chris, and they both roared with laughter.

'What'll you do if you've got the sack?' Syl asked, sobering up the atmosphere. She absent-mindedly heaped a third spoonful of sugar into her coffee, then grimaced when she tasted it.

Chris shrugged. 'Go on the dole, I suppose.'

'They're looking for a barmaid at the White Hart . . .'

'That's no good. It's in the evenings, and I play with the band in the evenings. I need a daytime job – part-time, preferably. If only I could type better,' Chris sighed. She munched into her cheeseburger, thinking that food had never tasted more delicious. Her last solid meal had been sausage, egg and chips at six the previous evening, in a transport café. No wonder she was getting spots. Now that she was back, she must start eating plenty of salads.

'How about going on a college course? They'll all be starting some time in September,' Syl pointed out.

'I could do word-processing, perhaps,' Chris said ruminatively. She didn't really want to be stuck in a classroom all day, though. Fancy having a record out and having to think about taking courses! She wanted to be appearing on television, playing at the Hammersmith Odeon. Fame was so quick when it came, it happened overnight. When was it going to be her turn? She hoped she wouldn't have to wait for long . . .

It was with a sinking heart that Chris returned to her parents' house to await the ordeal of the inevitable cross-questioning and upset. There were a couple of letters for her, which she hadn't noticed, either when she had crawled in in the middle of the night or that morning. She opened them. One was from an old school friend, Kim, inviting her to a party. The other was also an invitation – from her cousin Jenny, asking her to be a bridesmaid at her wedding.

I tried to reach you on the phone but Aunt Joan said you were never in these days, so I thought I'd better write, reported Jenny. Chris could just imagine the tone of voice in which her mother had complained about her absence. *The wedding will be on Boxing Day. That's the date Mother and Father got married, so Mike and I decided to carry on the family tradition. I was planning on crimson for the bridesmaids' dresses – nice and warm for winter. Do let me know right away if you can do it. I hope so. You were my first choice.*

Jenny, who was twenty-two, was the daughter of Chris's

father's elder brother, Joe, and her auntie Clare. She only saw them about twice a year as they lived in Devon, but Chris had always liked her cousin, and Jenny's two brothers: Jeff, who was in the air force, and Tim, who had just qualified as a vet.

'Wonder why it was Joe's children who got all the brains in the family?' Chris could remember her mother grumbling to her father when her O-level results came. Jenny was pretty brilliant, too. She had got a degree in maths and physics – she had met Mike at university – and had just finished her teacher's training. Chris felt a vague, sullen jealousy of people like her cousins, whose futures were assured, whereas hers was a straight choice between making it in the music business, or the dole queue. Yet she knew she would never want to swop with Jenny. Who would want to be a teacher, stuck in a classroom all day with thirty or more rebellious pupils, trying to find ways of shutting them up and getting them interested? Her own way of life might be riskier, but it was a lot freer and more exciting.

And as for getting married – surely that spelled the end of all your ambitions? Chris couldn't see any reason for marriage other than having children, and that was years off as far as she was concerned. Babies and bands didn't mix. She didn't think jobs and bands did, either.

She still had some faint hopes that things would sort themselves out at work, if only she could make up a convincing story, but they were promptly dashed when her mother came home from work.

'Mum, did anyone from the shop ring while I was away?' she enquired.

'Yes.' Mrs Lindsell's face was stern. 'Imagine how I felt when I found out you'd been lying, to me and to them. Holiday, indeed! The poor lady who rang was most concerned about you. "How is your daughter?" she said to me. "Perfectly well when I last saw her," I said. "She was on her way to Manchester. She was very pleased that the store could give her a holiday at such short notice."

'"Holiday?" said the lady. "She hasn't asked for any holiday. We all thought she'd been taken ill." I've never been so embarrassed, Chris. I could have curled up and died! I had to apologise and say I didn't know what had happened, and it was true. I *didn't* know. You've got a lot of explaining to do, my girl . . .'

Chris bit her lip, avoiding her mother's eyes. 'I – I just thought it would be easier,' she whispered, feeling quite sick. It had been such a perfect plan. If only it had worked!

'Easier? To tell lies to everyone? To risk losing your job in these days of unemployment? How long is this record going to take to become a hit? You tell me that! A year from now, you'll still be signing on down the dole office, still dreaming of fame and fortune. Oh, you silly girl!'

Chris raised her head defiantly. 'I wish I could prove you wrong, I really do.'

'So do I.'

Mother and daughter stood in silence, staring each other out. I wish she'd believe in me, Chris thought. If only she'd give me her support. It's not my fault that I like the saxophone better than any other instrument. Why can't *she* learn to like it?

It was Mrs Lindsell who turned away first. 'Oh well, it's your life,' she commented wearily, picking up one of the sofa cushions and pummelling it into shape a little too savagely. 'You've got to make your own mistakes. I can't say I never made any . . .'

Something about her tone of voice made Chris prick her ears up. What was she referring to? From the tinge of bitterness, she could mean marrying Chris's father. Chris swallowed hard. It was difficult trying to see your own parents, not as Mum and Dad but as Joan and Denis, a couple, just as Carol and Grant were a couple, or Jenny and Mike. She had to take a mental step backwards from them, then try to bring them into focus, like specimens under a microscope. If she were to be introduced to them, never having met them before, would she think they were compatible as a pair? She thought of her mother's moods and grumpiness, her father's cowboy films and manic drinking bouts. Had they always been like that, or had they driven each other that way? Whatever the case, they didn't seem to fit well together at all. Maybe they had only stayed married because of her . . .

No, that was stupid, Chris realised. Divorce was easy these days. No one had to stay with their husband or wife if they couldn't stand them. Children didn't come into it. Anyway, she was an adult now, so even that weak reason didn't count.

Her mother had sat down and picked up her library book. Chris still stood there awkwardly, not knowing whether or not the subject was closed. Then she heard the front door opening and her father came home, and her misdemeanours began to be gone over again.

'I think all you can do is go in there tomorrow and apologise, say you'll never do such a thing again and ask if they'll give you another chance,' said her father.

'I don't think they will,' Chris said doubtfully. 'They've already got someone in to do my job. They thought I wasn't coming back.'

'What else were they supposed to think? They'd seen that piece in the paper, knew you'd pulled a fast one . . . The main question is, do you want to go back to the store or don't you?'

Chris answered her mother's question immediately.

'No. I've had enough. I want to concentrate on music now. I've got lots of ideas and I need time to work on them. I've been looking through my old notebooks of poems. There are several things there that could be set to music –'

'But it's such a dicey business,' her mother pointed out. 'At least in the store you'd be secure and have a regular wage coming in –'

'And always be a titchy cog in a gigantic wheel, making money for somebody else,' retorted Chris. 'Don't you see the difference, either of you? Wouldn't you rather have a chance to do something by yourself, to make a go of it, achieve an ambition?' She recalled her conversation with her father when he had told her he had no ambition. Oh well! At least she was trying . . .

Mrs Lindsell sighed, a sound which coincided with the hiss as Denis Lindsell pulled back the ring on his can of beer. 'Of course your father and I want you to do well, love. It's just that you don't seem to have thought anything out properly. You're rushing at everything, acting too impulsively. I don't want you to do anything rash that you might regret – and I can't help repeating that we're terrified of you getting involved with drugs. We do read the papers, you know. I used to buy *Melody Maker* when I was your age.'

Chris boggled at her mother. It was hard to imagine her as a teenager, and even harder to picture her reading music papers. She said cajolingly, 'Maybe you'd better start reading it again. There could be something about me in it.' It was her way of trying to bridge the gap between them, but would it work? There were such vast gulfs of anger and misunderstanding in the way.

Her mother gave a little shiver and rubbed her arms, but she didn't take up the thread. The moment between them was lost.

'I'm going out for a while,' Chris decided. 'I'm going over to Linda's.' After the tense scene with her parents, she needed the happy chaos of Linda's home to distract her and help her unwind.

She rang Lee from Linda's, and he said that George wanted to talk to them all the next day. He seemed delighted when Chris told him about leaving her job. 'There'll be some money coming to you from the tour. That should keep you going for a while,' he reminded her. With all the furore over her job, she had forgotten about that.

George, looking even more Mexican than usual with his droopy moustache bristling, was sitting behind his untidy desk when his secretary showed them in at eleven the next morning.

'Right. Nice to see you. Glad the tour went well. The feedback's been good and I've got the write-ups here. They should help to convince the record company to shell out some shekels. As you know, they didn't put up an advance for the album because they felt they were testing the water, as you didn't have much of a following. But I feel sure I can persuade them to part with some pennies for the next one, particularly if the single does well.'

'Single?' Bonnie queried. 'We hadn't heard anything about that.'

'Well, I haven't exactly been able to get hold of you for a week or so, have I? They're releasing 'Johnson's Party' as an A-side, with 'Call You Up' on the B-side. Now, I've got some papers here that you've got to sign. You should have done them before the album was released, when you signed the contract with the record company. It's a publishing contract for the songs, some forms for PRS, and finally, I think it's time we made our own arrangement a bit more formal.

'I've asked a guy called Tom Mortimer to pop in. He's a

solicitor. He'll be here any minute. He'll go over the contracts with you, explain if there's anything you don't understand. I take it you do want me to manage you?'

His rather ferrety face grinned round from one to the other and when his thin-lipped smile reached Chris, she found she couldn't smile back. What was it her mother had said about rushing into things? She was being rushed now, all right.

'Er . . . how long do these contracts last for?' she asked.

'The publishing ones are for eighteen months. That's quite fair. In the old days, you used to sign away your songs for life plus fifty years, but a few big court cases have sorted that out! The management contract is for a year initially, with options on either side. Is that OK? Anything you're not happy about?'

Chris gulped. There was one absolutely enormous thing which she wasn't at all happy about.

'Yes. I'm not quite sure if I want to stay in the band . . .'

CHAPTER • 10 •

In less than twenty-four hours Chris had ended up minus both a job and a band. After the awful scene at George's, which she still couldn't face thinking about, she had fled home, put on a cassette of Sting's, *The Dream of the Blue Turtles*, placed her headphones over her ears, lain full length on her bed and cried.

It was the first good cry she had had in a long time, and all kinds of things, such as the endless arguments with her parents, the Howie drama, the collapse of her relationship with Ian Fowler and the impossibility of her situation with Lester, came welling up and spilling out onto her pillow.

It was a good hour before she felt her tears drying up and her mind going numb and blank. Then, like an automaton, she detached herself from her personal stereo and went to bathe her face. Feeling almost human again, she sat back on the edge of her bed and tried to make some sense out of everything, but her thoughts kept skittering away like a herd of nervous ponies every time she tried to catch hold of them. In the end she took a notebook and a pen, thinking that if she could see her problems in writing, she might be able to focus on them better.

Parents, she wrote first. Then she put down her notebook and thought. The problem of her practising wasn't going to get any better. The only solution would be to move to a flat where there were people who didn't mind musicians. That was going to take a while to find and in the meantime she was going to have to compromise at home, especially as she was in the doghouse over losing her job.

Money, she wrote next. Beneath the word, she jotted down the salary cheque she hoped to receive, for a week's wages plus any days owing to her for holiday. She optimistically added on three days. Then she wrote down the very disappointing sum they had received for the tour once their petrol and accommodation, general expenses and George's percentage which he had claimed for fixing up the tour, had been taken out. Two hundred and sixty pounds she had been left with, when she had hoped for nearly five hundred. What a rip-off! Another thought struck her with an uncomfortable jolt: how would she be able to buy her new sax on instalments if she didn't have a job? She would be refused credit straight away, and she wouldn't be able to save anything out of her dole money.

The next item on the problem list was *Music*. Unpredictably, Howie had been a pig. True, Bonnie and Lee had tried to speak up for her, but Curtis had kept very quiet, which was as good as admitting that he agreed with Howie. A tight-lipped little virgin, Howie had called her. She was a virgin, it was true, and she wasn't ashamed of it, and what difference did it make to her playing? Prick-teaser, he had accused, and at that she had seen red. She had not led him on in any way. Never! He was a selfish, spoilt male-chauvinist of the worst kind, and she had told him so in front of all the others.

'If that silly, sulky little bitch stays in the band, I'm quitting,' Howie had said. 'She's not much good, anyway.'

'And if that lying pig stays in it, *I'm* going!' Chris had thundered.

George had attempted to make the peace. 'Chris is a good composer. It's her number that the company have chosen for the single,' he said.

'Then they've got cloth ears. It's not even our style of music,' Howie had spat.

'On the other hand, Chris is a very recent member of the group and Howie has been in it for some time. And I must say that you seem to have changed direction slightly since those earlier tracks were recorded, and that's since Chris joined. Only you can work out where you want to go. A girl sax player is a plus –'

'Huh! She'll never pull in a male audience. You should see the way she dresses in those black sacks!' Howie interrupted.

'That was never what I was in the band for!' Chris said hotly.

'That's my job, anyway,' butted in Bonnie. 'I like dressing the way I do. It gives me a kick. I don't mind being ogled a bit, as long as they keep their gropy hands to themselves.'

'OK, OK,' George said. 'These papers here have to be signed. Chris, you must sign this publishing deal whether you're going or staying.'

Chris signed it savagely, almost tearing through the paper.

Howie got to his feet. 'I'm off. Plenty more bands are looking for a good funky bass player. I'll have no difficulty getting another gig. You can keep *that*.' He pointed at Chris and she flew at him, all set to hit him, but was restrained by Lee.

'*Let me go*!' she yelled, trying to wrench her arm free. Howie was still standing by the door. '*I'll* leave. He's more use to you than I am. I've never really felt part of this band, anyway. I never wanted to change your style. It was fun guesting on those album tracks, but I should have left it at that.'

Lee released her. Howie was still waiting, a faint smile of triumph on his face.

'You're not going to let her just walk out like this?' Bonnie appealed to the others. 'She was so good on the tour . . .'

'So were you,' Curtis grunted. 'You're all we need.'

Chris knew that by *all*, he meant 'all the women', and she gritted her teeth. 'Just send me any royalties that are due to me,' she said stiffly. 'You know my address.'

She shouldered her way past Howie, avoiding his face. 'I'll be in touch!' Lee called after her.

Well, it was an experience, she thought now. I learned a lot, gained a lot. That time on the road, learning to play to an audience . . . My first write-ups. They were worth having. Perhaps she would look through the *Musicians Wanted* columns in the music papers.

She was about to start a fourth subject, headed *Men*, when she stopped. They had done her enough damage for the time being. Ian had caused a wound which, while it had healed now, had left scar tissues of mistrustfulness behind. Howie was out of her life, but his attitude was still rankling. And Lester could never care for her. It was her own stupid fault if she was suffering from unrequited love. She was behaving like a stupid little girl.

Some lines from a poem by C. Day Lewis which she had done at school suddenly floated back to her . . . *I imagine you really gone for ever. Clocks stop./Clouds bleed. Flames numb.* It would be like that if she couldn't see

Lester, if she had to stop loving him, even in her silent, secret way. If someone ordered her never to have a warm, yearning feeling for him ever again, could she do it? Could she switch off, on pain of death? No. It would be like being told she must never play the saxophone again. Her playing came from her emotions – and emotions, music and Lester were inseparably linked. Without feelings, without Lester, without music, she might as well be dead.

Suddenly, all the other problems on her list became smaller and less important, and Chris smiled and reached for her saxophone case. The house was empty.

By mid-afternoon, Chris had completed her second full-length composition. Called 'Cry It Out', she felt it really had been torn from the depths of her heart. It was in G minor. It started on B flat, went down to A, then swooped down an octave and back up again, then up to D, C, then that swoop again, like the bottom falling out of her world. She had even begun to think of some words to it. She hadn't intended to but they formed naturally in her head once she started playing the tune – *Cry, cry it out, Whatever it's all about, just cry it out . . .*

That evening, she managed to separate Carol from Grant and went out for a drink with her.

'I'll ask around where mum works and see if there's anything going,' Carol offered when she heard of Chris's job plight.

'No, I'd rather you didn't. Thanks for offering, though. I think I'll wait a while. Who knows, I might get into a really top band, or get some session work, if I'm extremely lucky. Have you been invited to Kim's party?'

'Yes. Are you going? Are you taking anyone?'

'Like who? You know I haven't got a boyfriend at the moment.'

'There's always your older man,' Carol said impishly.

'Lester, you mean?' Chris could feel herself blushing.

'Got you! You *are* keen on him, aren't you?' Carol was jubilant.

'Look, if you've got five hours, I'll tell you about it,' Chris offered. Maybe it would do her good to get it off her chest.

In the event, her tale only took about fifteen minutes. There wasn't really that much to tell. 'So you see, I'm in a really awkward position,' Chris finished up. 'If I show my feelings and make a wally of myself, he won't want to teach me any more, and I couldn't bear that. Besides, he might be able to give me some work with his band . . .'

'But you say he kissed you that time,' Carol recalled.

'Yes, but it was only a social kind of goodnight kiss, not anything special.'

'Hasn't he done or said anything that might mean he's interested?' her friend persisted.

'There is one thing you've got to realise about Lester and that's that he's a man of the world, he's been around. If he wanted to show a girl he was interested, I'm sure he would do,' said Chris despairingly. 'He just doesn't see me in that light at all.'

'Do you think he's too old?' probed Carol.

'No. I've thought a lot about it, and I don't. It's because he doesn't *seem* old. He could be any age. And there's his music . . .'

'What are you really in love with, him or his music?' asked Carol searchingly.

Chris thought. Then she answered, 'Both.'

'Have you thought that he might be hanging back thinking, "she's not interested" and waiting for a sign from you, just like you're doing with him?'

'I've told you, he's not like that.'

'Oh, I give up,' declared Carol, sweeping her long, fair hair back from her face. 'Fancy another lager?'

It was Fate, Chris decided, that made the piece of paper turn up again when it did. It was such a glorious, hot day that she decided to lie out in the back garden, and she was just scrabbling through her top drawer, looking for her bikini, when the folded sheet of paper popped out and landed on the floor in front of the chest of drawers.

Chris knew what it was without opening it – the telephone number of Jan, the girl with the panda hair. Her heart thumped excitedly. Now was the ideal time to give her a ring.

There was nobody in, so Chris went and lay in the garden, from time to time experiencing little tremors inside when she thought of seeing Lester later on. The second time she tried the number, she got a reply.

'Yes?' barked a suspicious female voice.

'You've probably forgotten who I am,' began Chris hesitantly. 'It was a long time ago. I met you in the 100 Club, the night Soundwaves were playing. I played sax for a number and you were thinking about forming a band . . .'

'Oh yes. I've forgotten your name.'

'Chris Lindsell. Are – are you still looking for musicians?'

'No, not really.' Chris's heart sank. 'A lot's happened since then. Christ, it *was* ages ago, wasn't it? Reet's having a baby, so all her musical plans have been postponed for a while as she didn't want to be leaping in and out of transit vans on the motorway when she was eight months gone. And I've joined To Hell And Back. Have you heard of them? We're doing sort of gothic horror rock.'

Chris hadn't heard of them.

'They're looking for a really good girl singer. I don't suppose you can sing, can you?'

'Not very well . . .' She immediately thought of Bonnie.

'Let me know if you hear of anyone, won't you? And why

don't we meet up, anyway? We've got a gig at the Greyhound tonight. Why don't you come along?'

Chris thought quickly. Her lesson was at seven thirty, she would be free by half eight, and that would give her plenty of time to get up to Fulham and catch at least part of their set.

'OK, I'll be there. We'll talk afterwards. I've got a record out!' Chris said proudly. 'I'll tell you about it later . . .'

Lester seemed very preoccupied. 'I'm a bit pushed for time tonight,' he told Chris. 'Do you mind if we cut the lesson a bit short?'

Normally, she would have been upset at the thought of not having so long to spend with him, gaze at him, be close to him, and at the reminder that she did not come first in his life but that he had many more important things going on that she couldn't even begin to guess at. Tonight, though, it fitted in perfectly with her own plans.

'I'll give you longer tomorrow, as you're free in the daytime.' She had told him about losing her job. 'How about a quarter to twelve, and we'll have some lunch afterwards?'

She felt sure her beam of happiness told him far too much . . .

The pub was packed and she had to fight her way to a vantage point from where she could see the band. They came on, all dressed in long black robes, with stark white make-up on their faces, so that they resembled vampires out of a Hammer horror movie. Chris recognised Jan straight away, from her two-tone hair, and watched her sit down behind the drum kit.

Jan had been right about the vocals. The girl singer just didn't have the power to make the lyrics heard above the screaming guitar and thundering drums. But Jan was good, Chris could tell that; dynamic, energetic, right on the beat and, in the quieter passages, subtle, too; a good base for her own playing.

Afterwards, as the roadies were clearing away the gear, she asked one of them if she could go and see Jan, and he led her to the van parked outside, around which the band were disconsolately drooped.

Jan waved to her and pulled a face. 'We bombed out, didn't we?' she said.

Chris shrugged. 'Just one of those nights,' she said consolingly.

'If you give me a chance to get out of this lot, we could go for a coffee,' Jan suggested. Chris waited while she went back inside, and returned wearing a long, sleeveless T-shirt over ancient jeans.

'Let's go,' she said, linking her arm in Chris's and speeding her off without a goodnight to her fellow musicians.

They found a greasy-spoon café and ordered a coffee and a toasted sandwich each.

'Tell me about you, first,' Jan said. She still had her white make-up on and was gathering strange looks from the other diners, a weird collection of cab drivers and down-and-outs.

Chris gave her a brief run-down on the events of the past few weeks, culminating in her leaving the band. Jan was particularly fascinated to hear about the record, and made her go over every detail.

'When's this single being released?' she enquired eagerly.

'Next Friday. I've had to go to the record company offices and sign a publishing contract.'

'Wow! Aren't you thrilled?'

'No. I just feel depressed. Just imagine if it does well? I won't even get on *Top of the Pops* to play it – they'll bring some session person in. It's my number and I'll get no fame and acclaim.' Just talking about it made her feel worse.

'I'm thinking of leaving my band, too, after tonight. Are you still in the market for getting something together?' Jan's eyes were sparkling with enthusiasm. 'Just think of what we could do! Jazz, funk, heavy metal . . . we could turn our hands to anything!'

'Starting from scratch would take so long, though,' Chris complained. 'Jalova had something going, they were getting a following. But we'd have nothing. It might take a year or more to get to that pitch . . .'

'How about that manager, George Thingummy? And anyway, if the single does well, the record company know you wrote it, so they'll be behind you. They might even offer us a deal . . .'

Chris promised to think about it, then dashed off to get her bus home . . . and found her mother sitting with a glass of sherry, entertaining Bonnie!

'I've split up with Curtis and I've left Jalova,' Bonnie said breathlessly, as soon as Mrs Lindsell had announced that she was going to bed and leaving them to it. 'I just *had* to see you. You don't mind, do you? Your mum's really nice, isn't she? She's got such a sense of humour.'

Chris stared. Bonnie might have been describing a total stranger. Her mother wasn't a bit like that. Sense of humour, indeed? But this news of Bonnie's was riveting. 'Come on, tell me everything!' she urged.

Bonnie pushed her half-filled sherry glass away from her across the coffee table. 'Yuk!' She grimaced. 'Much too sweet for me. It's like honey.'

Chris felt she was deliberately delaying things. 'Come *on* . . .'

Bonnie leaned forward and hugged her knees. She had a white dress on with a colourful silk scarf tied in a wide band round her waist. 'All men are rats!' she declared vitriolically.

'Don't I just know it!' Chris sighed.

'You don't know what happened after you went the other morning, of course. I've been trying to phone you but you haven't been in. There was a real battle and Howie was horrible.'

'Don't tell me!' said Chris emphatically.

'Lee and I were completely on your side, but Curtis has been really peculiar lately. He and I have had a lot of problems, which I won't go into now, and I think that's why he decided to take the opposite side to me, and side with Howie.

'The strange thing is, he's said loads of times how much he likes you, and how good your music is, but right then he started agreeing with Howie that the band had changed and it was all your doing.

'I said that if it hadn't been for your sax playing and songs making us sound different, we'd never have got our recording contract, and Curtis said Jalova was great as it was, and we'd have made it anyway, without you.

'I was so fed up with it all that I said I was leaving the band, too, and you should have seen their faces! George leaped up from his desk and I thought he was going to have a heart attack, thinking of all those percentages he wasn't going to get if there was no Jalova.

'Curtis said if I was leaving the band, then our relationship was all over, so I said OK, if you only wanted me for my singing, then I don't wish to know. Doesn't love come into it anywhere? I asked him, and do you know what? He never answered. So that's it.'

Although Bonnie shrugged it off, Chris knew that the

split-up with Curtis had hurt her a lot more than she was admitting. She reached out and gave Bonnie's arm a little squeeze.

'Plenty more fish in the sea,' she said.

Bonnie gave a wry grin. 'For both of us,' she grunted.

'Yeah,' Chris agreed. 'For both of us.'

Then she told her about Jan. 'I don't know how good she is, because she was playing with a pretty awful band, but it would give us a drummer, a saxophone player and a singer –'

'That's a pretty weird combination,' observed Bonnie.

'It's a start,' said Chris hopefully.

'Well, horrible though this sherry is, let's drink to it!' She raised her glass and passed it to Chris, who took a sip, shuddered and passed it back to Bonnie.

'Here's to fame and fortune and no more lousy men!' Chris declared stoutly.

'I'll second that,' said Bonnie.

Chris suggested Bonnie should sleep the night on the sofa-bed in the lounge, and fetched her some bedclothes. As her parents had long gone to bed, she taped a note to the door, saying: *Bonnie's sleeping in here – ssh!* because she knew her father got up early and clattered around in the kitchen/diner which was next to the lounge. Then she went up to bed, but lay awake for a while, wondering how to set about finding more musicians. If only the album had got somewhere, that would have helped, she knew. But it had obstinately refused to sell. Not only that, they hadn't heard one track played on the radio. As for the single – *her* single – she might as well forget it. An exercise in recording technique, that was all it was.

Lunch with Lester! In the fun of having toasted bacon sandwiches with Bonnie in the morning, she had forgotten all about her arrangements for the rest of the day. She needed to talk to Jan, too. She was dying to introduce her to Bonnie.

Although it was drizzling and chilly, and she kept getting spider threads in her face, a September hazard, Chris nevertheless felt quite lighthearted as she turned down Lester's wide, tree-lined street.

Someone had been through the house with a duster and a vacuum cleaner, she noticed as soon as she was inside. It was supiciously tidy, and she couldn't quite believe that he had done it himself. Did that mean . . . ?

'I thought we'd get down to some work before we stopped for lunch,' Lester said. 'You need to improve your octaves and intervals, getting up to those high notes from the low ones. It's OK to scrape up there some of the time, but other times you may want a clean sound. I haven't got much for lunch, I'm afraid. Just some salad and we could have a glass of wine. That OK?'

'Yeah. Fine.' Funny how she almost went off food when Lester was around. He was wearing all black today, like her – black cords and a sweatshirt with a white saxophone stencilled on it. She asked him where he had gone it from, and he told her that he'd bought it in Milton Keynes, when he was there teaching and performing at a weekend jazz course.

'Black suits you,' she told him daringly. 'It makes your hair look fantastic.'

'I'd like to see you wearing another colour occasionally,' he replied. 'Why do you always look as if you're in mourning, or trying to disguise yourself? I know fifties jazzmen all seemed to wear black polonecks, but by and large, they weren't attractive young women. I hate to see all these young girls in the street, all looking like Italian grandmothers. Why don't you try a nice bright red, or a blue?'

She had worn her blue dress for her eighteenth party, but he hadn't been there to see it. She was glad he had called her attractive, rather than pretty. She wasn't the pretty type, and she was glad. She hated stuck-up girls with blonde curls and snub noses whose only interest in life was getting off with boys. Why *did* she wear black? She wasn't quite sure. Because it didn't look dirty as quickly as light colours was one slobby reason . . . but maybe he had hit on something. Perhaps she *was* trying to hide behind it, inasmuch as she didn't like drawing attention to herself. She wanted people to like and accept her for herself, not for the clothes she was wearing.

These thoughts were far too complicated to relate to Lester, so she ignored his remarks and raised her saxophone to her lips instead.

Over lunch, she told him about Jalova, and Bonnie and Jan.

'It's not going to be easy getting ourselves off the ground, even if we manage to get a decent band together,' she said glumly. 'I don't want George to manage us. I don't like him. Do you know any managers?'

'You don't need a heavy manager at your stage of the game. All you need is someone who knows about the business, to get you some bookings in and look after the money side. That's not difficult –'

'Then why couldn't *you* manage us?' She had spoken the words the instant they formed on her lips, without spending even a fraction of a second thinking. She nearly choked on a piece of celery as she waited to see what he would say.

'*Me*? I wouldn't have the time, Chris. I've got my teaching . . . my band . . .'

'Oh. Well, it was just an idea.' Chris felt crestfallen. Being able to work with him would have been so wonderful. All those extra hours with him! And what if they went on tour and he came, too? She had a brief fantasy of sitting next to him on a jet bound for America, his arm round her and her head on his shoulder, the way it had been in the taxi that night, as they watched the in-flight movie. The fantasy led on to a vision of the lights being dimmed and his lips coming down on hers and she shivered, then gave a little cough.

'You all right? Not coming down with a cold, I hope?'

Chris shook her head.

'More wine?'

'Yes, please.' Please let this lunch last for hours – through till dinner, till supper, even. As he poured out the wine, she marvelled at the shadows beneath his cheek-bones, at the way his eyebrows and lashes were still jet black. He was so lean, so fit. From the back, if he dyed his hair, he would look like a twenty-year-old. He was a titchy bit like Bruce Springsteen, even more so in some of his photos from years ago. If they had their arms around each other, she knew his body would feel taut and young, his ribcage hard, his shoulders and back strong. She longed to know what it would feel like to hold him. He was so close now – so tantalisingly close. She could reach out right now and run her fingertips very lightly over his forearm where he had his sleeve rolled up, just touching the fine dark hairs on it . . . if she dared.

She looked up at him and caught him looking at her and he smiled, causing a miniature explosion inside her, as if the wine she had drunk had ignited like a sparkler and was fizzing in her middle. She felt faint, she loved him so much. Yet she knew she must never let him know, for fear of spoiling things, of having him say that it would be too embarrassing to teach her any longer – of having him reject her. That would be worst of all. If he already had a girlfriend who was a mature woman, he might laugh at her, think she was just a silly kid, and not take her feelings seriously, even though they were the deepest she had ever had in her life.

Her half-written song, 'Cry It Out', suddenly came into her head.

'Hey! Do you want to hear something I'm working on?' she asked him, and stood up. Anything to break the unbearable tension she felt when he was too close for comfort.

Lester said her song had a lot of potential and he really liked the melody, but it needed some more work, which she already knew. 'Why don't you try an F sharp here?' he suggested, and they passed the rest of the lesson experimenting with her melody, trying different key changes and modulations, until Chris was really excited with the way it was shaping up.

'If this ever gets recorded, I'll have to give you a share of the royalties as co-writer,' she offered.

He grinned. 'I'm going into the studio with Soundwaves soon. I might ask to record it myself,' he said, and she knew he could not have complimented her more.

One disadvantage of Lester's forthcoming album sessions was that he had to cut Chris's lessons down to two a week – but as he generally let their lessons wander on way past the regulation hour, she didn't mind quite so much. In any case, she soon had a lot on her own mind. Next time she saw Jan, she had three other girls with her, defected members of To Hell And Back. Chris had taken Bonnie along with her and the six of them sat down to work out whether or not they had the basis of a band.

They now had a drummer – Jan – a lead guitarist, Anna, a bass player, Dee, and two singers, Bonnie and Laura, the girl whose rather weak vocals had let down the heavy rock sound the band had striven for. However, it was soon apparent that her voice blended extremely well with Bonnie's when they tried some harmony singing, and she said she could play electric piano as well.

'What we need is a run-through to see what we all sound like together,' Jan said. 'It would be fine to have it here, but we just haven't got room.' Jan shared a house with two other girls, both musicians. The rooms were small and unbelievably cluttered with clothes, books, records, instrument cases, practice amplifiers, microphones and all kinds of personal and musical paraphernalia.

'If only we could use the studio,' sighed Bonnie, 'but I know Jalova are down there auditioning new singers and Don is definitely off me since I left.'

'Couldn't we hire somewhere else?' Chris suggested.

'What with?' Anna, the guitarist, retorted acidly. 'I'm skint.'

A wild idea was running through Chris's brain. Her parents were out in the daytime, the house was empty. If they kept the sound level well down . . .

'Let's have it at my house,' she invited daringly. 'As long as we finish by four, to give me a chance to clear up before Mum gets back.'

That Mrs Levy next door should have chosen that afternoon to develop a migraine was extremely unfortunate for Chris . . .

CHAPTER · 11 ·

'Oh God,' Chris moaned, 'where am I going to go? She might at least have given me time to make a phone call!'

She had the clothes she stood up in, her toothbrush, which she had grabbed at the last moment, and her saxophone, and she was standing in the High Street with Bonnie, Jan and Laura.

'I'd ask you to stay at mine, but you know my house is bustin' at the seams,' Bonnie said dolefully. She lived with her family and there were nine of them, plus two dogs and a cat.

'I suppose I could try ringing Gemma or Carol, but it would only be a sofa for the night, and I need several days somewhere, to sort myself out. My mother's mad!' Chris added furiously. 'She's always hated me. I think she wishes my brother had lived instead of me.'

'Oh, hush up!' said Jan in her flat northern accent. 'Stef's away in Germany for three weeks. You can have her room. She won't mind.'

'Are you sure? After all, you don't know me,' Chris pointed out doubtfully.

'You play good music. That'll do,' said Jan, and Chris voiced her thanks.

When she got back to Jan's, her new friend made them both coffee and toast and Marmite, and they sat talking over the afternoon's events.

'I thought we were playing quite softly,' Chris recalled ruefully. 'When the old cow hammered on the wall, I thought she was just being a nuisance. After all, it wasn't as if it was late at night. But fancy going and ringing Mum!' Chris threw up her hands in exasperation.

Her mother had come charging in on them shortly after three o'clock, at a point when they had discovered that Anna was tone deaf and couldn't tell that her guitar wasn't in tune, and the bassist, Dee, couldn't keep proper time.

'That poor woman next door!' Mrs Lindsell had shrieked. 'It's a wonder she didn't call the police! How could you do this, Christine?' Chris knew it was a very bad sign indeed when her mother called her by her full name. 'You've let me down and made my name mud with the whole street. Get out of my sight and don't come back until you've got this music business right out of your system!'

In the middle of this scene, Anna and Dee had slid out muttering that it wasn't their type of music, anyway.

Now, Chris was suffering from shock. To plan to leave home was one thing, but to be booted out when you weren't expecting it, when you had had no time to make any arrangements, was something entirely different and not in the least welcome. Quite apart from that, she felt hurt and rejected. What would her father think when he came home and was told that his daughter had been kicked out? Would they have a big argument about her tonight? She would ring her dad at work the next morning and have a talk to him. Perhaps her mother would have calmed down by then, too.

Jan had switched the radio on and it was playing softly as they spoke. Suddenly, Chris yelled, 'Turn it up, turn it up! That's my tune!'

She bounced up and down on her chair with excitement as 'Johnson's Party' blasted out of the tinny tranny, and she tutted loudly when the DJ faded it before the end.

'That was the first single from a London band called Jalova and I think we're gonna be hearing a lot of it. Don't forget, you heard it first on this show . . .' said the DJ pompously.

'Wow,' said Jan, gazing wide-eyed at Chris.

'Yeah. Ironic, isn't it? Obviously nobody knows the band's changed a bit. What am I going to do if it's a hit?' Chris made a hopeless gesture.

'No point in worrying about that. Chances are it won't be. Don't want to bring you down, but let's be realistic. You've got more important things to worry about right now, such as finding a flat,' Jan pointed out sensibly. 'I'll see what I can do to help tomorrow.'

Sometimes, Chris thought, your life got out of control and you were like a leaf that had dropped off its tree into a fast-flowing river, and were being spun and sped along, twirled in whirlpools and tossed against rocks and unable to see an end to your journey.

The next day, it felt as if she travelled about ten thousand miles and lived ten years in twenty-four hours.

She rang her dad. 'Have you got somewhere to stay for a while, love?' he asked. At least his tone was kind and loving.

When she told him she had, he said, 'Best not to come

home till your mum's got over it. She's very upset. I don't think she's very well at the moment. Change of life . . . you know. You're an adult now, we can trust you to take care of yourself. Any problems, ring me, and I'll come and see you whenever you want.'

She still had her doorkey, so she made a raid and collected clothes, her personal stereo, some tapes and her sheet music and manuscript books, and took them back to Jan's. Then she rang her closest friends, to tell them what had happened and where she was. Lester was on the list, but he wasn't in and she had to leave Jan's number on his answering machine. She hated answering machines because she never knew what to say on them. When it said, 'Speak after the tone,' she was afflicted with a kind of stage fright, and couldn't get her words out.

Bonnie wasn't in, either, so she left her number with Bonnie's eldest brother. Halfway through the afternoon, when she and Jan were right in the middle of playing saxophone and trumpet together – trumpet was Jan's second instrument – Bonnie rang to say she had to talk to Chris and it was really important. When Chris asked where they should meet, Bonnie insisted that she should come to Don's studio.

'No! I can't possibly! Won't the others be there? I don't want to go within a mile of Howie. Can't we meet somewhere else?' Chris appealed, but Bonnie was adamant. Chris *had* to come to the studio, and she had Bonnie's guarantee that Howie would not be there.

Chris asked Jan to come along for moral support, just in case. All the same, she was quaking as she reached the door just past the giant woman on the motorbike.

Don let them in. 'Great to see you, Chris,' he said, with a friendly grin. He was, if anything, even thinner than when Chris had last seen him.

Chris stepped into the main room cautiously – and all six feet four inches of Lee uncoiled from a corner and leaped up to kiss her on the cheek and give her a rib-cracking hug.

Bonnie was perched on a stool, wearing bright pink leggings and a short white top with pink spots that showed a snatch of gleaming midriff. She always looked as if she had just stepped out of a magazine fashion page. She had a smug kind of smile on her face – and Chris realised why straight away. Curtis was sitting cross-legged on the floor next to her, his head resting against her legs. They were obviously together again.

'Hi,' he said, in his usual cool fashion. 'Meet all that remains of Jalova. Anyone want to form a band?'

It was a very odd line-up. For a start, they had two drummers, Lee and Jan, and the two of them started fighting it out to see who was going to play.

'Oh, come *on*!' drawled Lee, looking up from his position sprawled on the carpet of the studio. 'Look at this.' He flexed a bulging bicep. 'All this power goes into the sticks. Look at your puny little arms. What can you do with those?'

'This!' declared Jan. She sprang behind the drum kit that stood in the studio and beat out a furious tattoo with just one drumstick which she found lying on the floor. 'And that's only one-handed!'

'OK, OK, but have you got the stamina to keep going for two hours?' Lee challenged her.

'You bet! Want me to start now, so you can time me?'

'Why don't you two take turns?' suggested Bonnie. 'Swopping places would look great on stage.'

'What are we going to do about Laura?' said Chris anxiously. They had promised to fit the sweet-voiced singer into whatever they decided to do. 'If only she could play bass . . . that's what we need. We've got everything else.'

'*I* can play bass,' Lee said suddenly, and they all turned to stare at him.

'I never knew that,' Chris said.

'Well, I don't show all my talents at once,' replied Lee, with a smirk and a suggestive leer.

'Bloody good job too!' said Jan tartly.

'Right. That's settled then. Lee plays bass unless he's taking a turn behind the drum kit. Jan plays drums, and trumpet when it's Lee's turn on the drums.'

'I could do percussion, too,' Jan suggested.

'Fine,' Chris continued. 'Then we've got Bonnie singing and Laura doing harmonies and whatever else she can do.'

'Keyboards,' Jan reminded her.

'And Curtis on guitar. Two guys and four girls. How does it feel to be outnumbered, boys?'

'I'm not complaining,' said Curtis, grinning up at Bonnie.

Jan then went and phoned Laura, who said she'd really like to sing with them. She came down to the studio as soon as she could, and they spent a couple of hours running through some of the old Jalova songs, teaching them to Laura and Jan. After that, Chris had to leave because she had an appointment with Lester . . .

She felt that familiar leap of excitement inside her when she walked towards his door; the closer she got, the bubblier she felt, as if her blood had turned to fizzy lemonade. She had taken one of the things he had said on their last meeting to heart.

'Hey!' he said appreciatively, as he opened the door to her. 'You're looking really lovely.'

The familiar blush swept up from her shoulders to her

forehead in a pale crimson tide which she could do nothing to control. She just had to try not to mind. The jade-green shirt had been among the items she had grabbed from her wardrobe. She wore it loose over a denim skirt, and her feet were clad in multi-coloured plimsolls.

'Tea? Juice? Glass of wine?' he offered.

'Orange juice, please,' she accepted gratefully, noting as she entered the lounge that it was back to its normal untidy, lived-in state. Good!

'Obviously a lot's been happening,' he said as he carried two tall glasses of orange into the room. 'What's this new phone-number business?'

She told him. 'That's tough,' he commented. 'I hope you'll make it up with your folks soon. Are you OK?'

His concern pleased her. It showed he cared, even if only as a friend. 'Yes,' she assured him. 'That's not all, though . . .'

The break-up of Jalova was quite complicated to relate.

'After I went, it seems all hell broke loose. Curtis sided with Howie, Bonnie walked out and George said he couldn't handle it and had changed his mind about signing us now. He said he couldn't bear clashes of temperament in a band because it made them hard to work with.

'Anyway, Curtis came round to see Bonnie yesterday and said she'd got it all wrong and he wasn't particularly taking Howie's side, he was just trying to remain neutral and keep Jalova together. Then Lee apparently told Curtis that if he'd been a bit more supportive, Bonnie and I mightn't have gone. Lee, Curtis and Howie had a huge row and Howie stalked off, saying they were a load of losers and he couldn't be bothered sticking around.

'Now Bonnie and Curtis have made it up, we've still got Lee, and we've also got Jan and Laura. Phew!' Chris grinned up at him, wondering if he'd been able to follow her confused narrative.

'Are you keeping the name, Jalova? Doesn't exactly stick in the mind, does it? If you just saw it written down, you wouldn't know how to pronounce it,' Lester said, frowning slightly.

'Well, we should, because we've got the album and single out under Jalova. But it doesn't look as though they're going anywhere. And I think you're right about the name.' Chris took a lengthy swig of the refreshing juice. 'Have you got any bright ideas?' she asked him.

'I'd really have to see you and hear you first,' he said diplomatically. 'Now come on, let's think about those saxophone exercises . . .'

Chris was too excited by recent events to be able to concentrate on technical exercises, and she kept making silly mistakes. In the end an exasperated Lester asked her to play 'Cry It Out', and Chris found she could only half remember it.

'I'm in the wrong mood,' she said in excuse. 'It's a moody, sad song and I feel all quick and boppy and, oh, you know!' She made mad gestures with her hands and gave a little jump.

Lester looked at her sternly, and her heart missed a beat. 'A professional performer has to be able to play all kinds of different moods of music, no matter how they may be feeling. You should know that,' he rebuked her.

'Of course I do. I'm just a bit . . . distracted.' She sighed and put down her sax, resting it against the arm of the sofa.

'You can say that again!' She risked a glance at him and, thank goodness, he was smiling now, not scowling. She felt weak with love for him, and doing anything to displease him really made her upset.

The perfect relationship is mainly a fifty-fifty one, with both doing an equal amount of pleasing and compromising, Chris had decided some while ago. Though it could become sixty-forty sometimes, either way, otherwise things might get boring. She fancied that if she were in a relationship with Lester, they would know telepathically what each of them wanted, so that nothing would ever go wrong between them. They were twin souls. They would spend hours playing music together, they would play in the same band, travel together, share friends, enjoy the same food, books and records. She felt they knew each other perfectly. All she needed to do was convince him that they were meant for each other, and that had to be done very subtly, over a long period of time.

Chris felt she didn't mind how long it took. One year . . . two years . . . Just until he could view her as a mature woman, one he could spend the rest of his life with. She couldn't imagine going out with a boy of her own age now. He would seem so uninteresting, such a kid. Lester had spoiled her for anyone else. And surely, if she showed no signs of having a boyfriend for ages and ages, he would begin to wonder why? Then, maybe, the penny would drop.

All six of them were squashed into Jan's room, drinking coffee and eating chocolate digestive biscuits.

'Mustn't have too many of these or we'll have to call ourselves the Fatsos,' Bonnie said, scoffing another one.

'There used to be a band called the Average White Band. We could be the Above Average Black and White Band!' joked Lee. It was true, they were perfectly divided, the three black musicians, Bonnie, Lee and Curtis, and the three white ones, Jan, Laura and Chris.

'Perhaps we should avoid the colour thing anyway,' Bonnie said. 'It's a cliché. We should find something that expresses our kind of music.'

'Like what?' said Jan. Nobody could come up with anything.

There was a big mirror on Jan's wall. Chris pointed towards it. 'Just look at the lot of us,' she said, with a giggle. 'What a shower! We've got every kind of hairstyle, every kind of fashion style, we're all kinds of shades of skin, our heights go from six foot four down to . . . what *are* you, Bonnie?'

'Five foot one. Well, a smidgeon under, to be totally honest. Five foot and seven-eighths,' she confessed.

'There's been a band called Altered Images. That's a shame. We could use a name about the way we look, Vision-something. Something-vision,' ruminated Chris.

'*Tele*vision!' cracked Curtis.

'Ho-flipping-ho! Anyway, that's been done already,' Jan scoffed.

'*Super*vision,' put in Lee.

'Oh, shut up!' groaned Chris. 'How about Visual-something, then? We need something exciting, something disturbing, that'll make people –'

'Visual Disturbance?' suggested Laura, in her gentle voice.

The others mulled it over. Then it was decided that nothing better was going to come to them for now, and they could always change it in the future.

But somehow, Visual Disturbance stuck . . .

For the next three weeks, they rehearsed solidly. Chris patched things up with her parents as far as phoning and visiting was concerned, but her mother was still adamant that she couldn't bear to hear Chris practising.

One stroke of extreme good fortune for Chris was that Stef, the girl whose room she had been occupying, had met the love of her life in Cologne and had decided to stay on, and was only too happy to have Chris cover her rent. Chris found she could make ends meet out of her Social Security money, but only just.

Laura worked part-time for a cleaning agency, and she managed to get occasional jobs for the other girls, while Lee found lunchtime work as a barman in a busy City pub. So they all scraped by.

Chris was dying for Lester to hear the band. She was dying to *see* him, because he had taken a trip to the States for two weeks, to visit his daughter. Chris wondered if his ex-wife would be there, too, and felt a sharp stab of jealousy. He had that little boy, too – both boys, if he was stepfather, or honorary dad, to the other one. When did he see them? He never spoke about them and Chris still wasted hours in painful speculation.

Finally, one afternoon she had a call from him. He was back and wanted to see her. He sounded very bright and bouncy, very young. If she only knew him as a voice on the telephone, Chris would have put him at no older than his mid-twenties.

'I'm rehearsing at the Blue Door Studios,' she told him – that was the official name of Don's set-up. 'Come and see us. We'll all be scared stiff of your verdict, mind!'

He arrived shortly after four. Chris wasn't aware that Don had quietly let him in. They finished their new version of 'Johnson's Party', worked through a changed arrangement of one of the old Jalova songs, did a number Curtis and Lee had written together, then ran through 'Cry It Out' and a new one by Chris called 'Avenue', inspired by things she'd seen and felt, walking through the city streets.

All this time Lester had been listening in the control room, and as they stopped for a rest, he came walking in, applauding, the sound strangely flat in the echo-less acoustics of the studio.

'I won't say there aren't rough edges and things that need working on and tightening up,' he said. 'You are new together – well, most of you are. But you've got one of the most bloody original sounds I've heard for a long, long time. It's fresh, it's different – I'm sounding like a TV deodorant commercial, aren't I? But it's true. I've got a buzz, goose-bumps down my arms. I always get that when I've heard something good. Make some tapes and I'll see what I can do with them.'

They looked at each other, pleased, excited, hopeful, each of them hugging their private dream of fame. Except Chris. Her private dreams didn't stop at that . . .

'Who wrote that last one . . . 'Avenue', was it?' Lester wanted to know.

'Me,' Chris admitted.

'Those lyrics . . . Did you do those as well?'

'Yes. Why? Aren't they any good?' She gritted her teeth and braced herself for the truth.

'Sing them to me.' He knew she could sing quite tunefully, though there wasn't much power in her voice, but she sometimes joined in the harmonies when she wasn't playing.

'Move your frozen lips a little, baby,
I'm afraid a smile might crack your face.
I've been doing a lot of thinking lately,
Think that we should get out of this place.
Not a sign of life among the paving,
Not a single grassblade pushing through,
Only mossy drains, a damp bouquet of decay,

Don't you feel the life draining out of you
Down the Avenue? Avenue,
Only statues move in the Avenue . . .'

Chris halted. 'You . . . Do you want me to go on? I mean . . .'

'Yes, I want to hear the rest,' he ordered her.

Chris took a deep breath and continued:

'*Our relationship seems well cemented*
But look at these fine buildings crumbling down,
And all our married friends who said they meant it
Are back there on the town . . .'

She stole a rueful glance at Lester, hoping he wouldn't think she was referring to his own broken marriage – which in a way she was. He was part of the point she was trying to make, as much as her parents, herself . . . anyone.

She carried on:

'*Let's invite a robot to a party,*
Let's find out what makes a lunatic.
And all those drunken ghosts who act so hearty,
They're so goddam sick, you can take your pick
Along the Avenue . . .

'Then it goes into the chorus again,' Chris said. 'And then it's all instrumental, with a sort of half verse at the end:

'*Take my hand and walk between the buildings,*
Try to find some moonlight pushing through.
Find a prayer to send up, to bring about the end of the Avenue.'

She half-sang, half hummed the final chorus. When she had finished, Lester stared at her, so hard that she felt herself flushing. Did his look mean the words were terrible and all needed changing?

'Did that start off as a poem?' he asked.

'No. It's strange but, now that I've started writing songs, I don't write poems any more. I get the words and part of the tune forming in my head at the same time. Do you know what I mean?'

'Not really. It didn't work like that with me. I was always a music person, rather than a words one. I always got the tunes, then had to fight hard for the words, or get someone else to write them. I envy people like you who have a natural ability for both.'

'Do you think I have? I mean, *can* I do both? Equally well?'

Lester looked at her amusedly. 'You should know that. What I want to say is, that song is something else. It takes the band into a new category, beyond mere pop. I think, with your songs, Bonnie's voice and the slight jazz-funk influence Lee and Curtis have brought in, you've got a whole new sound. I've never heard anything like it. With good management –'

'Ha ha!' said Jan hollowly. 'Wish we could find some . . .'

'You must have a lot of contacts in the music business,' Curtis said. 'Can't you think of anyone?'

Lee, meanwhile, had drawn Chris aside. 'This teacher of yours. He's not just a teacher, right?' Chris shook her head. 'He's a musician, he's been in the business a long time. Doesn't *he* know anything about management? I think I could work with someone like him. He seems a good guy.'

Curtis had come up and was listening. He took his shades off and polished them on his T-shirt. 'I'm with you. Why don't we ask the others what they think?'

'I already suggested it to him once and he said he was too busy. He's got his own band, he does sessions, lessons . . . He's even been asked to write a score for a movie,' Chris said.

Lester had to leave them in order to rehearse with Soundwaves. After he'd gone, Visual Disturbance held a meeting.

'I don't know if asking Lester to manage us is such a good idea,' said Jan. 'I know Chris has known him for a while, she can vouch for him, but we don't know if he's any good at business. If he was, then why hasn't he gone into management before? He doesn't even seem to have made all that much money for himself!'

Chris decided to keep quiet about what Marijke had told her.

'But there are people who have never done it before, who have ended up as good managers. What about Musical Youth? They had some big hits, and weren't they managed by the father of one of them?' said Laura.

'I was reading this book about seventies bands and the Bay City Rollers –' A chorus of *ughs!* from all round the room greeted Lee's words, but he continued, unperturbed. 'The Bay City Rollers had a manager, Tam Paton, who'd never managed bands before, but thought they had so much potential that he gave up his business and even drove their van to gigs.'

'I can't see Lester doing that,' Chris scoffed.

'The main thing is, getting someone we like and trust, who is 100 per cent behind our music,' Jan said. 'Now, I know we don't all know him, but I've certainly taken to him, and Chris can vouch for him, and we know he likes our sound. There's nothing to lose in asking him. If he says no, we can think again. If he says yes, we'll give him a trial period of, say, three months.'

They rang him next morning and arranged to see him at two. Lester listened intently while Lee put it to him. Then he shook his head dubiously.

'I've just landed a radio show to do, half an hour a week, mainly jazz. That's going to take up a lot of time. I'm very flattered to be asked, but I don't see –'

'A radio show? You could put us on it!' said Bonnie eagerly.

'That's a thought . . . But having to ring round, organise gigs, liaise with the record company . . . Hey, have you rung them to let them know about the new name and line-up?'

They all looked blank. 'I assumed George would have said something,' Chris admitted.

'What a shower!' Lester tutted and shook his head in hopeless amusement. 'How do you know there aren't magazines waiting to interview you? The album could be a smash hit in Finland and you'd never know. Somebody's got to get you lot organised.'

He paused, and gazed around the room and, yet again, Chris thought what a magnetic, commanding presence he had. 'Tell you what,' he said at last. 'I don't mind sorting out a few things for you, just for the time being, on an unofficial basis. I already get in the tours and gigs for Soundwaves; maybe I can get some for Visual Disturbance at the same venues. Mind you, you'd pull an entirely different audience. But we'll see. The main thing, as I see it, is to get those new numbers down on tape, to let the record company hear what they're dealing with, so they can make their decision whether or not to keep you. After all, you are presenting them with something very different. It may not be the kind of thing they want. But they must have put some money and work into Jalova, so you've got to give them the option.'

'You're very quiet,' Lee said to Chris, as they left Lester's that afternoon.

'Mmm. Just thinking.'

'Penny for them . . .'

'I wouldn't tell you if you offered me a million!'

'Oh! Be like that then.' Lee pretended to be offended. But, thought Chris, how could she have told him that what was on her mind was the prospect of seeing more and more of Lester, if he was to be closely associated with the whole band, but having him less and less to herself? Sharing him with the others, having to mask her feelings in order not to create problems in a business situation. Musical relationships of any sort, whether between artist and manager, musician and musician, composer and publisher, were so tricky and volatile. Would this particular one work, and how would it affect her? She felt as if she had lost something, rather than gained.

Lester quickly reported that their publishing arrangements were a shambles and they would be well advised to set up their own publishing company fast. He put some legal person to work on organising that. He also told them that XL wouldn't say yes or no about keeping them under contract until they had heard the new material. They decided to carry on working in Don's studio, and Lester generously agreed to pay the £10 per hour hire fee until XL, or another company, took up the band and paid an advance.

'What will you do if nobody likes us?' Laura asked him. 'You'll be out of pocket.'

'That's a chance I'm prepared to take,' Lester replied, with a dismissive shrug. 'With music, I rely on my gut reaction. If I get tingles up my back when I hear a record, I know it's a goodie. And some of your stuff rates high on the tingle scale.'

It was seven weeks before they were satisfied with their tapes. They were aware that they were only demos and that the record company might want them to do them all over again, with a professional producer. Lester spent as much time advising them as he could, though he was working hard preparing for his radio series. Chris wondered how he managed to keep control of everything. He's got no time for a girlfriend, she kept reminding herself happily. He spent more time with her than he could with any girlfriend. Except at night. Yet she couldn't imagine any girl being willing to put up with a relationship with a man who tumbled into bed in the early hours of the morning and was up working again by nine.

She was so immersed in music that she almost forgot Kim's party. Luckily, Carol rang and reminded her. All Chris's friends had been down to the studio to hear Visual Disturbance's new tracks and everyone was raving about them.

Chris walked into the party in a haze of weariness, having been recording all day. She slumped in a corner with a beer and various people came up and chatted to her. Suddenly, a voice she didn't recognise hailed her.

'Well, hello! It's the saxophone queen, isn't it?'

She looked up and, after a few seconds, recognised the owner of the voice as Mr Greenshirt from the 100 Club, the boy who had appointed himself as her very first fan. She struggled to remember his name. Dave – that was it!

'I'm afraid that autograph isn't worth anything yet,' she said.

'In that case, I'll have a dance while I'm waiting!' he insisted and Chris hauled herself to her feet. But once she got dancing, her tiredness disappeared and she thoroughly enjoyed herself, dancing a token dance with him, then moving on to dance and chat with friends. It suddenly struck her that she had become so saturated in Visual Disturbance that it was great to be in different surroundings with different people.

She didn't leave till two a.m., with Dave desperately trying to obtain her number.

'Look, there's no point,' she told him. 'I'm too busy to see anyone.'

'In that case, I'll write *my* number down for *you*,' he insisted.

She knew she would never call it.

CHAPTER · 12 ·

'We have to admit we're lucky,' Jan was saying. 'Most bands trail up and down the country, from grotty club to grotty pub, for months, even years, before they get the breaks we've had.'

'A lot of it's due to Lester, of course,' Laura pointed out, a statement at which Chris glowed. By now, her secret obsession wasn't so secret, the other female members of the band having noted how she always reacted when he was around. But they had promised to keep it to themselves – and Lee and Curtis were in blind ignorance of the fact that their sax player and chief songwriter was desperately in love.

Lester had featured them on his radio show and drawn a considerable mailbag from people keen to hear more of them. With that evidence, XL had offered them a generous contract for two albums and four singles, and had even given them a small advance, enabling them to put down-payments on some really good amplification equipment.

The company hadn't been quite satisfied with the quality of some of their tracks, however, and had booked them into a studio in the country, to re-record some of the material, and that is where they were when they received the news that a new television pop programme wanted to feature them on its opening show.

None of them had ever been in a television studio before.

'It'll just be like a recording studio with cameras,' said Curtis, cool as ever.

'I hope they're not going to pile loads of make-up on us,' said Jan dubiously. She hated putting anything on her face, especially if it smacked of animal products. Even her soap and moisturiser came from the Body Shop.

'I'll have to get my hair done, it's drooping again,' sighed Bonnie. Jan had given up having battles with her and had resigned herself to the fact that Bonnie was into image, and that it was just her. Her personality was so fantastic that Jan couldn't help liking her even if she disagreed with a lot of her views and beliefs.

'I'll just buy a new pair of shades,' drawled Curtis.

'Yeah, to hide your bloodshot eyes,' said Bonnie, in a barbed tone which didn't go unnoticed by the others.

Chris was increasingly worried about Bonnie. Although she was singing as well as ever, she was becoming a little withdrawn and remote away from work, and Chris suspected things were far from OK again between her and Curtis. She wished Bonnie would confide in her.

They were due to finish recording by the end of Saturday. They would then have Sunday off and had to be at the TV studio at ten the following Monday morning.

Lester, who had made many a TV appearance with his various groups, drilled them about what to expect.

'It'll be hot, and it'll be hard work. Do everything you're

told to do without argument, because these people don't have time or money to waste. Just act professional, and if you do make a mistake, keep calm and ask for a halt. It's only a recording, so you can always do it again. But don't stop just because of a slight fluff, because chances are no one will notice. Most of all enjoy yourselves – or at least look as if you are, because that will come across very strongly. Remember, TV is a medium of close-up, it picks up expressions and movements in a way the stage never does. If you're on stage and want to get a gesture or a mood over, you have to exaggerate. But not on TV. If a camera zooms in on you, even a twitch of an eyebrow will count.'

'Oh, blimey, I'll be too scared to scratch my nose, even!' moaned Chris.

'Just don't pick it, that's all,' grunted the irrepressible Lee.

Saturday ran into Sunday, as they snatched just four hours' sleep, and it was six in the evening by the time they pronounced themselves satisfied with the final track. Then they had the drive back to London, which took almost five hours as it was an unseasonably hot autumn Sunday and everybody in Britain seemed to be returning from a day out. By Monday morning, they were drained and exhausted – but they all managed to congregate in the modern leather-and-chrome reception area by quarter to ten, as arranged. All except Lester, who had a meeting about his movie soundtrack.

Chris felt as if a bit of her was missing. How could she play, if not for him? Her feet felt leaden and she couldn't stop yawning; she felt sure she was about to give the most uninspired performance of her whole life.

The director of the show was so chirpy and boppy that Chris felt quite ashamed of feeling so lethargic. They were to record two numbers, to be screened at different points in the show.

'Right, Visual Disturbance. Let's set our lighting director onto you and we'll see if we can't make you even more visually disturbing,' he punned. His name was Pip, which they all had a secret snigger about, Lee coming out with the obvious groan-worthy pun about the guy giving *him* the pip.

The studio was much smaller and more cluttered than Chris would have imagined. Great black cables snaked all over the place, and the cameras had a disconcerting habit of moving at great speed so you never knew quite where to look.

'Don't look at the camera at all,' instructed Pip. 'Just get on with your act and leave all the rest to us.'

Both Chris and Bonnie refused paper cups full of strong machine coffee, for fear of burping down the microphone.

They were playing Chris's song 'Avenue' and the number written by Curtis and Lee called 'It's Plain To See'. One or other was to be the single. XL Records hadn't decided yet, but said they would before the programme was actually aired.

As Bonnie and Laura sang their haunting harmonies and echoes on 'Avenue', Chris felt an ache inside, wishing she could be singing it herself. In her limited experience of composing, she had always found that other people never performed your material in quite the way you would have done it yourself. There were shades of expression which she alone felt, but other people had to give their own interpretation to the number, that was only fair. Still, she couldn't help wishing that it was absolutely perfect – *her* kind of perfect.

Laura sang flat on the last chorus and Chris winced, wondering if the director would call for a re-take. He did, but not just for that.

'There are a few problems with the sound,' he explained. 'Just run through it again for me. Watch for the signal . . .'

The second version was more technically perfect, but Chris felt it lacked the feeling the first one had had. She was boiling hot, sweat pouring down her forehead, and the Quentin Crisp-style hat she had taken to wearing made her head even hotter, but she refused to take it off, as she felt happy in it. Laura had her small teddy-bear mascot, Chris had her hat. Curtis had his hip flask full of vodka. She knew better than to mention that, especially to Bonnie, although it was obvious to all that he was drinking far too much these days, though it didn't seem to affect his playing. One of these days Chris quite expected him to keel over suddenly on stage – though, knowing Curtis, his hands would probably go on playing guitar automatically, even in a drunken stupor.

Lee had a very distinctive twangy bass style, bending the strings and pulling them between finger and thumb. It took a lot of physical strength to do that – Chris knew, because she had tried. Their sound was miles away from the Jalova style now – less funky and more sort of experimental. There was no term to describe it that she knew of. It wasn't New Wave, rock, pop or jazz, but a mixture of many things, with lots of vocal and electronic effects. 'Surprises,' was how they described it in their record-company biography.

Chris had felt quite shaky with nerves during the first run-through, but that wore off as soon as she managed to lose herself in the music she was playing. However, she noticed that Laura's voice sounded wobblier than usual, that Bonnie's top notes were definitely squeaky, and it was only Lee who seemed to be as relaxed as if he was playing in his own room. In fact, he even had the bravado to chat up the make-up girl.

'Does that man never give up?' she whispered to Jan, during the break while the lighting was changed for their second number. She had seen one of the huge lighting plans and been amazed at the complexity of it, all the changes and instructions worked out on graph paper.

'Nobody ever seems to say no to him, that's what boggles me,' Jan hissed back.

'*I* did,' Chris informed her, not knowing whether she felt proud or churlish. After all, Lee had always seemed especially fond of her, in a way which now was brotherly, but may not always have been so.

Jan's approving 'Good for you' reinforced her faith in her own instincts. Lee was a born ladykiller, and would be until he fell genuinely and heavily in love some day, when it might do him good to be given a taste of his own medicine, Chris sometimes thought.

They played 'Plain To See' three times before the various television experts pronounced themselves satisfied. Then they were taken on a visit to the press office, and finally to the cafeteria, where they were treated to an early lunch.

XL Records had sent one of their own publicity people along to the recording, a young guy called Rog who had hardly said a word all morning. But suddenly, faced with a plate piled with egg, bacon, sausage and mushrooms, he became talkative, prattling brightly about various ideas he had to get Visual Disturbance in the national newspapers.

'I thought you could all take part in this sponsored parachute jump which a mate of mine's organising,' he said.

'Eek!' squeaked Bonnie. 'I get dizzy changing a light bulb!'

'And I get vertigo tying my shoelaces,' grunted Curtis, whereupon they all burst out laughing and Rog silenced himself with a giant mouthful of food.

'Twit!' Chris hissed to Laura.

'Yes, isn't he?' she replied in an undertone. 'I thought the record label wanted to make money out of us, not kill us!'

The album, entitled *Visual Disturbance* in order to introduce the band, was scheduled for release the third week in November, to get ahead of the annual rush of Christmas releases. As for their single, it was to be a double A-side, so neither Chris nor the Lee–Curtis songwriting partnership had reason for disappointment.

Lester's album which he had recorded with Soundwaves was being held back until January. He was with a different record company and they wanted to avoid the Christmas period altogether as far too many records vanished without trace in December. Chris had had to put up with seeing him only once a week for lessons for a period of about six weeks, while he was working on the film music. Then suddenly, marvellously, he was freer, and invited her for lunch, to hear the tapes of his album.

'I would have invited the others, too, but I didn't think they'd be interested,' he said as soon as she arrived, and her heart sank. Was that the only reason? Hadn't he particularly wanted to be alone with her? She felt so desolate that she could hardly eat a thing, even though he had prepared a fantastic winter stew, chock-full of vegetables and chunks of chicken.

He looked thinner and rather tired, she thought. She worked at trying to distance herself from him, at seeing him just as a musician and their manager. But it was impossible. Her dreams had been nurtured over too long a period. If anything, his shadowed eyes and hollowed face made her long to look after him, see he ate good food and got early nights, and relaxed in a pair of soothing, loving arms . . . hers. His hair was ruffled, and her right hand ached to stroke it back into place, then continue downwards, tracing the outline of his temple, his cheekbone, his jaw. Then she would gather his face in both hands and draw it gently towards hers.

The muscles of her midriff tightened and she could hardly breathe as she imagined kissing him delicately, tenderly on the forehead, then on the lips, then on each closed eyelid.

Music that gentlier on the spirit lies / Than tired eyelids upon tired eyes. Tennyson's 'The Lotus-Eaters'. She had done it for O-level English. She would sing him a lullaby while he lay with his head on her lap, almost asleep as she passed her hand hypnotically over his hair and forehead, easing away strain and tension. Oh, he needed her . . . If only he would realise it.

She surfaced abruptly, registering that the tape he had been playing her was almost at an end and she would be expected to comment on it. The music hadn't been easy to get into on first hearing, and she told him so. His eyebrows twitched. 'Then maybe you won't want to tour with us . . .'

'What?' she cried.

'It was just an idea. Soundwaves is touring Scandinavia soon and I was going to suggest to your record company that Visual Disturbance played some of the dates with us. Of course, my own record label may disagree. They'd probably prefer to get one of their own acts on the tour. But I'll try my best. After all, I am your manager!'

He grinned wryly, and Chris couldn't help thinking how different he was to the sort of man she had always imagined a group manager to be – old and untrendy, concerned only with money and deals.

'Now that you've finished the record, I'm arranging for

you to play some British dates, too, and I'd like you on the radio show again. My producer was delighted at the response we got. If you tell Jan and Laura and I ring the rest, we'll call a meeting tomorrow afternoon, round here, and sort everything out then, after I've had time to talk to the record companies. Hey, do you know something?'

His voice had suddenly softened and Chris felt a great jolt shoot through her. Was he going to say something about her? She looked nice . . . he liked her a lot . . . loved her, even? Her heart was pounding like a hailstorm on a windowpane and she was frightened to meet his eyes.

'I'm really enjoying being a manager for the first time . . .'

Oh no! Was that it, the revelation she had been waiting for in such excruciating tension?

'. . . I never thought I would. But then, thinking about it, I suppose I've been more or less managing Soundwaves all this time. And do you know something else?'

A heatwave suffused her entire body, inside and out, a pulsing heatwave, like music. He *was* going to say it . . . tell her he loved her! Or, at least, that he felt a lot for her.

'You have got such a great future ahead of you. Don't tell any of the others, but if anybody's going to be a solo star, it's you, Chris.'

It was what she had always dreamed of, so how could she be disappointed in his remark? Yet she was; bitterly so.

'This is the life! It can't compare with Jalova, can it?' crowed Lee, as the roadie organised by the record company drove them up the M4 towards Cardiff. They were due to play as the support act to a really big chart band and it seemed a world apart from the kind of gigs Jalova used to play. It would be the first time they had appeared in a big hall and they knew it would be a challenge. If they could get themselves established with large audiences, it would mean all the difference to their record sales. But would this kind of audience accept them?

They ran into a patch of fog, which slowed their pace right down.

'We're never going to get there in time!' wailed Laura, as they crawled along with the headlights full on, obeying the flashing hazard signs. Then the fog lifted and miraculously they were soon picking up speed, and arrived in time for a sound check.

They were due to start playing at seven thirty. The doors opened at seven and people started pouring in in their hundreds. Chris and Lee peeped into the auditorium from backstage and the sea of bobbing, chattering faces seemed endless.

'I'm terrified!' Chris clutched Lee's arm. 'Help!'

'I don't feel so good myself. I feel quite sick,' he admitted. 'Let go, you're making me worse.'

Chris reflected wryly that it was probably the first time ever that Lee had told a girl *not* to touch him.

They walked on stage at twenty to eight, to a smattering of polite applause. The hall was still by no means full, many people having decided not to arrive until the main band were due on. Visual Disturbance had already encountered them; they had been pushed off stage by them after a scanty sound check, and their 'We're the big stars' attitude had got right up everyone's noses. However, they were allowing Visual Disturbance to use their PA system as there wouldn't be time to change sound systems between sets, and it proved to be brilliant, so they had that to thank them for, at least. But not for their audience, who had plainly come to see the superstars and not some unheard-of band from privileged London.

It was the first time Chris had played her new sax in public. She had got it just before the start of their second lot of recording sessions and she was thrilled with it. It was so reliable compared to her old one, and the tone was much better. As they neared the end of their opening number, though, she felt she might as well have been playing a tin whistle for all the impression they were making on the unresponsive audience, who were almost ignoring them.

The opening number finished, the applause was almost inaudible, and the members of Visual Disturbance glanced apprehensively at one another. Did they really have to keep going for a whole hour? Couldn't they just sneak away now with their tails between their legs? The audience wouldn't notice . . .

Jan started beating out the rhythm of their second number, an old Jalova tune. Chris looked at her and was treated to a broad grin. She stepped over to her.

'Let's just have fun ourselves and pretend that lot aren't out there, eh?' she called above the sound of the drums which were amplified by the stage monitor system.

Curtis's guitar cut in; then, after four bars, Lee's bass. Chris remained at the back, near the drum kit, and raised her sax to her lips. The riff she blew was unrehearsed, but it pleased her so she repeated it.

'Hey – great!' Lee yelled.

Bonnie started singing then, and Chris instantly noticed something different in the air, a current of crackling energy. She stared out into the audience. Could she be mistaken, or were there signs of interest on their faces, grins, rhythmic noddings, alert eyes following the band's movements?

Chris felt the band tightening up and beginning to work together. It was the most supreme feeling in the world, like well-oiled, perfectly integrated machinery pouring out power. And no, she wasn't mistaken; that energy interchange between band and audience had definitely started. She started playing louder, giving herself to the instrument; and when it was her turn to step to the microphone and sing harmonies with Laura, she did so with feeling, looking at Laura, exchanging triumphant, happy grins, hearing their voices blend as one with Bonnie's louder, soaring one.

And this time the applause was worth waiting for, worth coming all this way for. They had won a hall full of strangers over.

Yet, in spite of feeling high with happiness after the show, Chris still couldn't help noticing how Bonnie's radiant smile dissolved within ten minutes of coming back into the dressing room. Chris went over to her.

'Look, what's wrong?' she asked.

Bonnie shook her head and pulled a face. 'Just Curtis. Nothing anyone can do. It's between me and him. I don't want to spoil the tour so I'm trying to hold things together, but . . .' She shrugged and refused to say any more.

But that night as Chris lay asleep in the hotel room she was sharing with Bonnie, she was woken by a commotion out in the corridor. The next minute Bonnie burst into the room crying and fumbling for the light switch. Chris found the bedside lamp and turned it on.

'Oh, *no*!' she cried as her eyes took in the sight of Bonnie with her dress ripped and her face scarlet and puffy all down one side. 'What happened?'

'Curtis was drunk again. We had a fight. He says if I finish with him he'll quit the tour. So what can I do? I don't want to ruin our careers . . .'

'You can't put up with that sort of thing, though, it's ridiculous. No man has any right to knock a woman about – or vice versa,' Chris pointed out sensibly, trying to sound as calm and practical as possible. It was lucky Bonnie wasn't sharing with Jan, she thought; Jan would have gone straight out and punched Curtis on the nose, making things ten times worse!

Lester was their manager. Chris knew it was late, but they desperately needed advice, so her hand only hesitated over the phone for half a second before she called reception and gave them the number.

The phone rang for a very long time before Lester answered sleepily. Chris felt a knot of anxiety in her stomach; what if he had a girl with him? No, that's just my jealousy, she told herself firmly. Briefly, she told Lester what had happened, then put Bonnie on the line. They had some local press interviews to do the next morning, so it was vital that Bonnie was soothed and her bruises disguised.

'He says he'll be up here in the morning,' Bonnie said as she replaced the receiver. 'He's going to talk to Curtis.'

Chris's spirits took a leap. So she would see him in the morning! It took her ages to get back to sleep, she felt so excited. It had only been two days since she had seen him, but that had been just for a briefing before the tour started.

They were all having breakfast when Lester strode in, looking tired and unshaven, as if he had driven through the night. He had a coffee with them, then disappeared with Curtis and Bonnie, who were glowering mutinously at each other.

'I gave him a real bollocking last night,' Lee told the rest of them. 'He was completely legless. I mean, we all get a little drunk from time to time, but he was really out of it. He can't be allowed to go on like that. It'll affect his health soon, never mind his music. He's doing a bottle of vodka a day! I used to think drink was less dangerous than drugs, but now, after being around him, I'm not so sure.'

'Did he drink heavily when he was with Jalova?' Laura asked.

'I don't think so,' Chris replied. 'He seemed fine then.'

'I gather from Curtis that when they had that bust-up when Bonnie left Jalova, he got back together with an old girlfriend for a couple of nights. Bonnie didn't find out until recently, when she met a friend of the girl's, but she wasn't very happy about it,' Lee told them.

'I can imagine!' said Laura darkly. 'If Rod did that, I'd kill him!' Laura and Rod had been going out for a couple of years and she spent all her free time with him.

'I do wish Bonnie had confided in one of us. I remember how much better I felt after I'd told her about Howie. She shouldn't have bottled it all up,' said Chris.

'She's a funny girl, really,' Lee said. 'I've known her for about eighteen months and I don't think I've ever seen the true Bonnie in all that time, just the surface, the happy face she puts on. Who knows what's simmering away underneath . . .'

'I think everyone ought to be honest and up-front – like me,' Jan said, with a lift of an eyebrow. No one could argue with that! Her bluntness hurt sometimes, but her straightforward approach to everything was like a breath of fresh air, and they all appreciated it.

'Think I'll go for a jog to wake myself,' Lee announced. 'See you later.'

'I fancy a shower,' Chris said, then realised that Lester might be holding the summit meeting in the room she shared with Bonnie.

'Come and use ours, then,' Jan offered, so she went up in the rickety lift with Jan and Laura, used one of their already damp towels, and then they sat around feeling vaguely disturbed and unhappy, wondering what was going on.

Eventually, there was a loud rap on the door and Lester called, 'All decent in there? Can I come in?'

'Sorry I had to wake you up last night. I couldn't think what else to do,' Chris said.

'That's OK. I should have come with you, instead of carrying on with my own projects and leaving you to sort yourselves out.' Lester plonked himself heavily on one of the twin beds. 'Well, I'm here now, and I'm staying till you finish the tour. OK?'

'We're not children,' Jan said sharply and Chris tightened her lips in annoyance. Didn't she realise that Lester was only trying to help them over a difficult period?

'I know you're not, but tell me, could you handle the Curtis–Bonnie situation? If so, be my guest!' he said laconically, and Chris loved his coolness. He wasn't rising to the bait at all. 'I've had a lot of touring experience – more than twenty years of it. I know what to do on the road. I've had to handle rock-star crises and temperament attacks, drug overdoses, nervous breakdowns, stolen instruments – you name it.' He grinned wryly and rubbed his slightly stubbly chin and Chris thought how easily he fitted into any circumstances, and how ageless he looked. He was just like one of them – but with twenty-five more years' experience of music, recording . . . everything.

And relationships . . . a little voice tried to remind her, but she beat it back.

'So what's happening with Bonnie? How is she? What have you said to Curtis? He's not leaving, is he?' Laura enquired anxiously.

'I've arranged for the interviews to be with you lot, Curtis and Lee, if he gets back in time. He's gone jogging. I've said eleven o'clock. There's a room downstairs which is available. I suggest you get yourselves ready now. Bonnie's lying down with various medications on her face to bring down the swelling. I've had a doctor check her over, but she's OK, nothing broken.

'And as for that idiot Curtis –' Lester's tone grew exasperated – 'I've warned him that if he doesn't control his drinking on this tour, it'll be the last tour he does with this band. And I won't stand for him knocking Bonnie about any more. I'm sure we all agree about that. If it's the drink making him act like an animal, then the drinking must stop. And if he *still* persists in his brutish behaviour, then he must expect to be treated as a subhuman.'

'They used to be so happy together,' Chris said, sighing.

'I know a lot of people who could say that,' Lester added, and the sudden bitterness in his voice made Chris stare hard at him. He was looking away from her, his eyes focused on the window. Then he stood up. 'Well, better go and be there to greet the journalists. Don't be nervous of them,' he advised. 'Tell them what they want to know, but don't tell them anything you wouldn't like to see in print, OK?'

He laughed, and left the room.

'Oh God, I'm terrified!' Laura said, in a trembling voice.

'They're probably just as scared of us as we are of them,' said Jan soothingly. 'Mind you, if they dare ask me about my love life, I'll bite their pens in two!' she snorted, and Chris fell about laughing as she pictured it.

'They'll probably ask you about your hair,' Laura pointed out.

'I'll just tell them my father was called An-An,' Jan joked. Chris was grateful to her for lightening the gloomy atmosphere. Then she went off to her own room, stealing in quietly so as not to disturb Bonnie too much, and put on a clean black poloneck and black denims, which she had brightened up slightly, with Lester in mind, by stitching over the outer seams in vivid green cotton. She added emerald green socks and black plimsolls, and then she was ready for the fray.

As she had been interviewed once before, when she was with Jalova, she felt quite an old hand at it, especially having seen Soundwaves being interviewed as well.

Lee arrived in a grey jogging outfit shortly after the interview commenced. All the young guy from the paper wanted to ask Chris about was her songwriting, even though she kept trying to switch the subject to saxophones. She wasn't that wonderful a songwriter. Why was he bothering with all these stupid searching questions about inspiration and imagery? She hadn't time to think up any deep answers, so she just replied with the first things that came into her head.

At last, he *did* get onto talking about the sax, though not at all in the way she would have wished.

'You must know men find the sight of a girl playing the saxophone very sexy.' This was said with a cross between a wink and a leer. Chris bristled. She had a vague memory of Jan bringing up the same subject on the night they met. 'Tell me, when you're up there on stage blowing on that instrument, you must surely be aware of the effect you're having. Do you get a lot of propositions?'

Chris wasn't prepared to let him go on. She was furious. 'Are you insinuating that I took up sax just so I could play the role of a musical hooker?'

The guy had the decency to look slightly abashed. But he quickly recovered his composure – and, she noticed, kept his small tape recorder running. She hoped he would print her response in full.

'C'mon now,' he said wheedlingly, 'all the *big* names in sax playing are male. Surely that's not just a coincidence? Couldn't it be because women take it up more for the image than for musicianship?'

She could have hit him, struck that whirring machine right out of his hand. Controlling herself with difficulty, she asked icily, 'Have you never heard of Kathy Stobart? Gail Thompson? Barbara Thompson? Vi Reed? You wait! You've got a shock coming, mate. Lots of women are taking up the sax now and they're going to be making mincemeat of little nerds like you in a few years' time. And as for looking sexy, so what? Guys ogle us up on the stage . . . Well, let them. I can look after myself.'

'I can see that,' the reporter said dryly, clicking off his cassette recorder. 'Would you like to be my bodyguard?' Then he added, 'It works both ways, you know. I've had to interview quite a lot of nerds in my time.'

Chris thawed a little at his attempt to come out to her and be humorous. 'Sorry,' she said, 'I didn't really mean to call you a nerd. But I did mean the rest.'

'Touché!' Then he started on Curtis, and Chris was free to drift over to the table where Lester was sitting, drinking what must have been his fifth cup of hotel coffee.

'What's up?' he asked. 'Your face was like thunder at one point there. Did he give you a hard time?'

'He seemed to equate sex with sax,' she grumbled.

'You just wait till the Fleet Street mob start on you,' he said darkly. 'That's when you'll really be given a hard time.'

'Why?' Chris asked interestedly. 'Did it happen to you?'

But his reply was cut off by Laura remarking, 'Aren't they in Wapping now, not Fleet Street? Hasn't got the same ring to it, has it?'

A lively discussion about newspapers followed, but although Chris joined in, she still wished she had heard Lester's answer to her question.

'Look, it can't be happening!' Laura shook her head in a daze of disbelief. The tour was over, Curtis had sobered up and caused no more trouble, they had had a huge argument with the headlining band they were touring with for being too popular with the audiences, and the single had reached number fifty-one. A long way off the top ten, but still progressing.

'Bands have to wait years for this. We're having the most phenomenal luck. I don't believe it. It's a bit spooky, really.' Laura dragged her fingers through her long, straight, dark hair. Her green eyes were troubled. She, Jan and Chris were all sitting in Jan's room sharing a bottle of sparkling white wine.

'OK, so we *are* lucky. What's wrong with that?' Jan said sensibly. 'Lots of bands have been even luckier. Back in the seventies, there were hit songwriters who got bands together just to record their songs, and they were instant smashes. Artificially created bands, who didn't even have to go out on the road and slog for it. I've been trekking up and down with various bands for three years. You've had a couple of years of it and Chris got lucky and only started this year. But she's still done the crap gigs, the sweaty pubs, the claustrophobic little clubs. We deserve it. Don't go all doomy on us, Laura. Look on the bright side!'

'I'm not doomy!' Laura protested. 'I just want someone to pinch me and tell me I'm not dreaming.'

'It's Lester,' put in Chris. The others stared at her. 'He's got the magic touch.'

'You could be right,' Jan said. 'He's a really great guy.'

Chris didn't need to be told that.

'I spoke to Bonnie last night,' Chris told the others, remembering that she had some news. Jan had been out all day, so she hadn't seen her. 'You'll never guess what . . .'

She looked around and waited for the others to urge her

to reveal her secret. They did, with a chorus of 'What?' and 'Don't keep us guessing!'

'Curtis wants to marry her!'

Screams filled the room. 'Is she going to?' yelled Laura.

'She thinks she will. She's going to give him her answer tonight,' Chris said. 'I hope she's doing the right thing . . .'

'How old is Bonnie?' Jan asked.

'Twenty-four, though she doesn't look it, does she?' Chris replied.

'That's all I want, really,' Laura said musingly. 'A really nice guy who really loves me.'

'Hmm,' put in Jan. 'I don't care if it's a guy. Even a goldfish would do!'

Chris thought hard about Lester. He was the only being she wanted, and there had been no progress on that front whatsoever.

Lester had mentioned the possibility of some gigs on the Continent. Apparently France in particular was going for 'It's Plain To See'. It had a disco feel to it, with a funky beat, and Chris felt it was probably more commercial than her song. *But mine's more original*, she wanted to shout. However, she couldn't tell the French that!

A teenage magazine had asked them to take part in a fashion spread for them, modelling garments, and that had been great fun. But as yet, nobody was buying their album. It was as if they were at a crossroads and everything depended on their single, which could go either way, up or down.

'I'm bored!' Jan suddenly announced. 'I fancy going out and doing something. How about you two?'

Chris felt her spirits lift. 'That would be great – but what can we do in December? We can't really go to the seaside . . .'

'Why not?' Laura shrieked suddenly. 'Raging grey waves, freezing winds – us against the elements. It'd be fantastic!'

'It's ten to twelve. Brighton's the nearest. It takes about an hour on the train,' Chris said thoughtfully.

'What are we waiting for, then?' shrieked Jan. 'Combat gear and hot water bottles, here we come!'

'I've got a better idea,' Chris piped up. 'My mate Carol's not working at the moment, and she's got a car.'

Carol was still going strong with Grant. It was his car really, but he parked it at Carol's, as she lived in an area where you didn't need a parking permit. Chris rang her and she leaped at the suggestion, and half an hour later the four girls were on their way.

'If there'd been more room, we could have asked Linda and Danielle,' Carol remarked as she drove.

'Danielle's got chicken pox,' Chris informed her. 'Poor little thing.'

'You must have seen her since I have, then,' Carol said.

'Yesterday. I hope I've had it. I don't want to catch it now. I'd better ask Mum.' Chris was on quite reasonable terms with her parents now, and her father had actually said that he liked the Visual Disturbance LP. ('I hate the name, though,' he had said. 'It sounds like interference on the TV set.'). Her mother had hinted once or twice that it would be quite nice if Chris came home, but Chris was enjoying the freedom which reigned in Jan's house. Stef still showed no signs of wanting to reclaim her room, and it was sheer bliss to be able to practise any time she liked between ten in the morning and ten at night.

They sang all the way to Brighton and when they got there, it was just as Laura had predicted – grey waves pounding onto the pebbles and a bitter wind blowing.

'Brrrr! Whose crazy idea was this?' Jan complained. She bent down, picked up a flat stone in her mittened hand and sent it skimming into the sea. It bounded high off the top of a wave, then sank without trace.

'Hard luck,' sniggered Carol. 'My top score's twenty-seven.'

'Bet that was in summer, though, in a calm sea,' Jan retorted.

A shout from Laura and a cry of 'Nine!' from Chris assured them that stones could be skimmed in rough seas, too, if you got the timing right between waves.

As they crunched across the stony beach, squealing each time a particularly powerful wave sprayed them with drenching foam, Chris lagged behind, her mood as grey as the weather. She imagined that the three romping figures ahead of her had nothing to do with her, but that she was here with Lester. And a dog. He didn't have a dog, but it would be great. She invented a slim, speedy black mongrel for which they could throw sticks, a dog which, overcome with excitement, would yap and leap up at them and chase its silly tail. Lester would hold her hand – they would be a couple, like the other couples and their dogs whom she had seen and envied so often. Later, they would call the exhausted mutt to heel and take refuge in a café; hot pie and chips and a steaming mug of tea, with their dog crouched beneath the table, warm against their feet.

This is all my fault, she berated herself. I'm eighteen years old – plenty old enough to have a serious relationship. I've got to do something soon, let him know how I feel, or I'll be *twenty*-eight and still in the same position, hankering after what I can't have. And he'll be fifty-six, exactly twice my age . . . Somehow, that sounded a lot better than eighteen and forty-six. But she didn't want to have to wait that long.

She thought of Viola in Shakespeare's *Twelfth Night*: *She never told her love,/ But let concealment, like a worm i' the bud,/ Feed on her damask cheek: she pined in thought;/ And, with a green and yellow melancholy,/ She sat like*

Patience on a monument,/ Smiling at grief. Chris wouldn't have described her own cheek as damask, exactly – more like wind-chapped cardboard. And as for the green and yellow . . . But the feel was right. If she kept on adoring him in secret like this, and letting it eat away at her, she would pine away just like Viola. Somewhere along the line, she would have to take a chance . . .

They did have pie and chips. It was great, really warming and filling. Then they sang all the way home. And when they got back to Jan's place, Karen, the other girl who lived there, told them that they had to ring their manager urgently.

Chris asked Laura to do it, for a change. Her beach fantasy was still too vivid to allow her to speak to him. She didn't want her voice to go all husky and peculiar so that he would suspect something was up.

The others gathered round as Laura's eyes went round like dinner plates rather than saucers and her eyebrows vanished beneath her fringe. Putting a hand over the receiver, she gasped, 'We've got that tour of the Continent!' Then they all clamoured for the details.

'I wish I could come,' Carol said enviously.

'Why can't you?' enquired Chris.

'Can't afford it. It's Christmas soon, in case you'd forgotten.'

Chris had. She wished Carol hadn't reminded her. The record company was giving them forty quid a week to live on, which certainly wouldn't stretch to presents. She would have to speak to Lester on the band's behalf, to see if he could get them some extra cash.

But – the Continent! She had never, ever been abroad in her life! Except for a week in Benidorm when she was ten, and she couldn't remember that. But she had never been abroad away from her parents, as a free agent. *Wowee!*

CHAPTER • 13 •

There were some hitches with carnets – the lists of equipment they needed in order to get their gear through customs – but Lester and XL Records between them managed to sort everything out. The record company had got their best promotions person behind the single and the resultant airplay, plus an appearance on *Going Live*, had got it into the top thirty. But there it seemed to be sticking. It had spent two weeks at number thirty-four. The UK seemed to favour Chris's song 'Avenue', and they had made a video to go with it, featuring the band walking through a deserted shopping centre, wandering round stone statues and fountains, the camera panning up to take in the dizzy, bleak heights of the modern, glass-walled buildings.

A journalist from one of the big music papers interviewed the band and when the article appeared, it featured, as well as a photo of the whole of Visual Disturbance together, a moody picture of Chris alone, and the caption: *Chris Lindsell, nihilistic avant-garde genius.*

Chris had killed herself laughing. 'Avant-garde? Jeee-sus! I just play tunes,' she had exploded. As for nihilistic . . . well, perhaps they had a point about that particular song. But while she still had her soft romantic streak that made her carry her unrequited longing for Lester, she would never become utterly sceptical as a person.

The article also likened them to the Velvet Underground. As they quite admired the cult underground band of the sixties, they were rather pleased about that, especially Chris, who the journalist thought bore some resemblance to the brooding, high-cheekboned Nico.

They were to play two dates in France and one each in Belgium and Holland, and they would be back the week before Christmas. Lester was coming with them. Chris got out a library book on Paris and pictured the two of them strolling along the banks of the Seine, visiting Nôtre Dame cathedral and drinking red wine in little back-street cafés. She had made a big decision. Some time during the tour, perhaps aided by that red wine, she would let him know how she felt, and to hell with the consequences. He could only turn her down, and if he did, she knew it would be with his usual tact and warm humour. But surely he wouldn't . . . ? After all, they had known each other for seven long months, seen each other as often as any boyfriend and girlfriend. Through her music, he had glimpsed her soul – and she knew he was sensitive enough to have recognised the insights she had given him.

She also felt that she had glimpsed his – a churning, restless, powerful, passionate soul. Well, hers might be more timid, but the potential for passion was there, like a fire which had been laid but not lit. And Lester could, at any time, strike the match . . .

It was the first time on a ferry for most of them, heading for the Hook of Holland. The sea was rough and Lester had warned them to take pills for travel sickness. Jan hadn't bothered, never imagining that seasickness could strike her, but it did; fifteen minutes out from shore, she was turning a delicate shade of green and spent the rest of the trip in the ladies', the conditions inside which were indescribable, she told them later, due to the number of other women in the same state as herself.

It was too rough to go out on deck so they found a quiet corner of the saloon and played a game of Travel Scrabble which Laura had brought with her. Chris glanced round from time to time, to see if any of their fellow voyagers had recognised Visual Disturbance, but it seemed nobody had. She wondered what it would feel like to be a real superstar, someone like Madonna, who couldn't set foot out of doors without being mobbed, pawed and asked for her autograph over and over again. She felt sure she would find it impossible . . . yct there was a little bit of her that would have got a buzz – just a tiny one – out of having somebody come up and say, 'Hey, aren't you the girl who plays saxophone with Visual Disturbance?'

The reception they received in Holland and Belgium was lukewarm, but the French audiences more than made up for it with their broad-minded approach to new sounds. They enjoyed themselves so much that they decided to treat themselves to a day's holiday in Paris and booked into a small, reasonably cheap hotel in the Rue de L'Echaudé on the Left Bank.

Chris was in two minds whether to go off round the shops with Bonnie and Laura or to the Louvre with Jan; the guys all seemed determined to check out the bars. She was just deciding on the Louvre when Lester announced that he felt like coming with them, and her afternoon was made.

Thank heavens she hadn't plumped for the shopping trip; to change her mind as soon as Lester said he was in the mood for culture would have seemed a bit too obvious.

The Mona Lisa was their first port of call in the gallery.

'It's got far more in it than you can see from reproductions in books,' Jan pointed out. 'It's got more colours and more detail in the background. But I don't think she's really smiling. I think she got fed up with sitting for her portrait, and that's a kind of frozen impatience on her face.'

'I think Leonardo just told her a rude joke and she's trying not to laugh because he told her to keep her face still,' was Lester's guess. 'What do you think, Chris?'

'Well, I certainly don't think she's beautiful. I don't know why people make such a fuss about the picture. What does it matter if she's smiling or not?'

'Oh, don't be serious, Chris. It's just a game people play, trying to guess why she's got that expression on her face,' Lester said, and Chris felt stung. He was telling her she was a spoilsport, telling her she was no fun. She wanted to run away, find another part of the gallery where she could be alone and nurse her wound. But Lester didn't give her a chance. When Jan had strolled ahead and was planted firmly in front of a massive Gothic canvas, he laid a restraining hand on her arm.

'Fancy going to hear some good jazz tonight?' he asked her.

From being right down at the bottom of the Slough of Despond, her spirits came rocketing back up again. He was asking her out! Maybe this was her big chance at last!

'Ooh, yes!' she replied eagerly.

The club, the New Morning, was packed with jazz fans who had all come to see Wailin' Johnny Lewis, a tenor player who originated from South Carolina. Lester had played her his debut LP, recorded for Blue Note Records in 1956, in New York.

'I met him when he was living in Copenhagen,' Lester told her. 'The Chestnut Valleys were doing a couple of gigs there and, as usual, I skived off to listen to some jazz. I was in my transit period then, wanting to move away from rock, but not quite good enough to start playing professional jazz. I bumped into Johnny at a jazz club and we got drunk together. He's living in Paris now, so he said I must look him up any time I'm over. I rang him yesterday . . .'

The club reminded Chris very much of something out of the film *Round Midnight* – and the tenor player, Wailin' Johnny, was reminiscent of its star. Chris felt overawed to be in such company. Here was a man twenty years older than Lester, who had played jazz all his life. And what sounds he coaxed from his battered-looking instrument! It made Chris feel almost ashamed of her shiny new sax; perhaps she would have looked and sounded more authentic if she had stuck with her old one. But then, she would never be in either Johnny's or Lester's league in a million years.

The club was so hot compared to the freezing air outside that Chris was drinking cold beer. There was no room to sit, so she and Lester were standing on one side, so close that they were almost touching. Chris could feel the heat coming off his body and it made her feel almost faint, being so near to him. The gap between them was a mere inch of air. He could span it easily, just by reaching out to her, putting an arm round her waist. She longed for him to do it, but he didn't. He didn't even talk much.

'Enjoying it?' he asked her once or twice, and she grinned her approval. Then he was lost in the music again, his head nodding and weaving as if he were tracing out the musical lines in the hot, thick, smoke-fugged air.

'I'm going to introduce you to Johnny,' he told her when the set was almost over. 'I said we'd have a drink and something to eat with him afterwards. You're not too tired, are you? You can always have a lie-in in the morning.'

'No, I'm not tired,' she assured him. She was, but she would never have admitted it and passed up an opportunity to meet one of the best ever exponents of her favourite instrument.

After he had finished playing, Johnny moved among the crowd, greeting friends and fans, and finally arrived where Lester and Chris were standing. He had a lined, very mobile face which screwed itself into interesting creases and furrows when he smiled. As he talked to Lester, he took a pair of black-rimmed glasses out of his jacket pocket and put them on.

'I can see you now,' he announced, with another face-furrowing grin. 'My, what a pretty young lady!'

'This is Chris,' Lester said. 'I'm teaching her to play tenor, but she's a natural. She's got the feel, all she needs is a few tips on technique. She's over here playing with a band.'

'A jazz band?' asked Johnny interestedly.

'No, a sort of . . . *avant-garde* one,' Chris said. How else could one describe Visual Disturbance? They weren't quite rock, or pop. That reporter had got it about right.

'I see.'

She saw plainly that he wasn't so interested now, and felt left out as he clapped Lester on the back and they went on gassing about old times.

'Right, we're off. Come on, love,' Lester said.

He'd called her *love*! A slip of the tongue. He had forgotten who he was with. Perhaps last time he was in Paris, he had been with Mary . . .

But Chris nevertheless trailed behind them to Johnny's

car, where two musicians from his band, the bass player and trumpet player, were waiting.

Chris lost count of how many bars they visited that night. She soon went on to Coke, but the men seemed to have an endless capacity for alcohol, and she grew quite worried about the amount Lester was drinking. He had gone on to Pernod. Chris had a sip but hated the pungent aniseed flavour. The men seemed to have forgotten about food, but she ordered a *Croque Monsieur*, a toasted cheese and ham sandwich, and devoured it hungrily. Every so often Lester would make an attempt to draw her into the conversation, but as it was mainly about people and places she didn't know, she felt more and more left out. It was a bit like the feeling she had had when she first got involved with Jalova – but worse, because Lester was part of it. If only it had been just the two of them out on the town! Not that it wasn't an honour to be in the company of Johnny, but really, she wasn't getting much out of it except a headache and an overwhelming need to go to sleep.

Lester must have noticed her yawns and drooping head because he suddenly said, 'I think we'd better get you back to the hotel, Chris.'

'Oh no, you can't go!' Johnny almost shouted. 'I've got Annette back in the apartment, just dying to meet you. You remember Annette – that chick I was living with in Copenhagen? You were after her yourself, remember?' He dug Lester in the ribs and laughed, a wheezing belly laugh.

'I'll come over and see the pair of you tomorrow,' Lester suggested, but Johnny, very drunk by now, refused to take no for an answer, and the next thing Chris knew, she was speeding through Paris in the back of a bashed-up Citroën at half past two in the morning, thinking that as soon as they discovered that Annette was soundly tucked up in bed, she and Lester would be allowed to go home at last. Surely there wouldn't be any more drinking . . .?

Annette, a slim blonde Danish woman in her early forties, *was* in bed, but she got up as soon as she heard them stumbling in, and appeared in a vividly embroidered kimono, full of smiles and greetings.

'Lester!' she called, in a deep, musical voice, and flung her arms round him. 'And this is your girlfriend, yes?'

Chris opened her mouth to contradict her, then waited for Lester to do it. But he didn't, and the moment was past. Still, did it really matter? They wouldn't be here for longer than twenty minutes, surely? Annette must want to get back to bed.

'I'll put some coffee on,' Annette insisted. 'You look as if you need it.'

'I've got the tapes of my latest album,' Johnny said. 'I'll put a cassette on . . .'

Chris's heart sank. The tapes would last for forty minutes at least. Why couldn't they come back and hear them tomorrow, when she would be in a better mood to appreciate them?

She couldn't see much of the apartment, as all except the large living room and the kitchen, which was at one end but screened off, was in darkness. She sat down on a squashy grey leather sofa and closed her eyes.

She must have fallen asleep, because she was suddenly aware of someone shaking her. It was Annette.

'I thought you would be staying the night, so I made up a bed for you,' she said. 'Come, I will show you . . .'

In a daze Chris followed her down a soft-carpeted corridor. 'Here is the bathroom.' Annette pointed to a door on the right, which had a poster of Courtney Pine on it.

'And here is your bedroom.' She pushed open the door next to the bathroom and switched on the light. The bed looked large, comfortable and very inviting and Chris couldn't wait to get into it.

After Annette had left her, Chris went to the bathroom and washed her hands and face, wishing she had a toothbrush. There was some toothpaste on the shelf above the washbasin. She squeezed some onto her finger and rubbed it over her teeth, then rinsed her mouth out. She went back to her bedroom and was about to climb into bed when she noticed something was missing: her shoulderbag, containing her notebook full of scribbled song ideas, impressions of the tour and Paris, and some of her thoughts about Lester. She didn't think for a moment that anyone *would* trespass in her bag, but all the same, being apart from her notebook made her feel uneasy. Stifling a huge yawn, she pulled her sweatshirt and jeans back on and padded barefoot towards the living room, from which the sound of jazz leaked down the corridor.

She was in the act of pushing open the door when she heard her name mentioned and froze, her hand still on the doorknob.

'But Lester, Chris is a pretty girl and you are certainly not past it!' Annette's tone was roguish. Chris held her breath, waiting for Lester's reply, her heart thudding, all her senses suddenly wide awake and alert again.

'Maybe, but that doesn't mean I'm sleeping with her.' Lester's voice was slightly slurred.

'Why not? Don't you fancy her?' Annette teased.

'Of course I do, but I'm not into cradle-snatching.'

The blood was pounding so loudly in her ears that Chris could barely make out Annette's next statement, which was about making Lester up a bed on the settee. So he *did* find her attractive and fanciable, and the only reason he hadn't made any move towards her was because she was too young . . . It was almost too much to take in. She needed time to think about it before she could face anybody, especially him. Backing silently away from the door, she turned and sped down the corridor into the safety of her room.

She sat on the edge of the bed, still fully dressed except for her shoes. The room was warm, the old-fashioned radiator making occasional clanking noises. She took deep breaths, allowing her eyes to roam. The bedroom was minimally furnished, with just a bed, a chair, a chest of drawers with a small mirror in a pine frame standing on it, and a couple of framed watercolours of Paris; obviously their guest room. She was calming down a little now, her thoughts were starting to happen in logical sequence.

Maybe some people would say she *was* too young for him. But years meant nothing. Some people were old at twenty, others, like Lester, still young in their forties. She had always thought of herself as mature for her age. Surely writing poetry gave you an insight beyond your years? But could she make Lester see that? Could she open his eyes to the fact that eighteen-year-old Chris Lindsell, to whom he was very attracted, whose music he thought held promise and talent, was closer to twenty-eight in the way she conducted herself and viewed the world?

Or was it because he guessed she was still a virgin? . . .

Rubbish! she berated herself. Nobody gained a certain wrinkle in their forehead or developed a giveaway look in their eyes just because they had slept with somebody. There was no way of telling. Linda hadn't looked any different. Apart from putting on a few pounds, she looked exactly the same as she did before she had Danielle.

Maybe it's my reserve about boys, Chris thought. She

had never chatted anyone up in Lester's presence . . . never mentioned a boy's name.

Yet surely he's seen the way I look at him. I haven't hidden that, Chris told herself. But maybe he was used to women who were far more up-front and sophisticated. Perhaps he needed the message spelled out: *I, Chris Lindsell, love you, Lester Mulley, and am sure you care about me. Why not do something about it?*

She would have to wait until Johnny and Annette had gone to bed. That could take ages, she realised. However, she didn't figure that she was in any danger of falling asleep. Not now. As soon as she had heard the last person vacate the bathroom, and the last door click shut, she would give it another twenty minutes or so, then she would go back down that long, narrow corridor, re-enter the lounge and face Lester with everything she knew.

Hours seemed to pass, though probably it was slightly less than one hour. Chris found a copy of the French magazine *Marie-Claire*, and lounged on the thick white cotton bedspread, flicking over pages without really seeing them. Finally, just as she had reached a point when she could have screamed out loud, the apartment fell silent. She glanced at her watch. Almost ten past four!

Fifteen interminable minutes . . . Then suddenly it occurred to Chris that Lester might have gone straight to sleep and might not relish being woken up. She rolled off the bed and leaped to her feet and reached the lounge door without being aware of getting there, so intent was she on the purpose of her journey.

She sucked in her breath in sheer suspense as she opened the door. The room was in darkness and from the leather sofa she could hear the sound of steady breathing. He *was* asleep! Her courage and sense of purpose began to ebb. She heard a rustling sound: Lester, turning to make himself more comfortable. Leather must feel horrid to sleep on, she thought inconsequentially. Her heart was beating quickly, like drumming fingers against her rib-cage. She hardly dared to breathe for fear of waking him. She would go. It was the only thing to do. There was no point –

'Who's that?'

Chris let out a stifled gasp. The sofa crackled and creaked and, in the gloom, she made out the dim shape of Lester standing up.

'Chris? Is that you?' He was coming towards her. She wanted to run but her feet felt superglued to the carpet. She was trembling violently all over. Even her lips were trembling, and she couldn't get a word out.

He came over to her, took hold of her arm. 'You're shivering.' He sounded concerned. 'Are you OK?'

He reached past her to the light switch, and the spell was broken as she blinked in the sudden glare.

'I . . . I wanted to talk to you, that's all,' she mumbled. 'There's nothing wrong. I just . . . just couldn't sleep. I had . . . things on my mind.'

'Come and sit down.' He yawned unrestrainedly, like an animal, not bothering to cover his mouth. He was wearing the red sweater he'd had on all day, but had taken off his jeans and Chris averted her eyes quickly, but not before she had noticed his blue briefs and how well-shaped his legs were.

His hand was burning her arm. She shook it off, annoyed at her hypersensitivity, and followed him to the sofa.

'You haven't been to bed?'

'No.'

'What is it? God, I'm shattered!' He yawned again and sat down. Chris sat next to him, drawing her legs up under her, the way she sat on her bed at home.

It was now or never. She couldn't keep both of them sitting here all night.

'I heard what you and Annette were talking about. I mean, about me. When you said you weren't into cradle-snatching.' She felt almost faint. There was a current coming off him, something so intense that she felt her skin tingling with it. Her breathing was constricted. She wanted desperately to touch him, or for him to touch her, put his arm round her, pull her close. She ached with wanting him. Compared to what she had once imagined she felt for Ian, this was like a raging toothache to a grazed knuckle. She remembered a record she had heard once, which repeated the words 'love hurts'. It did; it was agony. When was he going to do something? Say something? Why was he looking away from her like that, down at his feet, across the room – anywhere, it seemed, to escape her eyes? She wanted to tug his arm, say, 'I'm here.'

He sighed deeply, then twisted his hands together. Then, as if reaching a decision, he turned his head. He looked at her and she felt as if her bones were melting, leaving only her eyes and her mind functioning.

'Chris . . . Oh, Chris, I'm sorry.'

Sorry? For what? For forming the wrong impression of her?

'I could see this happening. I tried to stop it, tried not to give you any encouragement, but it was very difficult. What I said to Annette was true. I do find you very attractive, and very sexy. It hasn't been easy for me –'

'But why?' she burst out, seizing the hand that was nearest her. '*Why*? You could have –'

'Look, Chris, I'm human –'

'I know.'

'That's not what I meant. I meant, middle-aged men like me have a very soft spot for young women. And if they know a girl finds them attractive, it flatters them; it kids them that they're still young, too. But it's an illusion. It rarely works. It can lead to heartbreak on both sides.'

'But I'm not just any young girl!' Chris felt furious with him. It was as if he were trying to brush her off, class her with the vast mass of females out there in the world, when she was unique, her emotions strong and real and unafraid.

'I know, and that makes it worse. You're very special, Chris.' Lester spoke in such a soft, slightly regretful tone that Chris felt as if all the breath had just been squeezed out of her. Her eyes stung, yet she didn't feel like crying.

'Am I?' she muttered, gazing reproachfully at him. Then, gaining courage: 'Then why don't you show me?'

This was it! Surely, if he cared anything for her at all, he would make a move now. But he was still sitting motionless at her side. Kissing wasn't enough any more. She wanted him to make love to her. She was certain of it. It would be her first time, but she felt ready for it, in the right setting with the right man, someone who would never be just a one-night stand, but a man she knew she could share her life with.

He still needed persuading. That was it. He felt guilty about her age, about the fact that she was a student of his so he would be breaking some kind of code of ethics.

'Lester . . .' She put her hand on his shoulder, gave him a little shake. 'Look at me.' He did, slowly, and she felt that habitual shock and tremor inside as their eyes locked. She slid her arm down, so that it was round his back. He felt bony and firm, and so warm. She had to do it . . . had to press herself against him, swivel round so that she was almost lying across his lap, straining up towards his lips. He had to kiss her . . . Oh God, he *had* to!

'I love you . . . I really do.' She closed her eyes, waiting; then, with a great draining away of her spirits, a hurt, stinging wash of incomprehension, she felt herself being prised away from him.

'No, Chris. No.' His voice was firm but she didn't feel he was telling her off. There was too much sympathy there. That just made it worse. 'Look, there are lots of things I haven't told you. I've got lots of complications in my life.'

'Mary?'

'Yes, Mary's one. And I have a son only four years younger than you, and a daughter who's even older.'

Marijke had tried to warn her of this, but she had just passed it off, refused to take note of it. And even now, she still she wanted to fight. She was halfway there, she knew. Why was he so obtuse, so stubborn? Maybe she wasn't trying hard enough . . .

'But you're not living with Mary.' She hated the petulant note in her voice.

'I see her every Monday. I go and visit the boys, take them out to a movie, or for a pizza. I sometimes have them for an evening, or take them out over a weekend . . .'

'But one of them's not yours! And you've split up with Mary!'

'I know one of them's not mine, but that doesn't mean I can't love him, does it? Mary and I lived together for nine years. She left me . . .'

Locked though she was in her own emotional turmoil, Chris still couldn't fail to sense the implication: she left him, he didn't want her to leave, therefore he still loved her. By not putting it into words, he thought he was sparing her feelings. It was the first time Chris had ever felt genuinely bitter. She drew away from him, swept a hand through her hair, drew in a sharp breath.

'Yes. Well. Sorry about this –'

'Chris!' Lester sounded stern. 'Never, ever think that I

don't care about you. It may not be the sort of caring you want, but it'll probably last a lot longer.'

He was right; it wasn't what she wanted. Not one bit. As disappointment washed over her, she became aware of the aching tiredness in her limbs. She felt cold now – that deep, bone-chilling cold born not merely of a drop in the temperature, but of utter weariness and misery. She wished she were a small animal with a hole to burrow into.

She got to her feet. There was nothing more to be said, though no doubt she would think of plenty once she was alone. She was turning away, about to take a step towards the door, when she found herself restrained. Lester's arms went round her in a gentle embrace which was profoundly more moving than if it had been urgent and sexual. She felt his fingers slide under her chin, tipping her reluctant face up to his.

'You've got it all to come,' he said. 'You've got fantastic times ahead. Just think of that.'

His lips touched hers and left them in almost the same instant. It was just a brief brush of a kiss when she wanted so much more. But *he* didn't; she had to keep reminding herself of that.

He released her, but he was still looking at her with that sympathetic expression that was somehow far more hurtful than anger or straight rejection. 'It would only have complicated things,' he said. 'What you're going to need more than anything is a friend who understands. And I'll always be that.'

She felt too choked to say goodnight to him. She managed to twist the corners of her mouth into a caricature of a smile, then stumbled out of the room towards her bedroom. She was too wiped out even to cry.

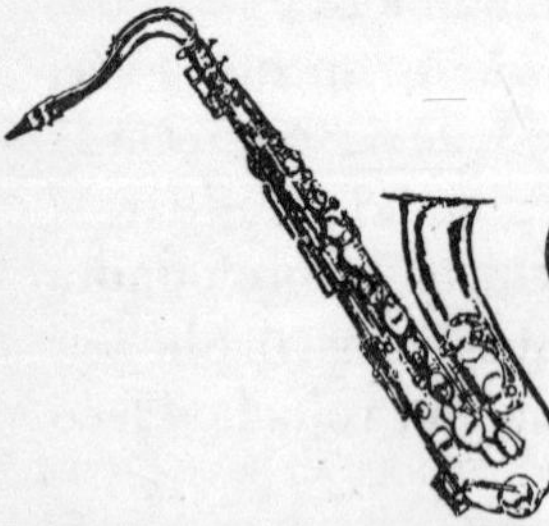

CHAPTER • 14 •

Next morning, she awoke to the sounds of music and cheerful voices. Annette, Johnny and Lester were already having breakfast. Feeling a bit like an intruder into the private world of their long-standing friendship, she joined them in the living room, hoping she had given Lester enough time to tell his friends the various pieces of news he might not want her to hear.

The coffee and hot, fresh croissants provided by Annette tasted very good. In fact, Chris ended up eating two, one with thinly sliced, tangy cheese and the other with raspberry jam. She realised that she could get fat very easily if she lived in France.

She was expecting something different in Lester's attitude towards her that morning, but there was nothing. He was cheerful and friendly, talking as much to her as to anybody else . . . but no more. Her spirits were a curious mixture of depressed and determined. Depressed, because she had not achieved what she had hoped for with Lester; today was not the first day of the love affair she had wasted so long dreaming about. Her determination was to carry on without letting her disappointment show; to live up to his faith in her, to be that big star, to have those good times. And who knew, but maybe, one day . . . After all, she hadn't stopped loving him. Love couldn't be switched on and off like a lamp. She glanced at him now, at the unshaven stubble on his chin, at his uncombed hair and rumpled clothes, and felt that almost pleasant ache of desire, but it was fainter than before, not quite so acute. She hoped it would stay that way and that it wasn't just because she was tired and had a lot on her mind.

When she got back to their hotel, Lee and Bonnie teased her, calling her a 'dirty stop-out' and insinuating that she had been 'up to no good'. Chris was short with them, and Bonnie looked a bit hurt.

'Sore head?' said Lee. 'Too much *vin rouge*? Or too much of the other?'

'Oh, leave her alone, Lee,' Bonnie snapped.

'Bonnie, I'm sorry but –'

Chris was just about to reveal that she hadn't had an altogether good night when Lester strode up to their corner of the guest lounge, looking very pleased about something.

'Where are Jan and Laura?' he asked.

'Gone down to the Seine for a walk,' Bonnie supplied.

'And Curtis?'

'Still asleep.' Bonnie grimaced. 'He's the one with the hangover,' she added.

'Well, I may as well tell you now. XL have just rung from London. The album's at number thirty-three –'

'Hey, that's good!' Lee said.

'Even better, 'Avenue' has reached twenty! What about that, eh? They're talking about releasing them in the States now. Oh, and you're to do a TV show in the New Year.'

After the excitement had died down, Chris went for a shower, then got changed. She was just plugging in her travel hairdryer when Jan came into the room. From the expression on her face, she had obviously heard the news.

'What a Christmas present!' she exclaimed. 'What are you doing for Christmas, anyway? Going home, or staying in the house with me? I'm not planning on going anywhere. Wellington's a bit far to go for Christmas dinner!' Jan's parents had emigrated to be near Jan's brother and his family.

Chris felt a twinge of disloyalty as she answered, 'I won't be staying. I've got some family things to do. Now that I've made things up with Mum and Dad, they're expecting me home, and I've got my cousin's wedding on Boxing Day, though God knows how we're going to get there.' She thought for a moment. 'Jenny said I could bring a friend. You wouldn't like to come, would you?' She knew Carol wouldn't want to go without Grant, and her other friends would be tied up with their own family get-togethers.

She didn't expect Jan to be interested. She waited for an answer along the lines of 'weddings aren't really my scene'. But, to her surprise, Jan's face lit up.

'Do you mean it?'

'Yeah.'

'Great! I don't have to get all poshed up, do I? I haven't got any weddingy-type clothes.'

'Oh, that doesn't matter,' Chris assured her. 'They know we're in a band. Come in what you usually wear. They'll love it. Actually, we'll have to leave really early in the morning on Boxing Day, so it might be a good idea if you came over to ours on Christmas Day . . .' Chris felt sure her mother wouldn't mind squeezing an extra portion out of the turkey. The thought of Jan being alone on Christmas Day would be bound to bring out her maternal instincts.

They had had Gemma over for Christmas dinner one year when her mother was in hospital.

Later that day, they packed up the gear and caught a crowded car ferry back to England. All of them except Lester, that is. Johnny and Annette had invited him to spend Christmas in Paris and he told Chris that he couldn't see Mary and the boys until the New Year, anyway. Something in his eyes made Chris feel a bit sorry for him.

The day after their return, 20 December, Chris rang the record company and found out that 'Avenue'/'It's Plain To See' was going to be released in the States as a double A-side at the end of January and the TV show they were to appear on was *Top of the Pops*. Even though they all thought the show a bit old-fashioned, they nevertheless realised how important it was to their career. Millions would see them and, hopefully, buy their records. In Curtis's words, 'I think we've made it, kids!'

When she rang her friends to tell them the news, they all sounded thrilled for her. Only Carol seemed a bit subdued, and when Chris pressed her on it, she confessed that she had rowed with Grant and they might split up. Chris went round to see her.

'It's all right for you,' Carol sniffed, staring gloomily into her cup of coffee as they sprawled on the rug in her bedroom, 'you've never really needed boys. You've always been so independent, so different to the rest of us with your poems and your music. Oh, I know there was *Ian*, but he didn't really count.'

'What do you mean?' Chris was both fascinated and slightly alarmed to be given this view of herself.

'We all thought he was a bit of an experiment for you. He was never right for you, he was far too ordinary.'

'You're making me sound like a real freak!'

'Well, you were a bit, at school. You weren't like anyone

else, you seemed in another world. We all admired you because you were so self-contained and you didn't seem to be affected by the things that got to the rest of us, like homework, exams and boyfriends . . .'

Chris suddenly realised that no one, not even Carol, had really known her. Perhaps it had been her fault, not confiding in people enough.

'You're acting like I don't have feelings,' she accused Carol.

'*Do* you?' Carol challenged.

'Oh, come off it! Of course I do! I was very hurt when Ian went off with Tracey. I mightn't have shown it, but that's me. I bottle things up and they come out in poems. Well, songs, now.'

'But Ian was ages ago, anyway. How have you managed to stay on your own since then? What's your secret?' There was envy and challenge in Carol's tone.

'Let's get a few things straight here, Carol. I've never felt the urge to have a boyfriend just for the sake of having one. I don't need a guy to improve my image. I don't feel a failure without one. If there's anything *different* about me, it's that not many guys appeal to me. Perhaps I'm too picky. I'm probably too selfish, too. They'd have to put up with my music, and all the time I spend rehearsing and playing. But there has been somebody . . .'

Chris ended up telling Carol everything about her and Lester that night in Paris. At the end, she half expected Carol to tell her what an idiot she had been, but in fact her old friend was very sympathetic.

'Neither of us is any good at picking men, are we?' she said.

'I'm better at picking saxophones,' Chris said ruefully.

'Oh, well, here's to better luck next time,' Carol said, and they toasted one another in cold coffee.

Chris's parents were fine about Jan coming over. In fact, she ended up staying with them on Christmas Eve, as they had decided to travel down to Devon on Christmas Day itself and stay overnight in a guest house which Uncle Joe had arranged for them.

Chris's Christmas shopping had been done in a terrible rush at the last moment, but it was great to have a bit more money to spend than usual. She had bought her mother some beautiful matching satin underwear in Paris, but her father posed a problem until Chris's mother said that he had mentioned that he would like a navy Guernsey sweater. She decided on a sweater for Jan, too, having seen her admiring one in holly-berry red in a shop window.

Everything turned out to be excellent choices, including the gifts she was given. After they had finished the unwrapping and admiring, Mrs Lindsell gathered Chris in her arms and gave her a big hug.

'We've missed you so much, love,' she said. 'Sorry I was so grumpy. I'm so proud of you now, I really am. It was never *you* I wanted to get rid of, please believe that. It was just –'

'*Just that wretched saxophone*,' Chris chimed in, mimicking her mother's voice exactly, so that they all laughed uproariously. But Chris's expression told her mother that she was forgiven.

The weather forecast threatened ice later on, so they were on the road by three, having had their dinner at twelve. Mr Lindsell was a bit gloomy, knowing that he couldn't drink at the wedding as he had to drive them all back. He hadn't even been able to enjoy more than one glass of wine with his Christmas dinner. Then Jan offered to drive home and he brightened up.

'I'm not that keen on booze, I can take it or leave it. I'll have one glass of champagne –'

'Shampoo!' Chris interrupted, remembering Lester's name for it.

'– then I'll go on to mineral water,' Jan promised.

It was a bit embarrassing at the wedding because the two members of Visual Disturbance were getting as much attention as Jenny, the bride, and the photographer insisted on taking several pictures of them, no doubt hoping that he could sell them for a lot of money once the band got really big. But Chris drew the line at signing autographs, even for insistent little cousins. It was Jenny and Mike's day and she had no desire to steal the limelight. She had to answer so many questions about the band, though, that she was quite hoarse by the time they left.

Mr Lindsell snored most of the way home, sitting next to Chris's mum in the back seat, while Jan drove carefully, especially on the country roads. They arrived just after midnight, without mishap, had a mug of cocoa each and fell into bed.

The day after Boxing Day, Chris went back to her room in Jan's house. There was a chance that Stef might be phoning and she was anxious to speak to her as she wanted to know how long their arrangement might go on for. Stef was talking about coming back, clearing her belongings out of the room and storing them at her mum's and then returning to Germany, but having witnessed so many ups and downs in relationships over the past few months, including Bonnie and Curtis's so-called 'engagement', which hadn't been spoken about since, Chris half expected Stef to announce that she was jumping on the next plane home.

Jan was wallowing in a foam-filled bath with the radio on when the phone rang, and Chris had just made herself a piece of toast and Marmite. 'Oh, blast!' she said crossly, knowing that, by the time she got back from the phone, the toast would be cold and soggy.

'Hello?' she said, rather sharply. There was a lot of crackling on the line, and some pinging noises. It sounded long-distance. It was probably Stef.

'Yes?' she added, trying to sound a little more pleasant. Maybe she had frightened whoever it was off by sounding so aggressive.

But when the voice came, it was quite loud in her ear, not filtered through loads of crackles, and had a foreign accent. It was a woman, but definitely not Stef.

'May I speak to Chris Lindsell?' the voice asked.

'This is me here,' Chris answered ungrammatically, wishing she had remembered to use the American phrase she rather liked because it had such a flourish to it: *This is she*.

'Chris, it's Annette. You remember? In Paris –'

'Oh yes!' replied Chris eagerly. Maybe Lester was there and wanted to speak to her.

But when Annette next spoke, there was no answering brightness in her tone. Her voice was low and a bit harsh, as if she had a sore throat. 'I . . . I'm afraid I have some bad news for you, Chris. Very bad news.'

She paused and Chris felt a chill creep over her. Nobody had ever spoken to her like this before. She rather hoped that Annette wouldn't say any more. Then she could just put the phone down and go back to her toast and pretend nothing had happened. If she didn't know about it, it *hadn't* happened . . . had it?

'Chris? Are you there?'

'Y-yes,' Chris stammered.

'There was a car accident. Last night. The roads were very slippery. Johnny and Lester had been playing at a private party in the country, about fifty miles away. I didn't go, I had a headache. It was about three in the morning. Lester was driving. They . . . what is the word for when you slip on ice? The car left the road and entered a field. I have just come from the hospital. Johnny is very sick, he has many broken bones –'

From Annette's dull tone and hesitancy, Chris sensed what to expect. Knew, and feared it, and was pushing the knowledge away with all her mental power. But Annette's voice, too loud in her ear, cut through her feeble resistance.

'I'm sorry, Chris, so sorry. Lester is dead. They say he was killed instantly, that he would have felt no pain. He had left his address book by our telephone so I called you. I know I am a long way off, but if there is anything I can do . . .'

'No,' Chris managed to whisper. 'I hope Johnny –'

She couldn't say any more, simply replaced the receiver with a hand that was shaking violently. Then she stood there in the hallway, waiting . . .

Nothing happened. The world didn't stop orbiting the sun, the room didn't sway around her or the ceiling crack open. But there seemed to be a silence everywhere, a deep hush as if a thick blanket had been thrown over the hallway, enclosing the spot where she stood, isolating her, muffling every sound.

She realised that she had stopped breathing; that her lungs, like the rest of her body, were frozen in a kind of suspended animation. It would be easy, so easy, not to start again but to bring her own life to an end. Because it *had* ended! What was there to live for now?

With that fierce, agonised thought came a struggling breath. Hoarse, audible gasps followed it in succession and there was a heavy weight crushing her throat and chest, a pressure which she knew could only be relieved by tears.

They wouldn't come, though. Nothing about her seemed to be working properly. With a powerful effort, she forced her legs to move her into her room. Once in, she clicked the door shut behind her and leaned her back against it as her body was convulsed with shudders.

No! screamed her mind. Say it isn't true, it didn't happen! Tell me I can press the rewind button, reel it all back.

Distractedly, she almost ran towards her saxophone case, fought with the clips, took out the instrument and stumbled to the window. There were birds out in the garden, bobbing about the lawn, but there were no leaves on the trees. Everything apart from the birds was bare and dead – and suddenly, even the birds looked unreal, like little, brown, battery-operated toys.

Dead. Dead. Dead. The word thudded in her head like the sound of an old, cracked bell. She forced the saxophone between her numb lips, jarring her teeth, then blew, her fingers working some automatic pattern. What was that tune she was playing? She had heard it before.

Cry, cry it out . . .

Pain hit her like a physical blow in the chest, winding her, sucking out her energy. On crumpling legs, she staggered towards her bed, somehow managing to unbuckle the sax and let it tumble onto the rug.

Her head landed heavily on her arms as she flung herself face down, but the pain in her flesh and bones was nothing like the pain in her heart, and she bit the pillow, pounded by waves of agonised, drowning tears. Lester . . . Oh, God, *Lester* . . .

It was very peculiar to be lying on one bed one minute, then to wake up and find yourself tucked up in another. Where was she? Chris lifted her head from her pillow and looked around her. A sloping loft window, an old teddy bear on a basket-work chair, a framed picture of a saxophone player . . . she was in her attic bedroom at home.

Boxing Day . . . the wedding. Was she just waking up from that? She had a feeling that she wasn't. She had an awful sense of doom, as if something dreadful were about to happen, or had already happened, but she didn't know what it was.

She swung her legs out of the bed and went to stand up, but her legs felt terribly weak and her head swam. She was desperately thirsty. She had flu – yes, that must be it. She got back into bed.

'Mum!' she called out weakly. Then her voice found extra strength from somewhere. '*Mum* . . . ?'

Footsteps sounded on the stairs and her mother came in, looking tired and anxious. 'I thought I heard you call, dear. How are you feeling?'

She fussed around Chris, plumping up the pillows, opening the curtains. Chris could see that it was daylight outside.

'I dreamed that I'd gone back to Jan's . . .' she said, feeling very confused. *Had* it been a dream?

Her mother moved the teddy bear to a shelf and sat down, drawing the chair up to Chris's bedside. 'You did go back to Jan's, love. Don't you remember?'

Chris shook her head and asked for a glass of water. When her mother came back with it, she asked, 'It is the twenty-seventh today, isn't it?'

Her mother had an odd, almost scared look on her face and hesitated before replying, 'No, it's the twenty-ninth.' Something about that hesitation rang a bell in Chris's brain but she couldn't quite make the connection.

'I don't understand. Mum, what's happened to me? Am I ill? I feel awfully peculiar,' she said.

Her mother reached for her hand and held it in her own.

'You've had a kind of black-out, a sort of collapse. The doctor gave you something to calm you down, that's why you feel so wobbly.'

'But what caused it?'

'You really don't remember?'

Chris shook her head.

'You had a telephone call. From France . . .' she prompted.

France . . . The tour . . . Annette and Johnny, the night with Lester – Chris jolted upright. It was coming back to her. *The phone call* . . . She gave a little moan.

'Sssh,' her mother calmed her. 'Take it easy, love. There's nothing can be done. These things happen. I remember how I was when your little brother . . .'

'Oh, Mum.' Chris made no attempt to restrain her tears and her mother moved to sit on the bed and put her arms round her daughter, rocking her like a baby. Above Chris's head, she filled in the blanks.

'Jan heard the phone go. Then about twenty minutes later, she heard you dash out of the house and slam the door. When you didn't come back, she rang to see if you were here. That got your father and me worried, of course. We rang Carol, Gemma and Linda, and Jan rang Lee and Bonnie. Then I thought of ringing Lester, knowing how friendly you were with him.

'A woman answered. She sounded terribly upset and she – she told me about the accident.'

'Did she say who she was?' Chris asked.

'Only that her name was Mary.'

Mary! The mother of Lester's son. If she still loved Lester even a little, she must be dreadfully upset. And the boy himself, how was he feeling?

'But how did Mary know . . . I don't understand, Mum.' Chris felt her lips wobbling. There was a great pit full of tears inside her chest. She felt as if she were choking.

'Mary went to get something out of her car and found you lying in the front garden. She called an ambulance and they took you to hospital and kept you in overnight for observation and we brought you back home this morning. As soon as she found you, she rang us. We'd given her our number in case you contacted her. She didn't know it was you at first, but she described you . . . Oh, Chrissy love!'

Chris was folded up into her mother's arms. She felt as floppy as a rag doll and allowed her mother to hug her and rock her. But she felt a thousand miles away. If she could remain like this, in a half trance, not feeling, not thinking, then the pain would leave her alone.

'What was it, love? What were you doing there?' her mother asked in a throaty, emotional voice. Her face was wet.

The pain washed over Chris in a salty, pounding tide. 'I . . . I loved him, Mum . . .'

Jan, Bonnie and Laura came round next day, bringing flowers and fruit. They didn't quite know what to say and there was an awkward silence. Jan broke it.

'It's awful. None of us can believe it. He was –' she eyed Chris carefully – 'such a terrific guy. He's done so much for the band. XL are pretty devastated. They say they'll help us find another manager –'

'*No!*' Chris rapped the word out. 'There can't be anyone else. No one could replace Lester. Don't you see? It's the end of the band. I don't want to play any more. I mean it. It's over.' How could she ever explain to the others that Lester had provided all her inspiration, tugged and teased the music from her, shaped and criticised it, speeded it and smoothed it? He had been the catalyst that she had needed in order to compose. Without him providing those goals for her to drive towards, she would never be able to get out another note. She had done it all for him. Because of him.

Well, maybe just a little bit for herself. But she needed his comments, and more than anything, she needed him to provide a focus for all those restless feelings inside her, that weight of love, misplaced though it may have been. And now that weight would drag her down, flatten her notes and her spirit. She never wanted to go on stage again. She had nothing to give.

The others were exchanging looks.

'"Avenue' is at eleven and may still go up. We've got *Top of the Pops* next week. We've got to do it,' said Bonnie urgently.

'We've got a hit, Chris. Isn't that what we always dreamed of?' said Laura, her big, shining eyes grave for once.

'I had . . . some other dreams as well,' Chris said quietly, almost to herself. She saw Bonnie look away and knew she was making her friends feel worse. She didn't want to let them down, but surely they could understand?

Bonnie clutched at her hand. 'Please, Chris,' she begged. 'I know I should have confided in you more about Jalova and Curtis but there were things that, then, I didn't think you'd understand. But don't turn us away, Chris. We're not just your fellow musicians, we're your friends. We want to help you over this, give you our support . . .'

Her brown eyes beamed sympathy at Chris. *Support* . . . she thought. Lester had offered her that, too.

She gazed at the three of them with tear-filled eyes, struck dumb. She didn't know what to say. She still felt that she never wanted to play a note again. Suddenly, a vivid picture of Lester came into her mind – Lester playing tenor with Soundwaves, as he had been the second time she had seen him.

'You're going to be a star,' Lester had told her. 'You've got it all to come . . .'

She saw those clear blue eyes gazing at her from beneath

that prematurely silvered hair. Who really knew about death, she thought? Perhaps a person's spirit, that electric charge that fired them through life, didn't stop but flew free, able to follow the lives of those the person had been close to, but unable to interfere. In that case, she couldn't let him down. Not now that everything he wanted for her was beginning to happen.

'OK,' she told the others.

Carol called round the next morning and told her how brave she was to want to continue with the band. 'Mind you,' she added, 'if I was about to be a superstar and make loads of money, I wouldn't quit no matter what happened.' Chris had never been able to convince her that she was in it for love of playing first, and all the rest second.

Chris didn't recover easily from Lester's death. Every time she thought about him, she felt as if she were sitting with her back to the engine on a fast-moving train, hurtling backwards away from everything that was familiar and loved. It was like a strange kind of vertigo and she couldn't really describe it to anyone, not even the doctor.

The day of Lester's funeral arrived. The rest of Visual Disturbance wanted to go and pay their last respects, and of course Soundwaves would be there. Chris had spoken to Marijke, who had said they felt they didn't want to carry on the band without Lester, but on the other hand they had the LP about to come out, which would be a tribute to his memory, so they would probably try to carry on for a while with a stand-in sax player, though it just wouldn't be the same.

That was exactly how Chris felt. Nothing could carry on the same. She didn't know how she could face the funeral, but felt she owed it to Lester to go.

She was amazed at the masses of people there – old friends from his rock days, newer ones from the jazz world, the members of Soundwaves, fans, people who had bought his records years ago, press reporters and photographers . . . She looked round for Mary, but there were so many people and so many dark-haired women that she couldn't be sure which one she was.

Annette had come over for it – Johnny was still in hospital – and she sat with them. Towards the end, Chris had to close her eyes. She couldn't watch what was happening to the coffin, didn't want to think about it.

It was drizzling as they left the crematorium. Jan and Chris were huddled beneath an umbrella, waiting for Annette who had promised them a lift back – the others were being driven by Lee in the band's van – when a small tabby cat appeared from nowhere and began rubbing round their ankles.

As she bent to stroke it, Chris suddenly remembered a larger tabby, a tomcat with one ear missing. Charlie, Lester's old cat. What would happen to him now? And what about Mary and Lester's son? Tears stung her eyes.

So many questions. She would never know the answers. Her innards seemed to have been replaced by a leaden weight, dragging her down. Where was that soaring feeling now? Would it ever come back again? How could she bear to hear a saxophone now when it would remind her so strongly of him?

Annette appeared and the three of them walked towards her hired car. She would be staying with them that night.

They drove back in silence, each wrapped in her own sad thoughts.

If she had made love with him, thought Chris, would she be feeling even worse now? It didn't seem possible to feel worse, but if they had begun a real affair that night, or even if they had just made love the once, would she now be feeling twice as grief-stricken, twice as bereft?

She would never know. Some part of her, deep inside, would always weep for him. Yet another part was making itself heard, too – a part that was going to be brave and strong for him, and try to do well for him. She had to carry on with Visual Disturbance, she knew that now. It was what Lester would have wanted.

Two days had passed since the funeral. Visual Disturbance met round at Jan's house to discuss their future and hold a kind of wake for Lester. It had been Bonnie's idea and Chris thought Lester would have appreciated it.

The single was sitting at number eight and the album had reached fourteen. Everything was happening just as Lester had predicted, Chris thought wryly. Even she realised that now it was vital for them to find a good professional manager to take over the business side of things, otherwise they could lose the momentum which they had built up. She even reflected that Lester may well have wished to hand his temporary management over at this point in their career, and remain with them in more of a creative capacity, arranging and producing their music, perhaps.

As she and Bonnie made sandwiches in the kitchen and Lee fought to pull a tight cork out of a bottle of wine, they had the radio on in the background. It was a programme about jazz and blues, and a guitarist was being interviewed.

'Some people say that white musicians can't play blues, as it is black man's music,' the interviewer was saying. 'What do you think?'

Chris didn't listen to the guitarist's reply. 'I think being black or white makes no difference,' she said to Lee and Bonnie. 'When you really think about it, only *blue* people can play the blues. It's a state of the emotions . . . of the soul.'

Suddenly, she yearned to pick up her tenor and play. She knew the music would come from deep, deep within her. 'Cry It Out' just had to be their next single. And once she had cried it out, perhaps she would be able to soar again.

'You've got it all to come,' Lester has told her. 'You've got fantastic times ahead.'

Bravely, knowing it would hurt her, Chris formed a picture in her mind of Lester that day they had first met, when she had sailed his white yacht on the shining pond on a blue and silver day.

I'm OK, she told him. *Don't worry. I'll sail on.*